SHERLOCK
The HOLMES
Back to Front Murder

ALSO AVAILABLE FROM TITAN BOOKS

SHERLOCK HOLMES
The HOLMES
Back to Front Murder

TIM MAJOR

TITAN BOOKS

Sherlock Holmes: The Back to Front Murder
Print edition ISBN: 9781789096989
Electronic edition ISBN: 9781789096996

Published by Titan Books
A division of Titan Publishing Group Ltd
144 Southwark St, London SE1 0UP
www.titanbooks.com

First edition: August 2021
2 4 6 8 10 9 7 5 3 1

A CIP catalogue record for this title is available from the British Library.

Printed and bound in Great Britain by CPI Group (UK) Ltd, Croydon, CR0 4YY.

For Luke, who asked for a mystery.

CHAPTER ONE

Upon my return to our shared rooms in Baker Street, I found my friend, Sherlock Holmes, sitting before the unlit fireplace opposite a stern-faced woman of no more than thirty-five years of age, whose posture was determinedly casual. Her attire was a fairly plain tweed walking-suit, and though she had slung her dark cape over the back of the chair in which she sat, I saw no evidence of a hat, and her copper-coloured hair was wild and untamed. Somewhat taken aback at her presence, I turned to face Mrs. Hudson in the doorway, ready to interrogate her for omitting to mention Holmes's visitor. Our landlady performed something in the way of a shrug of apology, then closed the door hurriedly.

Holmes raised a hand, perhaps as a greeting or simply to gesture in my direction.

"May I present to you Dr. John Watson, with whom you may find much in common," he said to his guest. "He will no doubt extend to you his apologies for his late arrival, which is on account of his having taken an unexpected diversion to Fairfield Road. However, as I expect he will assure you, he returns much refreshed."

His guest's expression remained placid, yet I imagine mine became that of a gargoyle, with bulging eyes.

"How the devil could you know that?" I demanded, in my amazement almost forgetting the presence of a woman. It was only at this moment that I registered that she was sitting in my own chair. A flush rose to my cheeks. "I gave no hint of my destination when I left this morning, and did not even know it myself."

Holmes leaned back in his chair. "Precisely so. Yet I would be remiss had I failed to observe your behaviour yesterday, which is pertinent to your behaviour to-day. You spent most of yesterday afternoon frowning at a blank sheet of paper placed upon your desk, occasionally turning to look at me as I performed my own work at my bench. Anybody might conclude that you were intending to write an account of another of my cases. Then, this morning, as is your wont when you are uncertain how to begin one of your lurid tales, you left the house without announcing your destination."

I nodded, no less perplexed. "But surely none of that gives you any indication about my whereabouts this morning."

"Perhaps not, but it is nevertheless a starting-point." He waved his hand again, this time towards my feet. "This morning you set off on foot, but the scuffing on the exterior of your left shoe – which you polished only yesterday in what I presume was act of distraction from a more important task in hand – suggests to me that you then boarded a hansom. Perhaps you are not aware of your tendency to favour one leg while boarding a hansom carriage? No matter, but it remains the case. There are a number of indicators that your journey was unplanned, the principal of those being the unfavourable weather forecast in to-day's *Times* as regards the late morning. I own that your luck held out, but the fact of your leaving without an umbrella is unusual considering your ordinarily punctilious character, and the faith you place in the forecaster's judgement. Your demeanour upon leaving and now, on your return, suggests no emergency has occurred, to which I add the observation that your journey was of no more than a half an hour's duration – any longer, and the practicalities and necessity for preparation would have overwhelmed the whim that came upon you."

I nodded. "But still, you are dancing around your most startling conclusion. None of this supports your pinpointing of my location."

Holmes smiled and turned to address the woman sitting before him. I blanched at the realisation that I still had not learned her name.

"I would like to assure you," he said to her, "Dr. Watson's customary aroma is not ordinarily so strong."

My mouth opened and closed impotently. I turned my head subtly to one side, so as to smell my jacket, but could detect nothing amiss.

The woman spoke for the first time. "I confess I smell nothing unusual."

"No?" Holmes said casually. "It strikes me as very strong. Rather like garlic, and if this were evening-time I might suspect the consumption of a well-flavoured meal. But any restaurant would be opening its doors to serve luncheon only now, and by my assessment, the nearest location in which wild garlic grows is far beyond the radius I have already identified."

"I confess I still smell nothing," the woman said, and despite her oddly clipped tone, I was glad of her statement. But then, after a moment's hesitation, she added, "Yet, yes, there is a trace. Not garlic, precisely. I believe it is the scent of white phosphorous when it is oxidised."

Holmes nodded in approval, and ignored my own gasp of disbelief. "Quite so. Therefore, to avoid drawing out my method more than is necessary, I conclude that Watson this morning took it upon himself to visit the Bryant and May match factory in Bow, in the hope of performing research related to a case of ours that was completed some eighteen months ago."

I bowed my head a little and considered interrupting my friend, but the rapt expression that transformed the face of his guest dissuaded me.

Holmes steepled his fingers and directed his entire attention to the woman before him. "The case involved the apparent elopement of a young couple, though, as it transpired, it was rather more in the vein of an abduction. While the woman in question was returned safely to her family, thanks in no small part to our efforts, the young man escaped only to drown in the Channel some weeks later.

"However, what concerns us this morning is the background of this man, the culprit of that crime. The physical characteristic that was to identify him and represent his downfall was a facial deformation – the result of the earlier removal of part of the jawbone in response to a case of phosphorus necrosis, which is sometimes referred to by less rigorous journalists as 'phossy jaw.' This deformation indicated that rather than possessing an aristocratic background as the young man claimed, he had in fact spent several years performing menial work in a match factory. This in turn provided part of the motive for the abduction. You see, the young woman was the daughter of a man of science tasked with the development of yellow phosphorus sesquisulfide, which, by all accounts, may soon allow for the creation of friction matches that can be struck without the requirement of a specially prepared surface."

I failed to stifle a groan. "I fear you have rather spoiled the story for Miss..." My words tailed off as I remembered that I was still ignorant of our guest's identity.

"Miss Abigail Moone," Holmes said.

Miss Moone rose from the chair and, without any display of

emotion, allowed me to shake her hand. "Please, won't you join us?" she said.

I cast around, once again thrown by the fact that my usual position was occupied by Miss Moone herself. After some deliberation, I moved a cane-backed chair to form a triangle of seats before the fireplace. As I deposited myself into the chair, I stifled a strange sense that I was the client rather than she.

"Well," I said. I attempted to ignore a cloying smell that now arose from my jacket, which only magnified my displeasure. I offered Holmes a tight smile. "The sole matter that remains, I suppose, is your correct identification of the factory in question."

"Then it was not the very same factory connected to the culprit in the abduction case?" Miss Moone asked.

Holmes answered for me. "That factory was Albright and Wilson, in Oldbury. However, even if Watson had returned to our rooms in a freshly pressed suit to disguise the pungent scent, the copy of *Baedeker's Guide to Great Britain* that he left open on his desk at the chapter devoted to the Black Country would have suggested his line of thought, and his preoccupation with that tale in particular."

Miss Moone nodded. "And yet visiting that factory in Oldbury would involve a journey of more than one hundred miles. So it seems that you, Dr. Watson, concluded that one match factory was as good as another, in order to observe its employees for the purposes of background detail for your story. Your choice of Bryant and May in particular…"

She rose from her seat and began to pace around the room. I watched in wonderment as she peered at my desk, then returned to the fireplace, whereupon she raised a box of matches from its place on the mantelpiece and gave a cry of pleasure. Indeed, the brand of matches I have favoured for many years is Bryant and May.

"There is also the fact that the Bryant and May factory itself may have lodged in Watson's mind since the matchgirls' strike of some years ago," Holmes added, "but I accept that your physical evidence is more compelling, Miss Moone."

"Well," I said, feeling more than a little foolish, and then attempting to inject levity into my tone, "it appears that I am the only person in this room ignorant of the workings of my own mind."

Holmes exhaled softly. "A trifle, Watson. Yet I hope that you will bear this lesson in mind when you are composing your accounts of our cases. You are predisposed to taking liberties with the truth, even if it is an unconscious process. I wonder what other liberties you will take with this particular case. A sensational title, perhaps." He pressed the tips of his fingers together once again, and his brow furrowed. "Something related to brimstone may be lurid enough to suit your tastes." He tapped his fingertips against his thin lips. "No. It will more likely be a phrase indirectly related to the young man's peculiar deformation, as well as hinting at his goal of securing the formula of phosphorus sesquisulfide – whilst also obscuring each of these details behind cryptic but grand-sounding nonsense. For example, 'The Problem of the Yellow Lucifer.'"

I felt heat rise in my cheeks. A very similar title had occurred to me on my return journey from Bow.

I cleared my throat and turned to our guest.

"I must apologise for interrupting you with this distraction, Miss Moone. I presume that when I entered you were in the process of relating to Sherlock Holmes your own story." Willing the blood to drain from my face, I added, "Please do continue."

Mirth flickered over the hard lines of Miss Moone's face, but she was kind enough not to voice her observations.

"In fact, I had not yet begun," she said.

"Indeed, I had simply had time to remark that it was a shame that you were not present to hear Miss Moone's case first-hand," Holmes said.

Perplexed but gratified, I turned to our guest and said, "I would urge you to explain your reason for visiting, then."

Before our visitor could speak, Holmes held up a hand. His lips were pursed and all his earlier amusement had left his face. "Miss Moone, I would be grateful if you would summarise your case as concisely as possible. I feel confident in placing my trust in you, of all people, to include all pertinent details."

Miss Moone bowed her head in acknowledgement.

"I come to you this morning concerning a death," she said. "It is my first association with death in the real world, as opposed to those in fiction. You have read this morning's newspapers, I trust? If so, you will have read of the unusual death of Ronald Bythewood."

Holmes only inclined his head subtly, so I took it upon myself to reply, "Indeed, Miss Moone. A suspected poisoning, was it not?"

"That appears to be the case, Doctor. And I am bound to tell you that I was responsible for devising the manner of Mr. Bythewood's death."

I leaped from my seat in alarm. "What?" I exclaimed. "And you are content to come here and confess as much?"

I spun around to see that Holmes's posture had not changed in the least.

"I suspect Miss Moone is not offering a confession, Watson," he said, "any more than you would confess to having killed more than half a dozen men this year alone, or having stolen countless riches. If you will be seated, you may discover that you and Miss Moone have much in common."

"I'm afraid you both have the advantage over me once again," I stammered. My mind reeled as I tried to resolve my friend's statement. "Are you a medical practitioner of some description, Miss Moone?"

"I am not."

"Then I am at a loss."

She drew herself up to an even more straight-backed posture. "Like you, I am a writer. And like you, I am preoccupied with mysteries and, frequently, murder."

I frowned and then spoke her name under my breath, but it agitated no associations.

"Do you read very many books written by women, Dr. Watson?" Miss Moone said lightly.

I suspected that my cheeks had coloured again. "I confess I do not."

"Neither do many men, I find. As Mr. Sherlock Holmes has already deduced, I deploy a pseudonym when publishing my work. You may have heard of *his* name. Damien Collinbourne."

"Damien Collinbourne!" I exclaimed. "Is it true? Indeed, I have read and enjoyed more than one of his – that is, of *your* – novels. In the name of professional research, I should add, and yet I own that I found myself engrossed. And even fellows at my club speak highly of him – of you." I took out a handkerchief and mopped my brow, then fell back. Once again, I found myself yearning for my usual seat rather than this cane-backed chair.

"Please, Miss Moone," Holmes said. "You had only begun your account."

"Indeed. Since the rise to fame of my stories, the success of which Dr. Watson has demonstrated, I have found it increasingly difficult to conjure new scenarios – at least, scenarios that satisfy me as to their complexity and interest. Furthermore, I admit freely that I have become ever more occupied with the workings of the criminal mind rather than the often-plodding procedures of investigating police officers. Perhaps that is a revealing admission? Regardless, it has been my custom during this last year to devise mysteries by first considering the actions of the culprit, and only then introducing an investigator to unravel the knot I have already tied."

I found myself nodding as I followed this account with interest. Such a manner of producing fiction had not occurred to me. I stifled the urge to turn in my seat to look at the bookshelf behind me, upon which it now occurred to me were copies of at least two novels attributed to Damien Collinbourne.

"I have become quite the daydreamer," Miss Moone continued, "as well as something of a *voyeur*. My custom each morning – I always work at my desk in the afternoon – is to watch people, and, invariably, select a likely looking victim, and then..." It struck me that her pause was in order to gauge my temperament rather than resulting from any true hesitancy on her part. "...I conjure a method of killing them."

Sherlock Holmes nodded sagely at his guest, as if this admission was a common one.

"Yet this occupation is entirely for the purpose of devising stories, I take it?" I said, feeling foolish at my need to secure this clarification.

"It is," Miss Moone replied without inflection. "And in this case, I selected Mr. Ronald Bythewood as a victim. I learned his name only this morning, when I received my *Times*, but my close observation of him this last week would have made him immediately recognisable to me from his description, even if I had not witnessed his death."

Again, I emitted a sharp sound at this new revelation. "You mean you *did* witness it? You were present when he died? This certainly changes things."

Holmes waved me away irritably and leaned forward in his seat. "In your arresting introduction, you stated that you devised the *manner* of Bythewood's death, and not only the fact that he would die."

Miss Moone nodded. "I suspect that I may have observed this rather unkempt elderly gentlemen in passing several times before I made the conscious selection of him as one of my victims. My recent habit has been to frequent the National Gallery of British Art each morning, due to the number and variety of its visitors. Have either of you visited the Tate gallery yet?"

Holmes did not answer, but I felt compelled to confess that I had not yet had the pleasure. The gallery had opened almost one year before, in the summer of 1897, and yet, to my chagrin, the idea of visiting it had not occurred to me.

"You must; it's a grand place," Miss Moone said. She inhaled deeply. "Having selected Mr. Bythewood, who at that point remained nameless to me, from the gallery's crowd, I followed him on several occasions. He proved a satisfying case study, in part because his actions each day remained unchanged, by and large – though at a glance one might summarise his movements as meandering or even confused, a conclusion that would be supported by the fact that he sometimes spoke to himself under his breath. Of his regular activities, the one that was of most interest to me was his habit of taking a drink from a public drinking-fountain each day, following his brief tour of the galleries. This fountain is to the south of the main entrance, and placed badly, in my estimation, as locating it requires performing two about-turns upon leaving the gallery. Consequently, I have seen no other person use the fountain during any of my visits. My invented method of murdering the gentleman, therefore, concerned secreting an amount of poison within the drinking-fountain. The poison would necessarily be rather slow-acting, in order for my victim to succumb to its effects elsewhere, to avoid exposing me – or, rather, the criminal within my story."

She turned to face me and continued, "Like you, Dr. Watson, I appreciate performing observations with my own eyes before setting pen to paper. Furthermore, as my habit is to identify myself with the criminals within my stories, I find that my *own* mannerisms can be as revealing as the people I study. This means that I am often compelled to enact my crimes physically, in order to record my mannerisms and movements. All of this may seem fanciful, but it remains a vital aspect of my research."

I considered all of this. "Then do you mean to say—"

"I assure you I conduct myself in a manner that ensures both my own safety and the safety of my unknowing participants," she said, interrupting me without so much as raising her voice. "Having determined that a soft gelatin capsule might be placed within the spout of the drinking-fountain, and once within the body would dissolve rapidly, I consulted a pharmacist acquaintance, who provided me with capsules which were unfilled and therefore harmless. On the day I instigated my 'criminal' plan, I followed Mr. Bythewood at a discreet distance during his tour of the gallery, and at the appropriate moment I contrived to pass ahead of him to the main entrance and then around to its south side, where the fountain is located. I placed the capsule into the spout only minutes before the time when I knew he would arrive. Then, having witnessed from a safe distance his operation of the drinking-fountain and – as far as I was able to determine – his swallowing of the empty capsule, I followed Mr. Bythewood along his usual route, across Vauxhall Bridge and into Vauxhall Park."

I saw that Holmes was once again leaning forward eagerly in his seat.

"As you so clearly anticipate," Miss Moone continued without hesitation, "it was in Vauxhall Park that I saw Ronald Bythewood collapse and die."

Then she clasped her hands in her lap, apparently satisfied with her telling of the tale. "Beyond that, everything I know is derived from the *Times* report, including, as I have already stated, the gentleman's identity."

Holmes raised a finger to tap at his lips. His eyes sparkled, betraying both his interest and his amusement. It occurred to me that Miss Moone and my friend were alike in many ways, not least their detachment from the horror of such a situation, which had resulted in a man's death.

For my part, the more I considered Miss Moone's story, the more preposterous it seemed. "But this is an outrageous coincidence!" I cried.

Both Holmes and Miss Moone gazed up at me accusingly, as if I had spouted the ugliest oath imaginable.

"My dear Watson—" Holmes began.

I held up both my hands. "I know, Holmes, I know. There are no coincidences. You have demonstrated that assertion to me many times over. Yet how do you account for the incredible similarity between Miss Moone's projected manner of death and the real one? The article in the *Times* made it abundantly clear that the man was poisoned, and for him to be attacked in that manner at the precise moment that Miss Moone was *pretending* that he was—"

"That is entirely the matter at hand," Holmes replied, "so let us consider the facts calmly."

It was only now that I realised I had leaped from my seat once again in my excitement. I turned around, only to be confronted by the damnable cane-backed chair. In my giddiness, I simply stared at it for several seconds.

"I perceive that I have inadvertently taken your chair," Miss Moone said brightly. "I would be happy for us to exchange places."

My cheeks flushed as I watched her retrieve her cape and

then move to sit in the cane-backed chair. Her graceful posture somehow made that lesser vessel seem immoderately grand.

I refused to meet Holmes's eye as I lowered myself into my usual chair, which was still warm from its previous occupant.

Nobody spoke, so I cleared my throat and said, "Well, Miss Moone, upon consideration of the matter, my immediate point of interest is this pharmacist friend of yours. Can we trust the fellow?"

"His name is Carsten Laine," she replied. "I trust his professionalism to a very high degree, and his wife is a close friend of mine."

To Holmes, I said, "I know the man myself. His understanding of pharmaceutical matters is second to none, and his reputation unimpeachable."

Holmes nodded in response.

"Furthermore," Miss Moone said, "Laine provided me with several of the unfilled capsules. As a precaution I selected one of them at random and swallowed it."

"That displays remarkable bravery," I said.

"Not in the least," she replied dismissively. "I had been assured by a friend that they were unfilled. A mistake might have been made – but would you prefer that I impose that mistake upon a stranger rather than upon myself?"

I held my tongue rather than point out that, to all appearances, it seemed possible she had indeed killed a stranger in precisely this manner.

"Who have you spoken to about your theoretical plan for murder, or your decision to enact it, or the outcome?" Holmes asked Miss Moone.

"Nobody on earth," she replied.

"Is it recorded anywhere that might be discovered?"

She nodded curtly. "In a note-book – but it never leaves

my house. Following my wanderings and observations each morning, my custom is to return home, record my findings in my note-book, and then resume drafting whichever manuscript currently occupies me."

"Your staff, then?" I interjected. "Might they have access to the note-book, particularly in your absence?"

Miss Moone responded with a smile that struck me as rather condescending. "I have no staff, Dr. Watson, and send out my laundry. I live alone, I am more than capable of keeping my own house in a tolerable condition, and I support myself independently, thanks to Mr. Damien Collinbourne, the only man who ever need cross the threshold of my house."

"Well, then, what about your friends?"

"Writing is a solitary occupation – that is to say, it is an occupation that rewards solitude. I have many friends, but I rarely entertain at home. For many months, nobody has had access to my house, either in my company or otherwise, and this particular entry in my note-book was written only three days ago. In any case, I am a zealous keeper of my professional secrets. The note-book is always held within a safe, along with my other important documents. Those notes are my livelihood, Dr. Watson, and retaining their secrets is vital to my professional success. I know that you would not expect me to be frivolous concerning them."

Once again, I was conscious that all eyes were upon me. Resenting the implication that Miss Moone's account might cause me discomfort or amazement, I said, "Am I to understand that you do not have the note-book upon your person to-day, then?"

"That is correct."

"And your interest in Mr. Bythewood's unhappy death is because you believe that you have directly inspired it?" I asked.

She stared at me, unblinking. "Given the facts of the matter,

I fail to see how another conclusion might be reached."

"Well, then." I cleared my throat once again. "I trust we shall take this case, Holmes?"

Holmes responded with a thin smile. "Miss Moone's account contains several points of interest, certainly. Yes, I believe we shall accept the case."

Miss Moone's reaction struck me as unusual among our clients. She bowed her head slightly to acknowledge Holmes's words, but gave no other sign of pleasure at his acceptance. It was as if she had known beforehand that the matter would inspire his imagination, and therefore the transaction itself was a mere formality.

"It is clear that you possess a great deal of knowledge about Ronald Bythewood's activities – far greater than the usual information a client might provide," Holmes said. "Therefore I would like to imitate your own approach, to a degree. Let us meet at the entrance of the Tate gallery at two this very afternoon, and we will begin our work reconstructing this crime."

Without a word, our guest nodded her assent, gathered her cape and made to leave, though not before casting a look of admiration at Sherlock Holmes, and a markedly more insolent flick of the eyes towards myself.

I escorted her to the door. In my determination to wrest some degree of control over the situation, I said hurriedly, "Miss Moone, these notes of yours may be a useful starting-point. Perhaps you would be so good as to show them to us later?"

She considered this, then nodded again. "Despite my earlier words, I am comfortable showing my notes to you and to Mr. Holmes. You were right: I should have brought the note-book with me this morning. I shall return home and I will give it to you when we meet. The harm contained within its pages has already been done, after all."

With that, she glided down the stairs, and I returned to my friend.

"Well, Holmes?" I said once I had heard the front door open and close. "What do you make of it all?"

"It is fascinating, but at this early stage it would be presumptuous to 'make' anything of it at all."

"But you have a notion of what truly transpired, I presume?"

Holmes rose from his seat and went to fetch his pipe from the mantelpiece. "Naturally. We will retrace Miss Moone's movements and we will endeavour to determine how the note-book could have been read by the true perpetrator of the crime. We will learn about the history, routines and eventual death of the victim, Mr. Ronald Bythewood, about whom I confess I know almost nothing. Using the outcomes of all of these observations, we will identify any differences, however small, between Miss Moone's projected method of murder and the one that was committed."

I nodded. "Unless it really is a coincidence, though I own that there seems a vanishingly small chance of that. Miss Moone's randomised manner of selecting her notional victim—"

I stopped speaking at a sharp movement of Holmes's hand.

"There are no coincidences," he said imperiously. "There is no such thing as random selection."

"But Miss Moone only moments ago informed us—"

Holmes crossed to his desk to rummage within its drawers. "We will soon know the truth," he said, "once our first-hand examination is allowed to commence." With an exasperated sigh, he turned, brandishing his unlit pipe. "At the present moment, Watson, a match is what I require most urgently!"

Rather sheepishly, I walked to the mantelpiece, retrieved the box of Bryant and May's finest, and passed it to my friend.

CHAPTER TWO

Not an hour after Miss Moone's departure, the sharp ring of the bell sounded. We waited as Mrs. Hudson attended to the matter, and presently, Inspector Lestrade of Scotland Yard emerged from the stairwell into our rooms, as furtive and ferret-like as ever he was.

"Well, then?" Lestrade said to Holmes sharply after coming to a halt in the centre of our rug.

Holmes appraised him with a wry expression. "I beg your pardon, Lestrade? I believe it is customary for the person entering another's home to state their business."

Lestrade's face fell. "Oh. I had just assumed that you would make some clever comment about my state of mind, or my recent whereabouts. That is usually what you do. It's most infuriating."

I did not allow myself to express any response to this statement, though I felt a great deal of empathy for the inspector, having been caught in such a trap earlier.

Holmes chuckled. "No, no. I'm sure that you'll tell us everything we need to know. You seem much your usual self, as far as I can determine."

I almost retorted that the heels of Lestrade's shoes were laden with mud of a particularly dark shade, and that surely that had significance for the great detective – but once again I held my tongue.

Lestrade cleared his throat. "Very well. I trust you have heard of the death of a man in Vauxhall Park which occurred yesterday?"

Now I was glad that I had not spoken at all before this point. Holmes merely raised an eyebrow. "Naturally."

"After all, it featured in the morning papers," I added hastily.

"An unfortunate gentleman named Bythewood," Lestrade said. "Not quite in his dotage, but equally not far from it. It seems he was poisoned."

"'It seems'?" Holmes repeated. "The *Times* article was very clear about that aspect."

"That is, the coroner has not yet pronounced as much, and there has not yet been time for a post-mortem," Lestrade replied. "But the evidence is clear. The man was witnessed convulsing, and he collapsed to the ground gasping and clutching his throat."

I interjected, "That might as easily be asphyxiation, from your description. The account in the newspaper gave no supporting evidence for the conclusion of poisoning."

Lestrade puffed out his cheeks. "I am told that his tongue was also coated with a white substance."

I considered this, and fell silent.

"You were told this by whom?" Holmes asked.

"The officer who was first on the scene. As luck would have it, my colleague was passing through the park at the time, so he was at the unfortunate man's side mere moments after he fell."

"And did anybody else observe him at the time of his death?" Holmes enquired.

"What about—" I began, but a sharp look from my friend halted my speech. Evidently, he preferred to withhold information about our most recent client, for the time being.

"Not to my knowledge," Lestrade replied, entirely ignorant of the silent exchange that had passed between us. "Though the park was as well populated as you might consider on a spring morning."

I looked at my friend, still curious at his failure to mention Abigail Moone.

Lestrade became more animated as he said, "It was a specific discovery of the officer that most aroused my interest, and which I hope will catch your own. It was not shown to the press."

Noting with pleasure that he now held our attention, from an inner pocket of his jacket he produced with a flourish a narrow scrap of paper some two inches in length.

Holmes darted forward to examine the note.

"Where was this found?" he demanded.

"It was discovered clutched tightly in Bythewood's hand."

"And was that where it became crumpled up?"

Lestrade stiffened. "I hope you would not suggest that I might damage a piece of evidence myself. I am not so clumsy as you believe, Mr. Holmes."

I said nothing. I knew that Holmes likely considered the simple act of Lestrade's carrying the piece of evidence loose in his inner pocket an unforgivable impertinence. He might as well have bunched it into a ball and simply tossed it through the window of our rooms.

Holding the scrap of paper lightly by one corner, Holmes moved to the dining-table and smoothed it flat, then used the weight of a lamp-base and a heavy microscope from his desk to prevent it from curling. For the first time, I was able to read the writing scrawled upon the paper. Written in a hand that immediately struck me as peculiar was the message: *D C DID IT.*

"Now, what do you make of that?" Lestrade asked in a distinctly triumphant tone. He liked nothing more than to surprise Sherlock Holmes.

Holmes did not answer, still bent low over the table to scrutinise the paper.

"What are your own conclusions about it, Mr. Lestrade?" I asked.

"Naturally, Bythewood wrote this message upon finding himself unable to communicate by any other means: an effect of the poison."

Holmes rose from his crouch. "And yet these letters are formed in a deliberate manner. Hardly the hurried scrawl of a dying man."

I looked again at the message and saw that it was true. Each of the vertical strokes of the characters was clean and unwavering. Despite this, the handwriting appeared erratic, the letters trailing oddly to the base of the note-card.

"To my eyes," I said, "it appears almost as if each letter were written by a different hand."

I was rewarded with a flash of a tight-lipped smile from Holmes, who had evidently noted the same irregularity.

"Does anything else excite your curiosity?" Holmes asked me.

I peered at the note again, bending low to mimic Holmes's earlier stance. I reached out gingerly with an index finger to touch the scrap.

"It is written upon card rather than paper," I said hesitantly, "and it has been torn from some larger piece." I pointed to the left-hand side, where a ragged edge was unmistakable despite the crumpling of the note, which had resulted in all edges of the card being curled inward.

Holmes nodded curtly, but I suspected that he was pleased with my observations.

"And what of the message itself?" I said to Lestrade. "Do you understand it?"

"The murderer's initials are D.C.," Lestrade replied promptly.

"And you are suggesting, I take it, that the victim did not write out the name in full because of his great hurry – because of the poison working its way through his body?"

"Exactly so."

"It is frustrating, nonetheless," I remarked, "though I have no doubt that Holmes will find the detail most invigorating."

"Then you will take this case?" Lestrade asked, directing his question to Holmes.

I watched my friend closely. Accepting the same case twice in one morning would be an undoubted novelty.

"Certainly," Holmes replied. "I trust I may keep this note?"

Without waiting for an answer, he retrieved a pair of tweezers from the drawer of his desk, moved aside the lamp and microscope, and lifted the scrap with the utmost care.

Lestrade appeared hesitant. I saw his eyes flick to his own jacket and suspected that he was, belatedly, suffering an attack of guilt for having carried the note loose in his pocket.

"Very well," he said finally.

"In addition, will we be permitted to be present at the post-mortem?" Holmes enquired.

"Very well," Lestrade repeated, sounding more wary. "I will inform you as soon as a time is set."

Holmes secured the note in a drawer and then paced to the window, staring out at the street and seeming to have forgotten our presence.

"Well, then," I said, and guided Lestrade to the door.

When the inspector had left, I was bold enough to approach Holmes. He remained deep in thought, still gazing out of the window.

"May I ask why you failed to refer to our other recent client – Miss Moone?"

Holmes turned to face me. "My omission was simply due to

the risk of implicating one of our clients before we know the truth. That is, before we know whether she is to be protected from harm, or whether we are to pass her over to the authorities ourselves."

"But there seems no relation between the two accounts of the case," I exclaimed. "Could we not have referred to Miss Moone simply as a witness to what occurred in the park, without making mention of the peculiar circumstances about the entry in her note-book? After all, Lestrade's message implicates somebody with the initials D.C., does it not?"

"Quite so, Watson."

"Then I fail to see…"

My friend watched me closely as my eyes darted. Then I groaned as realisation dawned upon me.

"Damien Collinbourne."

CHAPTER THREE

The very moment that our hansom pulled up before the National Gallery of British Art, and as I laid eyes upon Miss Abigail Moone standing at the head of the stairs before the grand Grecian columns of its façade, it was evident to me that something was amiss. In place of her earlier calm poise, her current manner – her neck elongated, her eyes scanning the road, her hands wringing – signalled deep concern, perhaps even panic. Though Lestrade's discovery of the note upon which was written "D C DID IT" had the potential to change everything we had previously understood about this case, nevertheless I found myself unable to behave coldly towards a woman so clearly in distress.

We ascended the steps hurriedly and I clasped Miss Moone's hands. She flinched only a little.

"My dear lady," I said, "whatever is the matter?"

She offered a weak, insubstantial smile. "Is it so obvious that something dire has happened?"

"One does not require my friend's deductive capabilities to determine as much."

Sherlock Holmes was standing apart from us, observing Miss Moone in silence. Then he turned on the spot to survey the area, particularly the south corner of the façade. Judging by Miss Moone's earlier description, it was around this corner that the drinking-fountain must be located.

"Can you tell us what has occurred?" I asked Miss Moone in a tone that I hoped was reassuring.

"I fear that I will soon be implicated personally in this matter." To my surprise, her voice was now level and betrayed nothing of her earlier panic, as if speaking it aloud nullified its power over her.

"Then you—" I began.

Holmes turned sharply to face me. His eyes flashed with warning. I understood his meaning immediately: he was instructing me not to reveal to our client the information provided by Scotland Yard. If Miss Moone noticed his glare, she said nothing of it.

"Then what makes you fear that?" I concluded.

"I am a fool for writing down anything at all," she said, more to herself than to me.

I frowned. My first response was to interpret her words to mean that she had written the note herself, though I told myself that that idea made not the least amount of sense. Then I wondered if she were referring to the work published under her *nom de plume*, Damien Collinbourne.

"It would be as well to tell us everything that has transpired, in order for us to help you," I said in the calm tone that I usually reserved for patients in a state of anxiety.

"It is my note-book!" Miss Moone replied forcefully, then clapped a gloved hand over her mouth and stared around her as if fearful of broadcasting her words to the people entering and exiting the gallery. In a much lower voice, she added, "It has been stolen from me."

I stared at her. "Your note-book? The one in which you noted your observations that prefigured Bythewood's death?"

Her gaze hardened. In a voice laden with scorn, she replied, "The very same. As you will appreciate, it has become ever more precious to me these last days."

"Was it taken from your house?" Holmes asked.

She shook her head. "From my person, immediately outside the house."

"And yet you were very clear in your statement this morning," Holmes said icily. "You claimed that the note-book never left your property, and indeed that it was held in a safe."

I released Miss Moone's hands and stepped back. "That, at least, was my doing," I said sorrowfully. "When I escorted Miss Moone to the door, I suggested that she supply the note-book to us for our examination. It seemed a key piece of the puzzle."

Sherlock Holmes is not a man generally disposed to displaying surprise or anger, and yet in his eyes I saw a flash of annoyance, though he recovered himself immediately.

"Yes, it is a key piece of the puzzle," he said, speaking slowly as though to a perpetually misbehaving child, "which is why it was imperative that it remained safely in Miss Moone's possession."

"I apologise," I said, hanging my head. "It was a gross error of judgement. I believed that whoever it was that read the note-book before performing the crime would have no further interest in its contents."

Even as I spoke, I recognised the folly in that assumption. I looked up at our client's pale face and noted the quiver of her lower lip.

"And now you believe that the note-book may be used to implicate you in this crime," I said to her weakly.

She only nodded in response.

"I do not know what to say," I said sorrowfully. "I am ashamed."

Abruptly, all trace of despair left Miss Moone's face. Now she regarded me with disdain.

Holmes ignored my distress. To Miss Moone, he said, "Tell me, what were the circumstances of the theft?"

Miss Moone now appeared to have gathered her wits entirely following her outburst. Without hesitation, she answered, "I saw no one. I turned my back to lock the front door of my house, and at that moment the bag containing the note-book was whisked away. I have no other information to give you."

Holmes's immediate response was to bound down the steps. Before I knew it, he was striding into the street to hail a cab.

I turned to Miss Moone and offered what I hoped was a contrite expression. "I take it that this means that our first line of investigation has changed. I hope you might allow us to visit and—"

But I was unable to finish my request. Miss Moone had left me gabbling on the steps. She was already climbing into the cab that Holmes had secured.

CHAPTER FOUR

"My bag was resting here," Miss Moone said, patting the top of a pillar to the left-hand side of the front door of her house in Cheyne Row. The house had an unassuming frontage, with mottled brickwork and thin vines forming a vivid green spider's web around the doorway. There was only a single ground-floor bay window and a narrow dormer window that protruded from the uneven grey tiles of the roof. The building was far lower than its terraced four-storey neighbours, appearing for all the world as if a country cottage had squeezed itself into the gap between its better-presented urban cousins. It occurred to me that Miss Moone may have purchased one of the more affordable houses in this area of the city at a point when her career was aspirational rather than yet a success. The cab had brought us along the riverfront and then the gentle curve of Cheyne Walk, a crescent which I knew had been home to many writers and artists before the time of Miss Abigail Moone and her prolific colleague Damien Collinbourne. However, I found it difficult to place this stern, strange woman within a lineage that included George Eliot and Mrs. Gaskell, and I found it impossible to imagine her entertaining like-minded artists in this squat, humble building.

"Why ever did you leave the note-book unattended for even a moment, knowing its importance?" I said, acknowledging that, to some degree, I remained eager to absolve myself of absolute responsibility for the theft. I felt that my face had not yet returned to its usual colour and that its flushed appearance must be clear for all to see.

Miss Moone stiffened. She handed me the keys to her house. "If you would be so good, perhaps you could open the door." Then she placed a hand on my arm. "Or rather, please take off your hat and *then* open the door."

Puzzled, I did as she asked. However, as I put the key into the lock and turned it, I found the door singularly unyielding. Gritting my teeth, I put my shoulder to the surface of the door and pressed, but found that in doing so I was no longer able to keep the key turned in the lock whilst also holding my hat. With a frown, I placed my hat to one side and finally succeeded in opening the door in a matter of moments.

When I turned again, my hat was no longer where I had left it. Then Miss Moone drew it from behind her back, a merry smile playing upon her face.

Holmes, too, was unable to hide his amusement. "Our client has demonstrated her point very well," he said, clapping a hand on my shoulder.

Then he spun around and walked the length of the path to the open gate – a matter of only three long strides. On the pavement, he looked along the length of the street in either direction, then turned to face a large ash tree that interrupted the paving with its broad trunk, and which cast the front of Miss Moone's house into dappled shade. Finally, he made the same three long strides to join us once again. He tapped the upper surface of the pillar beside the door, then returned to his position at the gate, and I realised he was timing his short journey.

"It would certainly be a matter of seconds for somebody to effect the disappearance of the bag," he concluded. "The aspect that most interests me remains the manner in which the culprit determined that the note-book was contained within the bag in the first place. Shall we go inside?"

He pushed past us to enter the house.

The interior was sparse and lacking in all usual traces of femininity. In every direction I saw hard, undecorated surfaces, and it struck me that our own Baker Street rooms contained more items of furniture designed for comfort than Abigail Moone's home.

Our tour of the ground floor took mere moments. Other than the entrance-hall and a small scullery, the entire floor was comprised of a single large room which contained only a dresser, an armchair, an emerald-coloured chaise-longue and a low table upon which were stacked half a dozen books. Discreetly, I glanced at their spines and was taken aback to discover that their lengthy titles evoked nothing so much as the books on Holmes's own shelves in Baker Street. One was a history of the Metropolitan Police Service, another an academic work concerning the pigments contributing to the colour of the iris. Many of them meant little to me, but the subject of one other seemed significant. It took me a moment to recall why I had heard of the name Mary Ann Cotton – then I recalled that she had murdered perhaps as many as twenty-one people in the middle part of the century, including three of her husbands, by poisoning them with arsenic.

Miss Moone was looking out of one of the pair of wide windows at the rear of the house, surveying a large, square garden that appeared singularly desolate and untended. Taking this opportunity, I caught Holmes's eye and gestured at the pile of books. Like me, he bent to examine the titles, but to my chagrin he plucked out the volume on Mary Ann Cotton – and he was still leafing through it when Miss Moone turned again from the window. For a dreadful few seconds I watched as he nodded approvingly at the contents of the book, and Miss Moone stared at him impassively, before Holmes placed it back on the pile without any display of concern.

"Is the safe upstairs?" he asked our client.

Miss Moone nodded and led the way. I followed at the rear to ascend the creaking stairs. At its head I saw that Holmes and Miss Moone had turned to the left, into a study. The door to the right was ajar and, though I flushed at the idea of spying into a woman's boudoir, I found my eyes straying in that direction all the same. To my relief, my glimpse of the room provoked not even a shred of embarrassment. Heavy-looking volumes were piled neatly on the narrow table beside the head of the large iron bedstead – and, as on the ground floor, there were no suggestions of a feminine touch to be found in any part of the room. The bedspread was smoothed and tucked in as neatly as a hospital cot and I saw no evidence of a so much as a dressing-table which might hold female accoutrements. Hardly flushing at all, I joined my colleagues in the study.

Unlike the other rooms, this one was in utter disarray – so much so that I stifled an urge to exclaim that Miss Moone had been robbed again in her absence, and that the study had been turned upside down during the ransacking. More books were piled on the desk before the window, and the shelves that lined three walls of the small space lacked any sensible arrangement, the volumes merely shoved in at any wild orientation – but the books were the least part of the mess. The desk was strewn with papers upon which were scrawled spidery handwriting and diagrams that meant little to me – some might have been untidy floorplans of buildings, whereas others were abstract or geometric pictures that suggested childish puzzles rather than meaningful notes. I summoned an image of my own neat desk at Baker Street, and even Holmes's chaotic arrangement, both of which must surely have appeared positively pristine compared to this. Even worse, the heaps of paper were interspersed with ceramic trays, plates and even glasses, all containing teetering piles of cigarette-ash. The sash window was closed and bolted, and consequently the air within the room was stifling.

"Here is the safe," Miss Moone said, indicating a squat metal box fixed to the floor, against the same wall as the door. She knelt before it, turned a key in the lock to open it, then retrieved a sheaf of documents contained within. She fanned them before us so briefly as to fail to reveal their contents, and then replaced them.

"There is only one key, which I keep upon my person at all times," she said with obvious pride. "There can be no suggestion that the safe has been infiltrated."

Holmes examined the integrity of the safe briefly, then nodded in agreement. "You say that the note-book did not leave the house – but was it ever taken out of this room, before to-day?"

"Never. It was restricted to moving between the safe and this writing-desk, and no further."

Without asking for permission, Holmes pulled back the wooden chair and sat upon it. From this position, he peered up and out of the small window, angling his head right and left. Then he stood and gestured for me to take the seat in his place. I did so and copied his actions, only to discover that the ash tree obscured all view of the houses on the opposite side of the street, from ground floor to fourth.

"Would it be nonsensical to suggest that somebody might have been within the branches of the tree itself?" I asked after a moment's hesitation.

"It would not be nonsensical in the least," Holmes responded.

"Yet, as you will observe, the lowest branches of the tree are a little over ten feet above the pavement, and there are no nearby structures that may be clambered upon to better reach the branches – which would make the route of a hypothetical climber somewhat more laboured. However, neither is it nonsensical to suggest the use of a step-ladder – though then, we must suppose the presence a second person acting as an accomplice, who would remove the ladder afterwards. We shall discount no possibility, however remote. For now, we can only tell ourselves that nobody might *easily* have observed Miss Moone writing in her note-book at this desk."

I watched Miss Moone. To her credit, she showed no dismay at Holmes's pronouncement.

Nobody spoke. To fill the silence, I remarked, "It's almost like something from one of Mr. Collinbourne's novels!"

Miss Moone smiled graciously. "Or from one of your own stories, Dr. Watson."

Holmes looked from one to the other of us. Then, without further comment on our awkward exchange, he said, "Perhaps we might retire downstairs to discuss the contents of your note-book, Miss Moone? I fear this room lacks the capacity for us all to remain here comfortably."

Downstairs, Holmes stood before one of the windows that faced the scrubby patch of grass at the rear of the house. His neck craned as he looked to one side and then the other. I fancied I could follow his reasoning: even if anybody had observed Miss Moone placing the note-book into her bag, having watched her from some hiding-place at the rear of the house, it would be no easy matter to skirt around to reach Cheyne Row itself in order to effect the theft of the bag, as the terrace of tall houses formed an unbroken barrier between the front and rear.

Presently, Miss Moone emerged from the scullery with a pot

and three cups and saucers, and she poured out coffee. I sipped my drink, but its intense strength of flavour compelled me to put the cup down on the low table and effect a permanent retreat from its noxious contents.

"We have spoken a great deal of your note-book," Holmes said, turning from the window, "yet little of its precise contents. In the absence of the item itself for us to scrutinise, perhaps you might furnish a description."

Miss Moone tipped her head back, draining her cup of the foul coffee. Without so much as a wince, she put down the cup, and then reached for a pack of cigarettes and a box of matches from the tabletop. "Certainly," she murmured, then she lit the cigarette in the languid manner of an action repeated many times each day, with no consideration of her present company. "The book was perhaps a quarter filled. You may have noticed that there are no other note-books held within the safe upstairs – that is because my habit is to burn them once the work in question is completed. No reader has any desire to observe the tortured gestation of a work of fiction. Most of the observations within my current note-book relate to potential settings and minor observations that might yet inform my ninth Collinbourne novel, and relate in no way to Ronald Bythewood, or the location or circumstances of his death. Only in the last week had I settled upon the Tate gallery as a place of particular interest, and therefore only the most recent few notes relate to the case that you have accepted. The pertinent notes are a detailed description of Mr. Bythewood – he was the first and only 'victim' that I committed to paper, despite having watched a great number of people coming and going during the week – along with an account of the hypothetical murder method. That is, a capsule of poison placed in the spout of the drinking-fountain which he would undoubtedly use. I even went so far as to sketch a map of Bythewood's movements within the Tate gallery and beyond, along with annotations indicating timings, and I marked the fountain clearly."

At this, I sensed that Miss Moone's façade was beginning to falter, though she regained control only moments later.

"And do you recall the wording of your description of Bythewood?" Holmes asked.

"I described him as a rather stoop-backed man in his middle sixties," Miss Moone replied without hesitation, "wearing an overlarge, heavy wool Norfolk jacket and unmatched black trousers." She paused, then added as an aside, "This description was written on the second day I saw Bythewood, but the description applies to all successive sightings of him, too – his manner of dress was unchanging. In my notes I went on to describe his facial features. That is, a hairline receding far from his temple, with short, startlingly white hair atop his head. I wrote a whimsical imagined account of his attempt to tame the whiskers around his mouth and below the ears, and his singular failure to address those growing from his chin. The result was a tufted crop of wild, wiry bristles that stretched far below his chin and brushed against his chest stiffly as he walked. The shoulders of his jacket and the lime-green scarf, which he unwaveringly wore despite the clement weather, were dusted with skin flakes."

I looked at Holmes. "That seems a particularly precise description of the victim, does it not? I imagine that anybody reading it, and knowing anything of Bythewood, would not fail to identify him."

"I agree," Holmes replied. "Miss Moone is to be congratulated on her precision."

"Though, for our purposes, that is not a thing to be celebrated."

"Quite so."

I looked at Miss Moone with a mixed sense of admiration

and wariness. Evidently, her powers of observation were second only to those of Holmes himself. Miss Moone's talents were fully suited to her occupation, and it dawned upon me that I could not hope to match them. I was forced to confront the truth that this pricked my professional pride to some degree – after all, nowadays I am a writer more than I am a doctor.

Before I could voice any concerns, or hint to Holmes at any misgivings, my friend said to Miss Moone, "Is it your custom to date each of the entries in your note-book?"

"It is, Mr. Holmes," Miss Moone replied.

Holmes nodded. "In that case, coupled with the fact that your handwriting is striking in terms of the formation of its characters, as I was able to examine at your desk upstairs, there is a strong possibility that you will be blackmailed or publicly implicated in the crime."

"I agree," Miss Moone replied in a remarkably calm tone. "I believe that was the exact conclusion I presented to you when we met outside the Tate gallery."

To his credit, Holmes did not react to this implied criticism in any way.

As I gazed upon Miss Moone's stern features, several notions occurred to me in quick succession. Firstly, Holmes had yet failed to mention to our client that he had accepted Lestrade's offer to investigate the very same case on behalf of the police – and, furthermore, that Lestrade had informed us about the note clutched in Bythewood's hand, which implicated somebody with the initials D.C. I supposed that Holmes must have his reasons for withholding these details from Miss Moone.

Another thought was more unsettling still. A combination of Miss Moone's oddly calm demeanour and her prodigious talent for observation – which implied a certain type of coldly logical mind – suggested the possibility that she might be taking us for fools. Was there not the remote chance that it was she who was responsible for the death of Mr. Ronald Bythewood, and that Holmes had been conscripted as part of her plan, perhaps to paint her as a victim of cruel chance? Holmes's failure to place his entire trust in our client supported this conclusion, however wild the idea seemed to me. I could not help but glance again at the book atop the pile on the low table, dedicated to the activities of a notorious poisoner.

"It is now late in the day," Holmes said, "and while I am eager for you to demonstrate the locations at which you observed Bythewood in the Tate gallery, it would be better for you to do so at the particular time of day you would ordinarily have seen him there, in order to recreate the circumstance accurately. At what time of day would have been your earliest sighting of him?"

"When I saw him enter the building, it was within a few minutes of a quarter past ten."

Her ability to specify such a precise time struck me as surprising and therefore important, but Holmes did not react.

"Then let us meet at ten tomorrow, at the same location as our previous rendezvous," he said.

Then he strode from the sitting-room and into the short corridor towards the front of the house, but turned before he reached the door.

"For the next several minutes, please do not be alarmed if you hear odd rustling sounds," he said calmly. "I shall merely be climbing the ash tree that grows outside your house."

CHAPTER FIVE

The next morning, Miss Abigail Moone was once again waiting for us at the Millbank entrance of the Tate gallery when we arrived at ten o'clock prompt. She stood before the leftmost pillar of the grand edifice, forming a black blotch against the white marble. Instead of her tweed walking-suit, to-day she was dressed in a long dark skirt, black boots and a charcoal jacket that enveloped the upper part of her body entirely. Once again, she wore no hat, and though her copper hair had been pulled back rather severely, several strands had come free to be tossed in the breeze.

"I am grateful to you for coming," she said without intonation as we approached.

Both Holmes and I bowed our heads graciously.

"Has the thief of your note-book yet made himself known to you?" Holmes enquired.

"In no way at all."

"Perhaps the robbery was a coincidence after all," I offered. "Perhaps this is simply a matter of an opportunistic thief, and the note-book was less his immediate concern than the purse within the bag?"

Holmes levelled a decidedly stern gaze at me. "I would prefer to gather all available information before we are compelled to fall back upon a conclusion of cosmic chance," he retorted.

I noted that Miss Moone, too, shook her head at my suggestion and now wore a contemptuous frown.

"I am sorry to learn that both of you would prefer to believe that a far worse outcome is the true one," I said stiffly. I walked left, passing the Grecian columns to approach the southern edge of the entrance that protruded from the building. "Shall we investigate the drinking-fountain, which I believe is just around this corner?"

Holmes put his hand on my arm to restrain me. "Having planned the timing of this tour to correspond with Ronald Bythewood's customary movements, it would seem appropriate to follow the path he took, and the correct order of events. Can we agree upon that?"

I assented, though with a superficial show of grumbling.

"So, Miss Moone," Holmes said. "To-day is Saturday. You say that you observed Bythewood within the gallery on more than one occasion – enough to determine his habits. Please, be so good as to tell us what you can."

Miss Moone nodded. "I saw Mr. Bythewood here on Monday, Tuesday, Wednesday and Thursday. Thursday, as you know, was the day of his death."

I glanced at my watch. "It is now five minutes past the hour. I believe you said that the gentleman in question arrived each morning at the gallery at a quarter past ten?"

The hardness of Miss Moone's expression, at least when it was directed at me, remained unwavering. "On the contrary. I stated that when I had occasion to *see* him enter the building, it was within a few minutes of a quarter past ten. There is a clear distinction. In fact, that observation applies only to Wednesday – though I am confident that on the two previous days he arrived at around the same time, as his subsequent movements remained unchanged."

I decided quickly that any interruption to her lecture would be unwise. "Please, continue," I said meekly.

"My very first observation of the gentleman in question was not here at the gallery, but rather in Vauxhall Park, where he would later end his life," Miss Moone said. "Even in an open environment such as the park, he stood out among the throng. Certainly, I noticed him there on Saturday, exactly one week ago, before my daily wanderings brought me over the bridge to Millbank. When I encountered him within the gallery on Monday, I recognised his lime-green scarf immediately, and noted the oddity of his continuing to wear it indoors. It is barely warranted out in the open, given the temperate days we have had."

"And before the week just passed, did you commonly frequent the Tate?"

"I had visited several times, like anybody else. But my visits had been at different times of the day – in the late afternoon, as far as I am able to recall – and before this week I had not visited on consecutive days. Therefore, I am unable to say whether Mr. Bythewood's habits extended before this week – though his familiarity with his surroundings would perhaps indicate as much." She offered a rather sweet smile, then added, "Last week my attention was centred on a number of bridges crossing the river. I had a notion that one of them might be more suitable than any other, if one was compelled to push a man over the side without attracting notice." Her eyes glittered, perhaps indicating that she was revelling in the idea all over again. "I speak merely of another idea for a work of fiction, if that was not already clear. Anyway, I would venture that I strode up and down all the bridges of the Thames last week. Ultimately, though, I put that idea aside. The method of murder was too blunt, too unsophisticated. I determined that it was not sufficiently complex to warrant the consideration of Damien Collinbourne."

"And did you note in your book that method of killing?" I asked. "Of course."

"Then let us hope that nobody falls off a bridge in the near future," I said hoarsely. "Otherwise you may be deemed responsible for their death—"

Though I stopped myself from continuing any further, Miss Moone was able to read my thoughts. "As well as Ronald Bythewood's death, you mean to say? That, I understand, Dr. Watson, is the very same wrongheaded notion that you have pledged to disprove."

I cleared my throat and checked my watch again. "Oh, look – it is nearing a quarter past the hour. Shall we enter?"

We passed between the tall columns and through a vestibule with a dizzying floor pattern, a labyrinth depicted in tiles. We emerged into an entrance-hall with a tall dome two storeys above our heads, light flooding through its glass panes. I found myself utterly overcome, as though I were entering St. Paul's Cathedral for the first time.

"It is rather grander than I had anticipated," I said to nobody in particular.

When I lowered my eyes, I saw that my colleagues appeared unaffected by our surroundings.

"It was in the Pre-Raphaelite room that I first saw Bythewood within this building," Miss Moone said. "This way, please."

She led us to the left and into the first of the gallery rooms, its walls crammed with canvases. I had little time to register more than a blur of paint, though in the next room I recognised one or two works by William Blake. Then we passed through several rooms dominated by large landscapes, then past works by Constable or perhaps J. M. W. Turner – or possibly both – before Miss Moone slowed her pace and announced, "Here we are."

The ceiling of the room in which we had come to a halt was

a long, semi-cylindrical arch that reminded me of nothing so much as Paddington station. Here, most of the canvases were large and predominantly depicted aristocratic figures draped in velvet and lace. I was grateful to Miss Moone for having identified the style as Pre-Raphaelite, and chastised myself for my ignorance. Holmes turned slowly in place, casting his eye over each work in turn, without the appearance of showing appreciation for any of them in particular.

"On Monday, I sat for some minutes here," Miss Moone said, pointing at a bench in the centre of the long room. Then she waved a hand to indicate the other patrons of the gallery, who moved slowly from picture to picture, either in couples or alone. "I confess that I was watching the observers of the paintings rather than scrutinising the works themselves. My mind was occupied with the concept of choosing a victim for murder at random – that is, I was in the early stages of formulating a novel narrative in which a criminal does just that. Mr. Ronald Bythewood passed directly before me, as did many others, and I noted his lime-green scarf, just like the one I had seen a gentleman – the same man, as I soon concluded – wearing in Vauxhall Park. I watched him from the corner of my eye, though without entirely giving up my search for other, potentially more interesting, studies. His manner became of some interest to me. At first I assumed his eyesight was poor, as he stood very close to each painting, and though at a glance anybody might assume he was an *aficionado*, his response when he came close to each work was cursory, as though reflecting his disappointment. All in all, I surmised that his movements were a product of habit as opposed to enjoyment. He remained in the room for only a short time, and when he left I found myself following him at a distance. To my surprise, when I entered the next room" – she pointed to the doorway by which we had entered – "he was nowhere to be seen. On this first occasion, I had no sense of urgency, but nevertheless I found myself peering into each chamber in the hope of spying him once again. Shall we follow his path?"

"I would be grateful if you would do so as accurately as you are able," Holmes responded.

Miss Moone led us out of the room and back through the one filled with landscapes. This time, Miss Moone turned from the main passage into a smaller room, lined with turquoise paper that lent it a regal air.

"I found him again here," Miss Moone said, "and despite my earlier assumption, now he did not stand close to any painting, but rather *here*, perhaps in order to observe the entire wall." She indicated a position close to the centre of the room, and then moved to that position and turned to face one of the two long walls of the room. "Rather than make myself known to him, I remained in the corner beside the doorway, half turned away. Evidently, he had already been in the room for some minutes before my arrival, as I overheard the final strains of an exasperated conversation between a lady and gentleman sitting upon the bench behind where Bythewood was standing" – she turned to gesture to the simple bench behind her – "obscuring their view of the works. Once they had vacated the seat, Bythewood took their place.

"The next day, Tuesday, I encountered Bythewood once again in the Pre-Raphaelite room. I anticipated his movements, arriving here promptly, and was able to confirm that he took a seat in this room immediately, as on this occasion it was already available. He also enacted the same routine on Wednesday, the day before his death."

I saw Holmes's eyes darting, but he withheld any questions for the moment.

"Please, continue," I said to Miss Moone. "What did you observe next?"

"Each of these days, he remained sitting on this bench for some minutes, perhaps to gather his strength, staring ahead of him. Then he stood and went on his way."

"Did he appear weak?" I asked.

"Let me show you."

Miss Moone sat upon the bench, ignoring the few other occupants of the room whose eyes flicked in her direction. It occurred to me that they were perhaps attempting to unravel the peculiar tableau of Holmes and me watching this young woman perform a pantomime of fatigue. Miss Moone slumped forward and crossed her arms in an awkward manner, placing each hand on the opposite upper arm, squeezing the flesh.

"Such a posture may indicate a weak constitution, or it may be simply a reflex action when preoccupied, conceivably," I said, glancing at Holmes.

My friend made no response.

"My assumption that he was exhausted was partly informed by his deep inhalation of breath momentarily before he stood," Miss Moone said. She mimicked the action as she rose from the seat. "At which time he seemed much restored."

"Then what did he do?" Holmes asked.

"He left by this door, to the west part of the central corridor," Miss Moone replied.

"Let us follow him," Holmes said with a grim smile.

We passed into the central hall – a tall passageway which I had glimpsed earlier – and Miss Moone led us along its west side, back towards the vestibule.

As she walked she spoke to us over her shoulder, in the manner of a tour guide. "On Monday, when I first saw Bythewood here, I remained in the room filled with contemporary works after he had left. I was no more interested in him than in any other visitor to the gallery. However, on the second and third days, I followed him in this direction as he made his way, in his wavering fashion, to the exit. He paid no notice whatsoever to the rooms containing watercolours, nor those dedicated to drawings, nor the special exhibitions."

We passed through the vestibule once again and then emerged into daylight. I stood between the columns, blinking rapidly to acclimate my eyes to the sudden brightness.

"Upon leaving," Miss Moone continued, "Mr. Bythewood turned right, then right again at this corner." She did so, too, and we followed. Once we had passed a long banner that stretched vertically along the side of the southernmost pillar and begun to make our way along the outer wall of the entrance-hall, which formed a promontory from the gallery proper, I saw embedded in the wall of the main building a stone, arch-shaped drinking-fountain, exactly as described by our client.

"He drank from the fountain on Tuesday and Wednesday – and on the day of his death, naturally," Miss Moone said, "and I am minded to state that he did so on Monday too."

"How can you possibly say that?" I said incredulously, "if you remained within the gallery upon his exit?"

She gazed at me, unperturbed. "Because I *did* see him less than an hour later, once I had made my way to Vauxhall Park. You are correct that it would be impossible to know whether he drank from the fountain – but, if you recall, Monday was particularly warm, and in the park I observed Mr. Bythewood pressing a damp handkerchief to his brow. I admit that it is certainly possible that he wetted the handkerchief at another location, even the one in the park itself, though at what point he could have done so, I am at a loss to say. However, given his unwavering routine on subsequent days it is more than a possibility that he dampened his handkerchief at this same drinking-fountain, before setting off towards the park."

"Upon my word," I said with a mixture of admiration and bafflement, and turned to Holmes, "you have met your match here. Perhaps Miss Moone ought to work as a consulting detective too."

Unperturbed by my jovial suggestion, Holmes replied simply, "It is gratifying to work with a client so precise in her recollection of events."

He turned to the drinking-fountain, whereupon Miss Moone indicated the place where she had lodged the gelatin capsule: between the jaws of a cast-iron lion whose mouth acted as a spout. I noted that Holmes pulled on his gloves before he operated the mechanism, and then he watched as the water came forth in an unbroken arc. He moved this way and that, observing both the water flow and the spout in minute detail.

Without turning, he asked, "Was it Bythewood's habit to run the water for any amount of time before drinking?"

"It would have been impossible for me to know," Miss Moone replied. She turned to point at the corner of the projecting entrance-hall. "From the position at which I observed his actions, his body always obscured the actual act of drinking. In more recent days, it bothered me that my hypothetical murder plot remained an imperfect one, due to this lack of certainty."

Holmes rose, nodding absently as though her statement was as commonplace as a comment on the weather.

"I assume, Holmes, you are suggesting that the capsule may have been dislodged before Bythewood even stooped to take the water?" I offered.

"It is certainly a possibility," Holmes said.

"Why, then the chances of the fountain being the source of the poison are even lower!" I exclaimed.

It was clear that Holmes did not share my sense of elation.

"What concerns us is not what is *likely*," he said sternly, "only what is the *truth* of the matter."

He turned to Miss Moone. "I would be grateful if you would continue your account of the victim's routine."

She bowed her head. "Having quenched his thirst, he would invariably walk directly to Vauxhall Bridge, though with a pace that lacked any suggestion of hurry, and then he would approach the park."

"Then we shall do precisely that, too."

As we set off down the steps from the gallery, I mused, "What strikes me about this case is that had Miss Moone selected a different victim for the purposes of her literary endeavours, then none of this might have been observed by anybody but the true perpetrator of the crime – and we would instead be beginning our investigation from a different direction entirely. And yet, here we are, retracing Bythewood's movements not only on that fateful day, but in the days preceding it. We have not yet seen his body, and we have not visited the place where he died. It all strikes me as profoundly back-to-front."

Miss Moone turned sharply. "But then, if I had not witnessed his death, I would never have arrived at your lodgings to contract you to investigate the matter in the first place."

I felt my cheeks flush. I had forgotten that Miss Moone had no knowledge of Holmes's services being simultaneously deployed by Scotland Yard.

I was immensely grateful when Holmes succeeded in changing the subject of conversation. "I confess that I am perturbed by the idea that the selection of Bythewood as a notional victim was a coincidence. Miss Moone, you have already told us that your observations of the man pre-dated your first encounter with him in the Tate gallery."

"Indeed – two days before, on Saturday last weekend, I saw

him feeding the birds in the park."

"Quite so. Moreover, you recognised him on your second encounter for more than one reason. His lime-green scarf may have been the most visible feature that registered in your conscious mind – and that alone might have accounted for your identification of him as a subject of interest. Yet there were other aspects, too. By your own account, when you first introduced this matter to us yesterday, you noted immediately that Bythewood was unkempt and elderly – and he was alone. All three of these factors already predispose him to be a suitable victim for violence – that is, to anyone minded to search for somebody for that purpose. His being alone is simply a matter of pragmatism, as there would be no need to contend with another in order to perform the deed. His advanced years suggest reduced facility of observation: another convenience for the would-be assassin. As for his untidiness of appearance, it would be natural for the unconscious mind to reach the rapid conclusion that he lived alone, and consequently that no other person would be likely to apprehend him as he wandered, nor take a personal interest in his fate – a conclusion that would be supported by the man's evident lack of urgency in his movements, and further evidenced by his preoccupation with an activity such as feeding the birds. Furthermore, you noted in passing that his manner of walking might strike the casual observer as meandering, and that he sometimes spoke to himself under his breath. I contend that your subconscious mind was itself such a 'casual observer' – that is, you might as well have been describing your own first impressions of Mr. Ronald Bythewood."

Miss Moone had been nodding as Holmes delivered this conclusion. "You are undoubtedly correct," she said. "I find it fascinating that even as I conjure in my mind characters who might err in their planning of their crimes, I myself am prone to making conclusions that are not based on dispassionate observation."

I smiled. "Nobody is," I reassured her, "save for Mr. Sherlock Holmes himself."

Miss Moone insisted on paying the penny toll for each of us to cross Vauxhall Bridge, noting as she did so that the fact of Bythewood's willingness to pay this amount each day might have acted as further evidence to her subconscious mind that he made a suitable victim, as he was clearly no pauper, despite his dishevelled appearance.

The bridge was replete with pedestrians and carriages, most of them passing in the opposite direction to us. Compared to the nearby Lambeth Bridge, with which I was more familiar and which was almost exclusively dedicated to pedestrian usage, my overall sensation here was one of crowding and claustrophobia, irrespective of the exposure to the elements and the wind that gusted through the railings. Neither did it escape my attention that the bridge was in poor repair. The piers had been removed some years earlier and replaced with a single central arch, though this work had been conducted far from satisfactorily and marks of the hasty repairs were abundant. I had read in the papers only recently that a temporary wooden bridge was to be erected alongside this one within months, in order for the bridge on which we now walked to be demolished, in preparation for a new span of concrete to be constructed. I knew that some would mourn the destruction of such a landmark; I recalled tales of crowds lining up along the bridge to watch hot-air balloons launch from the long-closed Vauxhall Pleasure Gardens, and even one peculiar account of a clown from a nearby amphitheatre sailing from Vauxhall Bridge to Westminster Bridge in a washtub towed by geese. However, such heady days were behind the city, though whether that was a cause for regret or celebration, it was not my place to determine.

Holmes and Miss Moone seemed entirely unaffected by the bustle, and I was obliged to hurry to keep up with them.

"Am I correct in concluding that Bythewood crossed the river by this same bridge each day?" Holmes asked.

"I can only say as much for certain on Wednesday and Thursday," Miss Moone replied promptly. "On Monday I failed to follow him after he rose from his bench in the gallery. On Tuesday, while I did indeed identify him in the park, that was a matter of coincidence—" She stopped speaking abruptly, perhaps self-conscious about her use of the word in Holmes's presence. "That is to say, I did not follow his precise route, and though I crossed the river by this bridge, the decision was of my own volition, as far as I can tell."

Holmes nodded and even went so far as to offer a smile to reassure her. "Then we may conclude that his route was unvarying. Except, I take it, on the day of his death?"

We had reached the eastern side of the bridge. Though I was walking behind Miss Moone, I noted her stride faltered. "But I have not yet spoken of it."

"True, but you have nevertheless told me a great deal."

When Miss Moone did not respond, he continued, "In your account of Bythewood's movements within the gallery, you noted that they remained unchanged on Monday, Tuesday and Wednesday. Due to your failure to include Thursday in that list, I conclude that on the day of his death his actions differed to some degree."

"Quite so," she replied. "Perhaps my reluctance is due to the fact that on Thursday I myself was in a heightened state of nervousness, partly on account of having the gelatin capsule in my pocket ready for deployment, and partly due to the consequent need to predict Mr. Bythewood's movements accurately. So, when he arrived at the gallery later than was his custom – at twenty-five to eleven rather than his usual appearance at around a quarter past ten – you can well imagine that I was perturbed and anxious."

"Where did you locate him, finally?"

"In that same room containing contemporary works – the room with the bench. Furthermore, he did not take a seat, despite the bench being unoccupied. Rather, he stood before it, with his hands clasped before him. As I have noted earlier, it was his custom to mouth words that were inaudible to me, and I saw him do so again at this moment. I was watching him from the doorway leading to the west corridor, ready to pre-empt his movement towards the entrance-way and the fountain – but when he made to leave, instead of heading in this direction, he walked further *into* the gallery, as if to take his usual route in reverse."

I exhaled in exasperation. This detail struck me as another aspect of events occurring back-to-front.

We continued walking along Upper Kennington Lane, and at Vauxhall Cross we turned right to make our way beneath the raised railway tracks. At each junction it was Miss Moone who determined our direction, evidently following the scheme laid out by Bythewood before her. Holmes's eyes were rarely directed ahead; instead, his gaze travelled across every building and landmark that we passed.

Miss Moone said, "At that point, on Thursday, my purpose was very nearly exposed – or at least it might have been had he not been so preoccupied. He wheeled around and stared in my direction. I froze, naturally. It took me a second or two to determine that he wasn't looking at me, but rather the doorway behind me – the one that led back into the room of contemporary works. His expression was... it did not seem to suggest suspicion, only confusion. Then he made his way to the west corridor after all."

"Then you were compelled to find a way to get ahead of him, to place the capsule?"

She nodded. "Confident once again of his destination, I passed quickly through the parallel rooms in order to emerge in the entrance-hall before him – and was able to insert the capsule into the spout of the drinking-fountain and then make my retreat, all in good time. I confess, however, that by this point my heart was racing."

Still plodding behind the pair, I wished that I could have observed Miss Moone's facial expression. It occurred to me that the racing heart of which she spoke might have been a key aspect of her custom of devising crimes. Perhaps the vicarious thrill of enacting a crime – and for the success of this undertaking to hang by a thread – might have fuelled her choice of vocation in the first instance. I confess that, in addition, another thing came to my mind: was the same conclusion, and its implicit criticism, true of my own latter-day career as Holmes's biographer? Was I equally as morbid as Miss Moone?

The entrance to the park was now in sight, which roused me from my discomforting meditation. We arrived by the north-west corner and Miss Moone led us along a curved path that took us to the rough centre of the parkland, where the path widened into a circular area containing benches and, in the middle, a tall drinking-fountain with spouts set all around its circumference. A man with a Pekinese on a lead strolled past it, his eyes flicking to the skies for a moment before he murmured in passing us that rain was overdue.

Both Holmes and I looked askance at the drinking-fountain.

"I never saw Mr. Bythewood use this fountain," Miss Moone said in anticipation of our question.

"But from the slowing of your pace, I take it that this location is significant?" Holmes asked.

"Yes. This is where he fed the birds each day. And furthermore, this is where he died."

"Let us approach these events in order," Holmes said calmly. "Precisely where did he stop to feed the birds each day?"

Miss Moone pointed to the south-west part of the open area, where a bench was angled to face the drinking-fountain from a distance of perhaps twelve feet. "He sat there and allowed the pigeons to come to him. He did not flinch even if they hopped up beside him."

We were still standing beside the bushes, where the path had brought us out. Holmes pointed at the ground. "Did you remain here, having followed Bythewood to this location?"

"Yes. That is, I did so on Tuesday, Wednesday and Thursday. When I first saw Bythewood on Saturday, I believe I was standing at the opposite side of the clearing. There was no impediment to my remaining in one place to observe people as they came and went – each day last week was far fairer than to-day and consequently there was a certain amount of bustle, but equally many visitors were content to stand by either in groups or alone, to watch others."

"He did not notice you?"

Miss Moone laughed hollowly. "I suspect that he noticed nobody, Mr. Holmes. If a herd of elephants had passed before him, it is conceivable that he might have paid them no heed."

Holmes indicated his agreement without humour. "Please, describe his actions after that point."

"There is little to tell – in relation to his usual actions. Each day he remained here for some five or ten minutes, until his supply of breadcrumbs was exhausted, and then he left by the opposite path. I do not know his movements beyond that." She pointed directly ahead, along the route that wound towards the southern gate.

"You did not follow him?"

"No. Are you about to chastise me, Mr. Holmes?"

It was clear to me that Holmes had been on the cusp of doing exactly that. It suddenly struck me as humorous that this woman's failure to stalk an innocent man might seem a matter of annoyance.

Miss Moone continued, "As I have told you, it has been my custom to stroll during the mornings, then to return to my home for luncheon and to write up my notes. Despite my selection of Ronald Bythewood as a case study, I was not minded to traipse all over the city in pursuit of him. Do not forget that no crime had been committed, and my interest in him was intellectual. Shall I now tell you of the events of his death?"

"I would be eternally grateful," Holmes replied with a warm smile.

"On Thursday he came along this path as usual – at only a little after his usual time, a quarter past eleven, despite the alteration to his schedule at the Tate. I remained standing here, as was my custom. I had observed that Mr. Bythewood's manner of walking had been more erratic than usual during his crossing of the bridge – at one point I almost called out to him as a passing carriage came a whisker's length from knocking him over. Once he entered the park, his odd movements became more pronounced, as if he were a marionette with its strings severed. Upon reaching this clearing, his gait became ever more loping, and occasionally he stumbled. I recall him crossing the clearing, passing to the right of the fountain, then veering sharply to one side. At that point, he fell to the ground. Though it may sound melodramatic to say so, he never rose again. Shall I show you the exact place?"

Holmes nodded curtly, his gaze darting around our surroundings.

Miss Moone promptly directed us to a location several feet from the fountain, approximately a quarter of the way between it and the bench on which it was Bythewood's custom to sit. There seemed nothing about the ground here to inspire interest. After several minutes of close examination on his hands and knees, watched impassively by the man with the Pekinese, even Holmes was compelled to conclude as much.

"I would be grateful if you would play the part of Ronald Bythewood," Holmes said to our client.

To her credit, Miss Moone was not at all startled by the request. "Very well," she said, and they both returned to the northern path. I watched, fascinated, and retreated to the southernmost edge of the clearing as Miss Moone emerged from behind the trees, followed moments later by Holmes, who stopped beside the bushes and monitored his quarry with narrowed eyes. Miss Moone had slowed her pace to match Bythewood's, and I saw that her face, too, was creased with concentration. At first she made directly for the bench, but then her body swung to the left, as though one of her legs was longer than the other. She corrected her course, but then swung her entire body around so that she was almost facing the fountain. At this point she staggered, swayed dramatically and slumped forward.

Despite the pantomime, I found that I could not restrain myself from darting forward to steady her. To my surprise, Miss Moone beamed up at me. As Holmes came to our side, she said, "Doctor Watson has inadvertently completed the tableau."

"Bythewood was approached as he fell?" Holmes asked in a sharp tone.

"Indeed, yes. It was a gentleman wearing an overcoat. I am afraid that I have no other description to supply – you can appreciate that my recollections are somewhat scattered."

"Is it so very unusual that somebody might rush forward to help him?" I asked Holmes, noticing his knitted eyebrows. "Anybody would act as I have acted this very moment."

The look that my friend directed at me made me reconsider my statement. I stifled a gasp. The note! Was it not reasonable to suggest that the note reading "D C DID IT" was pushed into Bythewood's hand by the very person who appeared to be helping him in his dying moments?

"Where had this man been standing before Bythewood stumbled and fell?" Holmes asked.

"By deduction, I may say that he was standing where Doctor Watson was standing – but I did not observe him before he ran to help."

"You say 'ran', rather than 'walked.'"

She considered this, then said slowly, "I believe that is correct."

Holmes turned to face the northern path. "Yet from the position in which you stood, you could have seen nothing of any interaction between Bythewood and this Good Samaritan."

I watched Miss Moone blink rapidly, and I presumed she was now gripped by this new idea – that the bystander might have played a greater part in the event than she had suspected.

"That is true," she said.

Once again, I wondered why Holmes chose to withhold the information about the note. Despite his obvious admiration for our client's faculties, it appeared that he still did not trust her fully.

Holmes turned to Miss Moone. "Thank you for the care you have taken in illustrating these most pertinent events. Now, if you will excuse us, Watson and I have some matters to address. I assure you that we will be in contact with you again very soon."

Miss Moone nodded. Then, after the briefest of hesitations, she set off along the path in the direction from which we had come.

When she was out of sight, Holmes turned and strode in the opposite direction, towards the Fentiman Road exit.

As I hurried to keep pace, a thought occurred to me. "Is it not possible that all this talk of drinking-fountains and the intricacies of Bythewood's route may be entirely misleading? Could this Good Samaritan not have administered the poison at the very moment Bythewood stumbled, at this precise location?

Bythewood was an old man, and Miss Moone has on several occasions intimated that he was frail and somewhat unsteady on his feet. Perhaps his veering from side to side was merely an indicator of age rather than poisoning."

Even as I spoke these words they seemed hollow. If it had not been for those elements of the case that I had just now suggested discounting, the very concept of poisoning would not have been our starting-point.

"We shall soon find out, Watson," Holmes replied. "This very afternoon, you and I will have the pleasure of attending Bythewood's post-mortem examination."

CHAPTER SIX

When we arrived at the examination room, we found that the surgeon had already begun his work, and was in the process of prising apart Bythewood's ribs to bring forth his heart. While I gazed upon this marvellous organ in admiration, Holmes darted immediately to the side of the body lying prone upon the table, as though Bythewood were a relation and this were a hospital bed – but though his stream of muttered words were unintelligible, I knew that he was cursing the surgeon for tampering with the body before Holmes himself had been allowed the opportunity to make an initial assessment.

"Why didn't you wait for our arrival?" I asked the surgeon, whose name was Twomey, as he lifted the heart onto a counter and raised a scalpel ready to make an incision.

Twomey performed an insolent shrug. "I am interested in this case. Regard this heart. There are few external indications of longstanding cardiac disease, which is to say, some calcification, but nothing that strikes me as significant. It is so entirely unremarkable in its appearance – at least, as befits a subject of this man's age – and yet this man's death was certainly a case of sudden arrhythmic death syndrome and a paralysis of the heart."

"But that is only a description of the manner of the man's passing," I said, feeling ever more set apart from my fellow medical practitioners. "It tells us nothing about the *cause* of his death."

"Next I shall examine the brain and we will learn whether it was damaged."

"But what of the poison?" I demanded.

"You are leaping far ahead," Twomey replied. "I have not yet concluded it was a poisoning."

I turned to Holmes, who was standing close to Bythewood's head, pressing down the chin lightly to observe the interior of his mouth. He inhaled deeply above the parted lips, then frowned.

"Is the tongue white, as Lestrade described?" I asked.

Holmes nodded and moved aside to allow me to take my turn at the mouth. Bythewood's skin was pallid, which was no great surprise given the interval since his death. His whiskers were wiry and matted, though I suspected that this dishevelment was customary, going by Miss Moone's description of his everyday appearance. I saw no lesions or extreme discolouration on his lips or around his mouth.

I confirmed that upon the tongue was a white coating.

"I believe I can detect some traces of corrosion," I said, angling the head so that light shone into the cavity.

Holmes nodded. To Twomey he said, "We must see within the stomach."

Twomey appeared surprised at this impertinence. I had never seen this man about Scotland Yard before; it occurred to me that he might not understand that he was speaking to Sherlock Holmes, or perhaps even that he had no knowledge of Holmes's importance to the police. This latter possibility filled me with discomfort. I had assumed that my accounts of Holmes's investigations had reached far enough to secure his reputation.

"As I say," Twomey said slowly, as though addressing a child, "next I will examine the brain to determine whether disease in that organ may have caused the arrhythmia which surely ended this man's life."

In my frustration I raised my voice. "But you are trifling with only the very final moments of his life. Surely what is more important is what *inspired* this death. That is, the poison that somehow made its way into his body. Whether it was his brain or his heart that failed is a secondary consideration."

I wondered whether my own attitude to such matters had changed by virtue of my association with Holmes. Might I have been as blind to significance as Twomey, before setting myself alongside the great detective and moving beyond the straightforward calling of medicine?

When I looked back at my friend I saw that he had moved around Bythewood's body to examine each of the man's hands in turn. The left was curled tight   this must have been the hand that had gripped the note that Lestrade had brought to us, and which now was in the throes of rigor mortis.

"Do not go to the trouble of scolding Mr. Twomey," Holmes said in an offhand tone. "Let him be methodical with the body. I am patient enough to allow him time to confirm what is already evident."

I sensed Twomey stiffen beside me. "You presume to have an answer so soon?"

"I will only say that I would be very surprised if my conclusion is not borne out by your examination."

Twomey snorted derisively. "Equally, I would be interested to know your theory."

Holmes took a breath as if to compose his thoughts, though I knew him well enough to be certain that they were already well ordered.

"For the last eighteen months," he said calmly, "Ronald

Bythewood has suffered from angina pectoris mild enough to have not caused cardiac arrest in the past, but conversely serious enough to inspire bouts of mild chest pain and to prompt self-treatment without resort to a general practitioner. On Thursday morning he ingested an amount of phenol that ordinarily might provoke no more than burning of the throat, but the obstruction of the blood supply to his heart amplified these existing symptoms and, after more than one hour, inspired severe shortness of breath, cardiac arrhythmia and the seizure that would end his life. When you have completed your study of the heart, an interior examination of which will reveal signs of angina pectoris, I would suggest a cursory overview of the arteries supplying blood to the heart, which will show signs of obstruction. While you may remove the brain if you so wish, I doubt that you will find anything pertinent to our case there."

Ignoring Twomey's scoffing at Holmes's statement, I looked at Bythewood's body afresh. The pallor of his skin was certainly consistent with angina, though the time that had passed since his death made that impossible to ascertain.

"These are all reasonable suppositions, Holmes," I said, "but I fail to see what gives you such confidence in your pronouncement. I suppose that you have smelled an odour coming from the mouth?"

Holmes bowed his head and stepped aside to allow me to come close to Bythewood's head once again. I leaned forward to inhale. Indeed, there was a faintly sweet scent of carbolic acid.

"Very well," I said, "but those other details elude me. How is it that you can diagnose angina so readily – and also the timescale and Bythewood's self-treatment of the disease?"

Without looking at the surgeon, Holmes replied, "It is a gross error to restrict oneself only to a narrow slice of evidence. You and I, Watson, are privy to one piece of information that supports my account – that Bythewood was prone to grasp his upper arms when at rest."

I recalled Miss Moone's playacting of Bythewood's posture when seated on the bench in the Tate gallery. It was true that an angina sufferer might experience his symptoms as a pain in the arms as readily as in the chest.

Satisfied that I had absorbed this information, Holmes continued, "But even with only this body as a source of evidence, much can be learned. The timescale, for example: regard the creases around the man's eyes. Most of these are lines gained simply by the passing of years, but observe these deeper creases that have not yet affected the elasticity of the surrounding skin. My wealth of study on the subject suggests to me that these cannot have been present more than two years ago, yet they are established enough to suggest they have been developed over more than a year – so my year-and-a-half is simply a sportsman's guess. Finally, I have said with some confidence that Bythewood has been treating his disease himself. The first two fingers and thumb of his right hand carry a sweet smell that is distinct from the odour coming from his mouth – rather more like burned sugar – which suggests the correct use of nitroglycerin to moderate his symptoms. And yet it appears to be self-administered, as—"

I clapped a hand to my forehead. "Because any general practitioner would prescribe a solution already mixed in alcohol, whereas the smell and… let me see…" I moved around to look at Bythewood's right hand. As I had hoped, the fingers that Holmes had identified had their tips stained faintly yellow. "The staining of the fingers is not attributable to nicotine, but rather nitroglycerin in its pure form."

Twomey was now standing before the body, his baleful gaze moving between the cadaver and the heart resting upon the counter-top. No doubt, after we left the examination room he would ask his superiors about Mr. Sherlock Holmes and would be told that he was far from the first to experience such marvels of ingenuity.

"By my estimate," Holmes said to Twomey, "when you examine the contents of the stomach you will find not more than a fluid ounce of phenol – an amount that might have placed another victim into a coma but would not necessarily have proved fatal. It is only due to Ronald Bythewood's particular medical circumstances that this poisoning resulted in death."

As Twomey rushed to and fro to ascertain the details that Holmes had described, Holmes himself spoke to me in a low voice. "Note also, Watson, that there is no burning of the lips. The corrosion is restricted to the tongue and, as we shall soon see, the throat and stomach."

I considered this. "Which suggests a vanishing likelihood that the poison was administered via the drinking-fountain, as there would have been some amount of droplets splashing the lips. We were told that Bythewood was not neat in his mannerisms."

As one, we turned to face Twomey, whose face was now almost as pale as that of Bythewood's corpse.

"I accept your theories as a sensible starting-point," the hapless surgeon said, "and yet I maintain there is much still to learn. For example, an inspection of the brain might provide evidence of degradation resulting in madness, which may have inspired this man to make away with himself. You cannot be sure that his death was inflicted by another."

After exchanging a glance with me, Holmes said in a forced tone of politeness, "Nevertheless, I would be grateful if you might begin with the stomach."

We moved aside and let the man proceed with his work, though I was entirely confident that his examination would only serve to prove the truth as outlined by the great Sherlock Holmes.

CHAPTER SEVEN

Once we had settled ourselves in our cab, Holmes, to his credit, did not gloat over his correct pronouncement of the conditions of Bythewood's death. He gazed out of the window, his fingers tapping constantly on the sill.

Reluctant though I was to break his concentration, there seemed too great a number of topics to discuss for me to allow silence to reign.

"Where does this leave our case, then?" I asked. "We have our method of poisoning, but doesn't that knowledge leave us further behind the truth than we had until now appreciated?"

Holmes turned to face me. Rather than scolding me for interrupting his thoughts, he nodded and I saw that his eyes were gleaming.

"I beg you, go on," he said. "It may be of some small help for you to outline the case as you perceive it."

"Well," I said, staring out of the window at the street as I recollected, "we know that Ronald Bythewood was poisoned, and yet it was cardiac arrhythmia and arrest that was the actual cause of death, as the dose of phenol was too small to cause anything more than severe burns in any other man. Therefore the poisoner must have known of Bythewood's predisposition to cardiac complaints – his angina." Now I raised my eyes to the featureless ceiling of the cab, urging my observations towards conclusions. "We can discount the administering of the poison by the drinking-fountain, and therefore we can absolve Miss Moone of any blame. However, her observations of his erratic manner after he left the gallery, and the time required for the poison to complete its work, mean that the poison must have been ingested by Bythewood before he entered the building on Thursday morning."

I lowered my eyes to see that my friend was watching me closely.

"Is there any more that we may say with assurance at this time?" I asked.

"Perhaps even less than you have already stated," Holmes replied. In response to my questioning look, he continued, "Your description of the effects of the poison appear inarguable. Yet the supposition of the timing of the consumption of the poison was not borne out by the autopsy. The burns within the throat were the principal evidence of the poisoning, yet they and the volume of phenol in the stomach tell us nothing about the time they were administered. As it was the heart that gave way, we have no way of correlating these two aspects."

I shook my head. "But you yourself warned of the importance of making use of all available evidence. Bythewood was watched by Miss Moone during his tour of the gallery. There would have been no opportunity for him to consume poison at that point."

Holmes exhaled sharply through his nostrils. "That, then, brings us to the final part of the puzzle. What is Abigail Moone's role in this matter?"

"Why, she was an innocent bystander!" I exclaimed.

Holmes laughed softly. "Need I remind you that Miss Moone was plotting Bythewood's demise?"

"That is a gross misrepresentation of her intent, Holmes," I retorted. "A simple coincidence."

Once again, Holmes stiffened at hearing the word. "It remains the case that her selection of victim was apt – more apt than I have yet demonstrated to you."

"How so? Do you have more information about Ronald Bythewood?"

"I would be a poor sort of investigator if I were incurious about the victim of a crime," Holmes said, though with no suggestion of being perturbed. "The answer to your question is yes, I have learned a little about Ronald Bythewood. Many of the details simply confirm the unconscious conclusions that Miss Moone reached through simple observation. He lived alone, at Wyvil Street, only a little south of Vauxhall Park. He was once moderately wealthy and, though he was an Englishman, he lived for the greater part of his life on the Continent, most recently in Paris, and he returned to England only when his wife died a little over three years ago. Bythewood's only son, born of a first wife who also died at a young age, twenty years before the second wife, appears to have been estranged from his father for a decade or more. In short, Ronald Bythewood lived an entirely solitary life. His suitability as the subject of a murder is unimpeachable, given his lack of any of the common relationships that may complicate such a crime."

"But it is absurd to say so," I scoffed. "You are ignoring the issue of *purpose*. Why would anybody wish to kill such a man?"

"Why did Abigail Moone wish to kill him?" Holmes replied calmly. "Her own method was back-to-front, was it not? She wished to kill *somebody*, and subsequently she selected Ronald Bythewood."

I clapped my hand to my forehead in exasperation. "But Miss Moone had no intention of actually killing the man! She had no true poison capsule. Her motive was only to map out a murder for the purposes of writing a story!"

"Equally, whoever was responsible for the actual poisoning may have had a similar motivation. Do not forget that the volume of phenol was relatively small."

I stared out of the window again, noting absently that I was no longer certain of our location. "Then it was a botched affair on the part of the attacker. Or else the phenol was self-administered by Bythewood, along with his nitroglycerin – whether by design or accident, who can say; though surely if he took it deliberately, he intended for it to kill him."

Holmes nodded slowly. "It is true that we cannot discount suicide, despite my reluctance to entertain any idea presented by that ineffective surgeon, Twomey. And yet there remains the matter of the note the Bythewood held tight in his hand, and there remains the matter of Abigail Moone."

I looked at him helplessly. "Can't you accept that Miss Moone's involvement is no more than…" I racked my mind for an alternative word to 'coincidence', and finally settled upon, "happenstance?"

"I confess that I cannot."

I groaned. "Then let us continue to approach this case back-to-front. To turn the matter around, can you not accept that the poisoner may have selected Ronald Bythewood by responding to precisely the same indicators that marked him out as a suitable victim for Damien Collinbourne's new novel?"

To my surprise, the cab came to a halt. From the window I saw the wide stretch of the Thames. I realised that we had stopped outside the Tate gallery.

"Now you are speaking sense," Holmes said as he leaped from the cab. "There are a great many more of these 'indicators', as you call them, than you realise. Come, and I shall demonstrate them to you."

By the time I had crossed the road Holmes was already at the top of the steps leading to the gallery, turning first one way and then the other. I presumed he was still preoccupied with determining Bythewood's routines before his arrival at the gallery each day.

Upon entering the building Holmes paused at each successive junction, looking along each passage and then in the direction of the rooms in which Miss Moone had told us she had first encountered her subject.

Like Miss Moone before him, Holmes led us to the Pre-Raphaelite room, then playacted being Bythewood, standing very close to each painting, pausing only for a moment, then moving along. After passing through the two connecting chambers, he emerged in the room populated with contemporary works. An elderly woman already occupied the bench; Holmes stood close beside her, at so minute a distance that she soon became uncomfortable at his proximity – but when she rose from her seated position, Holmes offered his arm to support her in a display of gallantry. As she left, he sat in her place, his body hunched forward and each of his hands clasping the opposite upper arm.

"Well?" I said testily. "You're showing me nothing I haven't been shown before."

Holmes did not react to my tone of voice. "Do you accept that Miss Moone's observations within this room were key to her selection of Bythewood as a subject of interest?"

"Certainly," I acknowledged. "He had roused her interest before this point, but it was here that she was able to study him closely and at length."

Holmes nodded. "And yet, there is far more within this room that may be observed." When I didn't reply, he added in a gentler tone, "You are in an art gallery, Watson. Look at the paintings."

I felt my cheeks flush as I turned slowly to regard the works hanging on the walls. Many were scenes from classical texts, others landscapes. I counted twenty-six frames in all, most upon the two longer walls which lacked doorways. To my untrained eye, the paintings seemed of no more interest than any of the others held within the building.

Resolving to piece together the puzzle set by Holmes, I moved nearer to the doorway leading to the west corridor, where Miss Moone had been accustomed to stand. On the wall directly opposite were two pastoral scenes – one spotted with hay bales, the other a nondescript display of rolling green hills – and a large portrait of an aristocratic character with three greyhounds at the foot of his gilded chair. I shook my head in dismay.

Of course, Miss Moone's attention would have been centred upon Bythewood. I turned to look at Holmes, who had remained in his slumped position on the central bench. Following his gaze to the wall to my right, I observed each of the ten paintings on that wall. Again, most were of rural or classical scenes that I felt I had seen many times over.

Finally, though, one caught my eye. I crossed the room to stand before it. The painting depicted a farmyard scene, with a glowering sky and a barn visible to the right-hand side. Close to the centre of the painting stood a single figure, a milkmaid. She faced away from the viewer of the painting, and the angle of her body suggested a route towards the barn, though her way was partially blocked by a group of placid-looking ducks. In one hand she carried a milking-stool; the other gripped a large metal churn. Rather than looking in her direction of travel, her gaze appeared fixed on the large pond that took up the left-hand side of the scene – almost a quarter of the canvas in total. I glanced down at the plaque below the frame to see that the work was entitled *Milking Time* and the artist was John Henry Yeend King.

I started at the realisation that Holmes was now standing directly at my side.

"How does this work strike you?" he asked.

I pointed at the figure of the milkmaid, whose face was only visible in its lower part and in profile, and the rest of her body only from the rear. Her copper-coloured hair was tied up in a loose bun at the back of her head.

"She looks the spit of Miss Moone," I said wonderingly.

"Do you think that Miss Moone herself might have noticed as much?"

I frowned. The answer to his question was less straightforward than I had anticipated. Would I know my own likeness, viewed from behind?

"It may have stirred some sense of recognition within her," I responded finally.

"I tend to agree. Now, please continue along that line of reasoning."

My eyes darted over the picture. Miss Moone, observing this scene, might have initially found herself taken by the figure – a lone woman, just as she was, and very similar in appearance – but then she, too, might have broadened her appreciation to the scene as a whole. The next most significant detail was the pond that reflected and enriched the light of the sky, and which certainly appeared to have roused the milkmaid's interest.

"Water," I said. "The body of water."

I felt Holmes's hand on my arm; he led me a few steps backward.

"Now, allow yourself to take in the other works on the same wall. Do any stand out to you in particular, now that your mind has dwelt on the figure in that first picture?"

Most of these were landscapes. Of the three that contained human subjects, one stood out more than the others. It depicted a fallen Icarus, the boy's great wings spread wide over a rock and his body slumped loosely upon this soft bed. Three nubile nymphs were in attendance, watching him with curiosity. I noted with interest that the figures were depicted at a gloomy lakeside, and that at least one of the nymphs was climbing from the water to see the fallen hero. The legend at the foot of the frame identified the painting as *The Lament for Icarus* by Herbert James Draper.

"I see that you have located it," Holmes said.

I nodded vigorously. "So is your theory that these two images, when viewed together, on more than one occasion, might have steered Miss Moone unconsciously to a method of poisoning? That is, the concepts of water and death were presented together in her unconscious mind at the very moment she was observing Bythewood?"

"Indeed. No doubt drowning would have occurred to her first – or perhaps death by failed aeronautics, if the Icarus happened to attract her before the wistful milkmaid. My expectation is that, consciously or unconsciously after following her quarry on Monday, Abigail Moone toyed with the idea of Bythewood meeting his end by toppling over Vauxhall Bridge and into the Thames. That fate would certainly have fulfilled the suggestion of a watery doom in both of these arresting images. Of course, this method of murder would present obstacles – the many people crossing the bridge at any moment, the necessity of considerable strength to push a man over its side – and we know that Miss Moone had already entertained the idea of such a manner of death for one of her stories, and then discounted it as impractical. So, naturally, her premise might stray, though with this first idea as a starting-point. A second visit to this room would undoubtedly reinforce the theme of water, and so what is left? Poisoning. Whether or not Miss Moone would have been conscious of the route of her ideas, I believe that we have described the twists and turns that her imagination took."

"It is certainly compelling," I said, taking a step away from the wall of paintings to look at them all anew. "I wonder, then, might Bythewood himself have been drawn to these same images for a similar reason?"

Holmes moved to stand beside me and surveyed the ten paintings with his arms folded – perhaps itself an unconscious echo of Bythewood's customary sitting position.

"To my chagrin, I cannot say," he replied. "Ronald Bythewood's mind remains impenetrable."

"Then what will be our next steps to learn more about him? I feel sure that that is the key to understanding the circumstances of his death."

"We will visit his rooms – but not yet. I am determined to follow the details of this case in the order presented to me, despite that order being back-to-front, as you have observed. Like you, I maintain that he was poisoned after leaving his home on Thursday morning, and before arriving here. There is more to be learned from Bythewood's daily activities, and I intend to deduce his complete habits."

"And I?" I said. "Shall I join you?"

Holmes shook his head. "We must not forget the other aspect of this riddle. Let us not discount the fact that somebody wishes us to understand that 'D C DID IT'."

"Then I should return to Miss Moone – to Damien Collinbourne?"

"I would prefer that she were under supervision, for now."

I bowed my head and left by the west corridor, my path to the exit wavering somewhat as I reminded myself *not* to ape Bythewood's movements.

CHAPTER EIGHT

Miss Moone received me with little show of surprise, and welcomed me into her home without ceremony. Nevertheless, I then found myself standing uncertainly in her sitting-room, kneading my hat in my hands.

"How was the post-mortem?" she asked, tilting her head back and yet continuing to watch me closely.

"Illuminating to some degree," I replied.

She laughed and shook her head. "That's not what I meant. I ask more about your enjoyment of the occasion."

I almost choked. "Enjoyment?"

"I have always longed to be allowed to observe an autopsy."

"Whatever for?"

"To see what you have seen. To glimpse the body long after death, to read the story that it tells over time, once the mind is departed."

I nodded, despite not agreeing with her sentiments one iota. "I can assure you that that grotesque vision is not suitable for women."

Miss Moone bristled visibly and turned away to pick up a packet of cigarettes. "And why is that?"

The rim of my hat actually buckled under the pressure of my

thumbs. "Well, because… I mean to say that nobody should be compelled to gaze on a cadaver – and yet it is necessary for—"

"For men to do so, whenever they please."

"Not in the least. Only professionals involved in the business of unravelling the cause of death."

"And yet they all are men."

I returned to the hallway and placed my hat on the rack, for fear of damaging it further. "It is a matter of suitability for the role, Miss Moone. I'm sure you are not campaigning for just anybody to be permitted into a mortuary, to indulge any whim that may enter their heads."

Miss Moone stared at me for a long while. The tilt of her head and her habit of gazing along the length of her nose reminded me of nobody so much as Sherlock Holmes, despite the dissimilarity of their features in every other respect.

"I would prefer you to call me Abigail," she said, "and if you do, I will call you John."

"I do not see why that would—"

"Sit down, John," she said.

She took the armchair that faced the window. I watched in mute shock as she lit her cigarette with a match, inhaled with a sigh of satisfaction, then leaned forward to push aside the tower of books upon the low table. As she settled back into the chair she placed her stockinged feet on the table.

I gulped audibly, then turned to the only other seat remaining: the emerald chaise-longue. Sitting upon it was an alien experience – I was reluctant to employ its curved headrest, and the result was that I sat perched upon its very tip as though it were merely a stool.

"We are on equal footing," Miss Moone said.

While I did not agree with her, I found myself bowing my head in assent.

She continued, "But you must accept that you have certain advantages over me. That includes access to the mortuary and other realms reserved for a certain type of gentleman. And it also includes access to the greatest mind in the city. I realise that I have not yet told you that I have enjoyed your stories very much, John."

I flushed. "And I yours, Miss Moone."

"Abigail."

"Abigail."

"I am interested in your work. To what degree is your work a transcription, and to what degree are you a compositor of fiction?"

"I have no claim to the art of fiction," I replied immediately. "I merely put down the facts in an orderly manner, as best I can."

"With no embellishments?"

Holmes had often criticised my accounts on these very grounds. "With as few embellishments as possible."

"You resist the lure of flourishes? Of insights that neither you nor Holmes possessed while conducting your investigations? Of neatness that exists only in fiction?"

"I certainly try to resist all of these."

Miss Moone's expression darkened. "Then perhaps we have less in common than I imagined."

I considered her words for some moments, then ventured to say, "Do you suppose that these embellishments that you are prepared to insert into your stories... that they are responsible for the great popularity of Mr. Collinbourne's novels?"

"Undoubtedly. But that does not make them valuable."

"From what I have heard of the royalties, that does not seem true."

A sly smile appeared on Miss Moone's usually stern face. "Surely a gentleman does not discuss money?"

"Yes, but—"

She held up a hand. "I understand. I have confused you, by

my frankness and by my being a woman."

Abruptly, I felt an urge to flee. Something about Abigail Moone's manner recalled a beast in its lair – lascivious and lazy, prepared to wait until its prey wandered near before striking. I told myself that this interpretation was inspired solely by my embarrassment.

Miss Moone continued speaking, ignoring my distress. "Perhaps we are inverted images of one another, John. I sense that you are in thrall to the idea of writing more popular works. I, on the other hand, have grown to disdain that sort of flim-flam. I confess that I would prefer to write more informed works – like yours."

A peculiar idea crossed my mind. Wishing to dispense of it as quickly as possible, I blurted out, "Anybody might conclude that you were petitioning to take on my role as Holmes's biographer."

She didn't respond immediately, but then the smile returned. It was wide now, rather than small and sly, and to my mind, entirely unreadable.

"Clearly, that position is not vacant," she said finally. She stretched her arms and slipped languorously further down into her armchair. The toes of her feet upon the table wriggled. "So, will you tell me what you learned of Bythewood?"

I almost thanked her for changing the subject of conversation. "It was phenol that killed him. A small amount, but enough to inspire cardiac irregularities and then total arrest—"

I broke off, gazing at her.

Her head tilted once again. "I believe I can read your mind, John. You're questioning yourself as to whether you ought to divulge this information to me. I am your client, but clearly I am embroiled in this case, and to some extent implicated in the crime."

I recalled the note reading "D C DID IT." Might she already know of its existence? Or worse still, might she have written it herself?

"Not at all," I replied. "As you say, you are our client and it is natural that I report to you. I am happy to say that the findings during the autopsy preclude poisoning by means of the drinking-fountain, as the span of time from that point to the moment of Bythewood's death would not have been sufficient."

"I am pleased to hear it," Miss Moone said, though in truth she sounded anything but happy. "Shall we drink to this development?"

Without waiting for my answer, she stood and padded in her stockinged feet to the scullery. Still thinking of the note clutched in Bythewood's hand, I reached out to pluck the uppermost of the volumes from the pile of books, which appeared to be a philosophical treatise whose title meant little to me. Nevertheless, I leafed through its pages, though only absentmindedly, and without paying heed to any page in particular. Before setting it down I stopped at the first page, where, as I had hoped, I found the name *Abigail Moone* inscribed. The handwriting was an untidy scrawl. While the words on the note found in Bythewood's grasp had been written in capital letters somewhat idiosyncratic in their formation, that handwriting had been a model of acceptability compared to this mishmash of left-slanting characters. I felt certain that a graphologist would conclude that Abigail Moone's hand made her a case ripe for study.

When Miss Moone returned, she carried a tray containing two glasses, a tall bottle and a carafe of water.

"For many years, Ardbeg whisky has been the only drink I have in the house," she said without any trace of apology. I imagined her, alone each evening, drinking whisky imported from the isle of Islay, surrounded by her books and nothing more. To my surprise, I attributed no shame to this vision. It was simply the life that she preferred.

She curled up in the armchair, now resembling a house-cat

rather than a ferocious beast. She nodded at the tray. "You can be mother."

Cheeks burning, I poured whisky into both glasses.

"Be so good as to add water to mine," she added. "I've had two neat already this afternoon."

Obediently, I added water from the carafe to one of the glasses. As I lifted both drinks and handed one to Miss Moone, I inhaled the distinctive scent of the Hebridean whisky, though I found its potency diminished as Miss Moone received her glass and raised it in a mock salute to me.

I sniffed at my glass again. It was a peaty single malt, with hints of smoke or even chocolate. Though I detected a trace of the same scent that I had noticed moments earlier, it seemed changed and certainly less powerful. My eyes raised to Miss Moone, who was watching me with a merry expression on her face.

I bent to the carafe of water and inhaled – then my eyes widened in shock when I saw that Miss Moone's glass was now touching her lips.

"Stop!" I cried out, lunging forward and almost upsetting the bottle on the table. I swatted the glass from Miss Moone's hand, sending it skittering onto the bare floorboards beyond the rug. Liquid sprayed from the glass and onto the wall of the hallway.

Miss Moone recovered herself quickly. "John, whatever is the matter?" she said in a remarkably cool tone.

I gaped at her. "I smelled phenol. I am certain of it."

She gave an indulgent smile. "Your mind is at work even when there is no requirement for detection. Phenol is released in the lighting of a peat fire, which makes its way into the malted barley. It is entirely safe, I assure you."

I shook my head vigorously. "I am speaking of the *water*."

With an expression of wonderment, she bent to the carafe and inhaled. Then she gasped in surprise, and nodded.

"But how?" she said weakly.

I rose and strode to the scullery, then immediately crossed to the sink and wrenched the tap. It juddered and spat out a thin stream of water. Careful not to come too close to the liquid, I lowered my head and inhaled. Then I turned to Miss Moone and gave confirmation with a nod.

"From where does your water come?" I asked. "Is it fed by the mains supply?"

Miss Moone shook her head. "The system has not been improved since the house was built – which was too long ago for mains supply, and yet it was built at a time too long after the surrounding houses to warrant the work required to access the nearby spring, as they do. There is an outside tank originally intended for collecting rainwater, which is nowadays kept replenished at frequent intervals with well-water."

"May I see it?" I asked grimly.

She showed me through the rear door into the bare garden. Its unloved lawn was surrounded by a path upon which were a collection of heavy ceramic pots that contained dry soil but no evidence of any plants. As I turned back towards the house, to my surprise, I discovered beside the door a large glass case with its base stained with soil marks and its walls streaked with glimmering lines of mucus. Within the case were several dozen small objects, all shifting noticeably as I watched. Noticing my amazement, Miss Moone said, "I have always kept snails. They are quite the finest pets."

Blinking in wonderment, I followed her indications to locate the cold-water tank on the far side of the rear wall of the building, above and to the right of the scullery window.

I was about to ask for some means of raising myself to look into the tank when I spied a step-ladder leaning against the wall.

"Is this ordinarily placed here?" I asked.

"Here or hereabouts," Miss Moone replied. "The only person who has use of it is the boy who brings the water. His last visit was on Monday." Then, pre-empting my next words, she ran her hand lightly along one rung of the ladder and said, "Yet I see that it has been used far more recently than that."

Indeed, while the ladder steps held nothing that one might describe as a footprint, upon the outer edge of more than one of its treads was smeared orange, claylike soil. A cursory survey of the garden was enough to satisfy me that this soil came from its bare centre, where the grass was particularly sparse.

I pulled on my gloves, then put the step-ladder in place to ascend it to the height of the tank. Its lid came free easily. The moment it was loosened, the now-familiar sweet smell of phenol assaulted my senses.

Miss Moone did not even ask for confirmation of the poison – my expression must have told the tale. She crossed the lawn to gaze along the length of the fencing at the rear of the property. I replaced the lid of the tank, then descended the steps to follow her. There were no gaps between Miss Moone's home and the buildings on either side that might allow access to her garden from the street. Close to the rear fence we came to a halt at a patch of trailing wild nasturtiums that appeared somewhat trampled. While there was no evidence of the fence above the plant having been climbed, there seemed no impediment to an intruder entering the garden by this route. Craning my neck to look over the fence, I saw a townhouse with a garden that backed onto Miss Moone's. Along the side of this building was an access route from the street beyond.

"I have never had been concerned at the notion of burglars attempting entry from the rear of the house, as the back door is very secure," Miss Moone said. "I had never considered that somebody might access only the garden in order to cause mischief."

Then she turned to me and took my hands.

"Thank you, John," she said simply.

I did not meet her eyes. "It was nothing at all," I assured her.

"What shall we do now?"

"I can arrange for the water to be purified, and this fence reinforced somehow."

"That's not what I meant."

The reality of the situation struck me finally. "You are under threat," I said, feeling foolish that the need to safeguard her had not been uppermost in my mind. Somehow she seemed capable of scrambling my wits.

"I must confess I find it rather exciting," Miss Moone said. In response to my questioning look, she added, "Any event in my life represents an opportunity to conduct research for my work, to some degree. But rarely do events adhere so closely to the tone and content of my stories. I am sure that I am learning a great deal, at this very moment."

"But it is not safe here. Surely that is more urgent than your research?"

"No doubt you are quite right. Then you are suggesting that we ought to leave, to find safer territory? If you will stay and guard the ground floor, I will go upstairs immediately to pack a bag."

I nodded stiffly, dimly aware that I was once again being drawn towards a conclusion that was not fully my own.

CHAPTER NINE

When we arrived at Baker Street, Holmes greeted us with polite formality and murmurs of sympathy as he listened to my account of the events at Miss Moone's house in Cheyne Row. His stiffness was mirrored by Mrs. Hudson when I asked her to replace the bedclothes of my bed, which would to-night be reserved for the use of Miss Abigail Moone. When Mrs. Hudson's work was complete I showed Miss Moone in, and she surveyed my room with a strange mixture of fascination and disdain.

"It is late," I said, "and you have had a trying experience to-day. I'm sure that you will prefer to go to sleep immediately."

"Not in the least," she replied curtly. "I always find that unusual experiences enervate the imagination rather than subdue it. Don't you?"

I glanced behind me to see Holmes seated at his desk, visible in profile as he bent over an open book. At that moment I felt unsure whether my desire to speak to my friend alone was a matter of professionalism, or simple pique at Miss Moone's impertinence with regards to my position as Holmes's biographer.

"I'm afraid that I don't," I replied. "I confess that I am very tired and will sleep as soon as I my head touches the—"

It occurred to me that I had not yet prepared a sleeping place for myself. In my embarrassment, I went so far as to perform a pantomime of a yawn. "Well, if you will excuse me."

Miss Moone did not retreat into my room far enough to allow me to close the door.

"As I say, my mind is alert," she said. "If I am to be relegated to this room, might I trouble you for something to drink, and a paper and pencil – and a book to read?"

I nodded and hurried to my desk, taking a pad and pencil from its drawer. When I turned I found Miss Moone standing directly behind me, one hand cupping her chin as she gazed at my collection of books in their case.

"What would you recommend?" she asked.

I cleared my throat. "Most of these are straightforward medical texts or historical accounts. I have little in the way of fiction."

Miss Moone traced a finger along the spines on the upper shelf, then stopped at a slim volume.

"Then I will take this one to read, if I may," she said.

To my surprise, I saw that the volume she drew from the shelf was a work attributed to Damien Collinbourne.

She gave a broad smile. "I find it very soothing to read my own work – it is like hearing the voice of a close relation. At first I will set my mind to writing, but this will be the ticket when I turn my ambitions towards achieving sleep."

She stood there for some moments, watching me and clutching to her chest the book she herself had written. Then she turned and made her way to my bedroom.

When the door had closed after her, I attempted to compose myself. Holmes's gaze remained fixed on the book lying open on his desk. I was just about to call out to him when my bedroom door opened again. I blinked at the sight of Miss Moone wearing a plain white nightgown, her hair loose around her shoulders.

Without saying a word, she crossed the room and passed through the opposite door. I winced at the sounds of the bathroom in use.

Finally, she passed me again, offering only a nod as a good-night.

After some minutes, Holmes rose from his chair and joined me before the fireplace.

"Well?" I said, then glanced at the door to my bedroom and moderated the volume of my voice. "Well, what do you make of it all?"

"I presume you are referring to the attempted poisoning of our client?"

Holmes seemed to possess a remarkable ability to speak softly but retain all of his usual clarity, as if his thoughts were being broadcast inside my head. I recalled Miss Moone's comment about the soothing qualities of the voice of a close relation.

"Naturally," I replied. "You have not told me what you believe it signifies. At the very least, it removes all doubt that Bythewood's murderer was inspired by Abigail's writings."

For the first time, I saw a hint of exasperation in Holmes's expression. "It indicates that our culprit is a poisoner by habit – which I agree is further evidence against the concept of random chance. However, I draw your attention to the fact that this course of events represents a further puzzle."

"It all seems quite straightforward to me," I said, "and though that doesn't make the situation any more palatable, at least our case has become notably less back-to-front in this respect. The culprit fears that Abigail may expose him in some way, and so he has resorted to silencing her." I grimaced, realising that I was continuing to use Miss Moone's first name, after her earlier insistence.

Holmes nodded, though it seemed far from a confirmation that he agreed with my statement. "That would be consistent with the outcome – the result of silencing Miss Moone, that is. While

Ronald Bythewood was killed by the phenol he ingested, Miss Moone, who has no weakness of the heart, would have suffered burns of the throat but certainly would not have perished."

In the flurry of the day's events I had not considered this fact. Certainly, the amount of poisoned water I had added to Miss Moone's whisky would have caused severe distress, but not her death. Had she drunk a full glass of water from the scullery tap it may have been enough – but in that case she would have tasted its peculiar sweetness immediately, and surely would not have consumed the remainder.

"Yes… silenced," I said wonderingly. "But only her voice would have been silenced. She would have remained free to tell anybody what she knew by writing it on paper – that is her trade, after all."

"Quite so. Perhaps that means that the murderer has no particular fear of her speaking out, after all."

"Then may this not be a simpler matter still?" I said. "Consider the method of murder detailed in Abigail's note-book. Having been inspired by this concept in some way, the poisoner then became determined to threaten Miss Moone, to prevent her from revealing the origin of the plan."

"For what purpose?"

I looked down at my hands in my lap. "I confess I do not know."

Holmes shook his head. "There remains the additional issue of the note gripped in Bythewood's hand. If indeed it was placed by our helpful bystander, our 'Good Samaritan' – who may or may not have been the poisoner himself – this seems to indicate an ambition of implicating Miss Moone in the crime in the first instance."

I continued along this same line of reasoning. "In which case, why then try to poison her rather than follow through with that plan?" I stared at Holmes, then gasped as a thought struck me. "Furthermore, why was the note-book stolen *after* the poisoning of Bythewood, and yet not exploited? Surely the note-book was taken as part of that original ambition to place all suspicion upon Miss Moone?"

Holmes did not respond, but it was clear that his mind was occupied with this same quandary.

"Holmes," I said slowly, hardly wishing to ask my question, "do you still fear that Abigail may have played a part in Bythewood's murder? That her plan was truly an intention to commit a crime, rather than an intellectual exercise?"

Again, Holmes failed to reply. He steepled his fingers and exhaled deeply, staring into the fire.

My eyes strayed beyond his bowed profile, to the closed door of my bedroom.

CHAPTER TEN

Despite the discomfort of my half-reclining posture in the window seat, I managed to sleep. The sun was already high in the sky when the clink of cutlery roused me from my slumber. I had slept in my clothes and the inside of my mouth had the texture of fur.

Pulling aside the curtain that separated the recess from the main part of the room, I saw Mrs. Hudson standing before the table, putting the final touches to the arrangement of breakfast-things. She had brought in a third chair, presumably taken from her own rooms downstairs, and had placed it opposite the one in which Holmes now sat.

Mrs. Hudson did not flinch as she surveyed my dishevelled appearance.

"I didn't know what the young lady likes, so I've brought more of everything," she said, indicating the array of foodstuffs on the table. "Perhaps you might ask as to her preference, if she's to stay another night?"

When Holmes did not reply, I was on the cusp of assuring our landlady that that would not be the case, but then something made me hold my tongue. However, a twinge in my lower back made me wish fervently that Miss Moone might be in a position to vacate my bed that evening.

"Thank you, Mrs. Hudson," I said as I saw her to the door.

I turned to Holmes. "How on earth did you pass me without waking me, when you left your bedroom?"

"I would have been surprised had you awoken even if I had fired a pistol," Holmes replied merrily. "From all appearances, your dreams were animated – you were murmuring in your sleep constantly."

"Nonsense," I said. "I have always been a light sleeper."

I glanced at the third chair at the table. "Our guest has not yet risen?"

"No – and it is fortunate that you have roused yourself before Miss Moone. It will give you the opportunity—"

He broke off as the door to my bedroom opened. Miss Moone emerged wearing a different outfit to that of the day before: a cream-coloured suit that, in my opinion, would have better fitted a man. Her collar was open at the neck. Miss Moone did not acknowledge my goggle-eyed stare, and Holmes seemed barely to notice the change in her appearance.

Miss Moone held before her a folded sheaf of paper, my copy of her own novel set on top of it like a paperweight. Addressing Holmes, she said, "Might I trouble you to place this in your safe? I am sure you must have one. Recent experience has made me only more cautious to protect my notes relating to my work."

Holmes stood stiffly and took the bundle from her, then nodded curtly and withdrew to his bedroom. I wondered whether he might leaf through the pages of notes before he placed them in the safe. Miss Moone must be aware that he might decide to do so at any time.

Upon his return, and without betraying any suggestion of his plans being disturbed, Holmes said, "Both of you would profit from reading the second page of to-day's *Times*." He indicated the newspaper set upon the table at his place.

Miss Moone reached the paper first and remained standing as she opened it, so I was forced to look over her shoulder to view its contents.

Even before I read the headline, the accompanying images told me everything I needed to know about the contents of the article. The first was a photographed reproduction of a handwritten list in which several phrases stood out immediately:

> - wears a lime-green scarf in all weather;
>   perhaps a gift from a loved one -

> - capsule containing poison [NB determine
>   type & dosage] placed in fountain
>   spout -

> - habitually alone and unnoticed by others;
>   nobody much would care if he were
>   killed -

The second image, perhaps even more alarming, was a faint oval portrait of none other than Abigail Moone.

The article was titled:

REAL IDENTITY OF DAMIEN COLLINBOURNE EXPOSED – INVOLVEMENT IN SUSPICIOUS DEATH

I cast my eye over the beginning of the article, which read:

The literary world has been shaken this morning at the revelation that the prolific writer Damien Collinbourne is nothing more than a *nom de plume* – and that the true author of the works attributed to that name is a Miss Abigail Moone of Chelsea. Furthermore, and representing a far greater shock to anybody of reasonable sensibility, newly unearthed evidence connects this secretive author to the death of Mr. Ronald Bythewood in Vauxhall Park, as was reported recently in this publication. Notes written in her own hand suggest the involvement of this 'ghost-writer' in the until-now mysterious crime – as the above reproduction of pages from the author's own note-book illustrates. Scotland Yard detectives are confident that—

I was prevented from reading further when the newspaper fell from Miss Moone's hands. She put one fist to her mouth as though she were choking.

This time I did not rush to support her, and I found myself standing inert, watching Holmes's reaction as much as Miss Moone's. He gazed at her, unblinking and clearly fascinated, as though he were a theatre director assessing the performance of his leading lady during a rehearsal.

"This is a double blow," Miss Moone murmured. After a few moments of silence she added, "But surely nobody would permit my note-book to be used as evidence. It was stolen from me, and must have been supplied to the police anonymously. I grant you, the similarities between my account and the crime are notable, which was why I was concerned in the first place, but—"

"The police possess other evidence that supports the conclusion suggested by the entry in the note-book," Holmes said, his eyes never straying from Miss Moone's face.

"Yes?" she replied weakly. "What is that?"

"Bythewood was clutching a note in his hand," Holmes replied. "This one, as a point of fact." He turned to his desk and took from a drawer the slip of paper that Lestrade had brought to Baker Street. When he spread it upon the table, Miss Moone gasped and tottered back, first one step and then another.

"Who wrote this?" she asked in a quavering voice.

Holmes did not reply. Once again, he was watching our client closely, his lips pursed.

I replied for him. "As yet, we do not know."

"You have had this paper in your possession for some time?" Now it was my turn to fall mute.

Miss Moone nodded rapidly, several times. "I understand. You do not trust me. That is only right."

Holmes said, "This scrap of paper alone meant nothing to the police initially – but in combination with the note-book furnished by whomever it was who burgled you, the note will now appear to be compelling evidence to support the notion of your guilt."

Miss Moone nodded again, this time sharply and lacking any trace of self-pity. "I know that you have a close working relationship with Scotland Yard. I am a fool for imagining that I might command your entire loyalty."

We all froze at the sound of the ringing of the bell downstairs. Holmes answered my silent question with a subtle shake of his head.

Then he said to Miss Moone, "You may be more comfortable resting a while longer in the room allocated to you." Without waiting for her response, he ushered her into my bedroom and closed the door firmly – then returned swiftly to the breakfast-table.

In response to a gesture from Holmes, I had just taken

my seat at the table when the door to our rooms opened and Mrs. Hudson escorted in none other than Inspector Lestrade of Scotland Yard.

"I apologise for interrupting your meal," Lestrade said. Then his eyes lit upon the copy of the *Times* still lying open upon the table. I grimaced as I realised that the newspaper was angled away from both Holmes and me, unnaturally so.

"Not at all," Holmes replied cheerfully. "It is always a pleasure to speak with you, Lestrade."

For the first time, Lestrade displayed a suggestion of wariness, and it occurred to me that Holmes might have overplayed his welcoming attitude. Crossing to the table and tapping the open newspaper with an index finger, Lestrade said, "I see that you have read of the recent developments in the Bythewood case?"

"It is a fascinating turn of events," Holmes replied.

"Beggars belief, doesn't it?"

"And you are quite convinced that this note-book points to the poisoner?"

"Naturally. Might anyone possibly suggest otherwise, having seen this evidence? Do not forget the note that was found in the victim's possession."

Holmes hummed thoughtfully. "I grant that it does appear straightforward."

"Perhaps not," Lestrade said, then appeared to relish making us both wait before he added, "One aspect in particular frustrates us."

"Oh?"

"The author in question – she is missing from her home. I came directly from there, having secured a warrant to enter and search the place."

Involuntarily, I glanced at my bedroom door. Surely Miss Moone must be listening to this conversation, her blood running cold at the idea of the police ransacking her home.

"It looked very much like a bag was packed in a hurry," Lestrade continued. "The bedroom wardrobe was open, clothes scattered on the bed. More unsettling still, there were signs of a scuffle downstairs. A smashed glass on the floor, and another untouched glass of whisky on the sitting-room table. So, not only did Miss Abigail Moone get wind of the need to flee, it would appear that she had an accomplice to boot. Or some sort of partner in crime, anyway. Given the signs of a struggle, it's possible that the relationship is far from harmonious. Perhaps…" His eyes lit up. "Perhaps that note was written by this other fellow, and he is actually an adversary of Abigail Moone's!"

Holmes received this information with a stoic expression, his eyes never moving in my direction. "There seems a great deal of conjecture in that proposition. What do you intend to do now?"

Lestrade gave a hollow laugh. "Well, here I am, aren't I? I hoped I might prevail on you to provide any new information that you have uncovered in the course of your investigation, which will now be directed towards securing the arrest of Abigail Moone." His eyes travelled over the open *Times* again, then settled upon the book that Miss Moone herself had placed there when she had emerged from my bedroom. He lifted the book, peered at the spine, nodded, then leafed through the pages. "I've read a couple of Collinbournes myself. Rattling good yarns, they were. Awful to imagine now what kind of a mind produced them. Then again, that's artists for you, I suppose. Writers in particular – lost in their stories, with no sense of the real world around them."

Silently, I prayed that he would not look at me. Then, when he did, I responded with an artificial smile that was little more than a baring of the teeth.

"So, gentlemen," Lestrade said, "what are your feelings towards Miss Abigail Moone? I mean to say, have you any ideas about how we might track her down?"

I tried to catch Holmes's eye, but he merely reached for a slice of toast and munched a corner of it. When he had finished chewing, he said, "My dear Lestrade, I know that I have provided you with swift results in the past, but do you now expect me to supply information about the location of a person of whose existence I have only this last hour been made aware?"

I froze. This was new territory indeed: Holmes was lying outright to the police.

Lestrade sighed and bobbed his head. "My apologies, Holmes. I'm rattled about the turn this case has taken, that's all. Anyway, now you know all that I know."

And a great deal more than that, I thought soberly.

"What about your investigation into Bythewood's death?" Holmes asked. "Has that yielded any results?"

Lestrade shook his head sorrowfully. "Much of it has been made irrelevant now that it is all but certain that Miss Moone poisoned the water of the fountain in Vauxhall Park – Bythewood would have passed through the same park after he left his home each morning, then again on his return journey."

Holmes's eyes flashed momentarily. "More conjecture?"

Lestrade's cheeks coloured. "We uncovered a number of witnesses who can attest that Bythewood customarily spent some part of his mornings on the west bank of the river."

"I would be grateful if you could supply precise details."

"Well… in actual fact, the witnesses are limited to three locations – firstly, a neighbour on his street maintains that he left his house at eight o'clock prompt each morning, and then there are the bystanders in the park itself, and in addition a couple in the Tate art gallery at Millbank. They were very clear about the matter, mind you, recalling Bythewood immediately when my officers provided the description of an elderly man wearing an overcoat and a lime-green scarf. The gallery is an irrelevance, though. If you know of a means of poisoning a fellow while he's strolling around looking at paintings, I'd be glad to hear it."

He drew himself up to his full height. "I have been talking a great deal. How goes your own investigation?"

Holmes grimaced wryly. "I regret to say that the details I have unmasked coincide entirely with those that you have just now provided. We, too, found evidence of Bythewood's visits to the Tate gallery, and as yet we have determined no other location – and, like you, I have dismissed the gallery as the location of the poisoning."

I could not prevent my eyes from widening, and I was grateful that neither Holmes nor Lestrade noticed my hopeless expression. If Lestrade had seen it, I felt certain that he would divine my guilt immediately; my restless mind conjured an image of him turning our rooms over in his certainty that we were hiding secrets from him, then finally flinging open the door of my bedroom and coming face-to-face with Abigail Moone herself. Surely then he would be compelled to arrest all three of us immediately.

Lestrade took a deep inhalation of breath and stuck out his lower lip in an expression of defeat. "I suppose I shall be on my way."

It occurred to me that his faith in Holmes had been severely shaken; he must have hoped that a visit to Baker Street might yield results where his own investigation had faltered.

"I trust I can continue to rely on your assistance in this matter," he added, "with our mutual attention now shifted to locating this authoress, Abigail Moone?"

Holmes bowed his head courteously. "Certainly. In the first instance, I would be grateful if we might conduct a brief examination of Bythewood's quarters."

"Why?" Lestrade replied bluntly. "We've passed that point, surely. We know who we're after."

"But there is the matter of her reason for murdering the man."

"Ah. Yes, my men have scoured the place, but you are welcome to visit it. If you will accompany me, I will arrange for one of my constables to escort you there and open the place up."

Holmes waved a hand at the overflowing contents of our table. "We have not yet breakfasted, Lestrade. Once we are finished here, we will be happy to meet your man at Bythewood's home – I am aware of the address already. Ten o'clock will be a suitable time."

Lestrade's cheeks flushed once again. After glancing at our breakfast-things as though he had never seen such foodstuffs before in his life, he paced to the door, an unsettled expression on his face. I could not recall a time when a visit by Lestrade to our rooms had rewarded him with less new information – nor a time when a meal had apparently formed an obstacle between Sherlock Holmes and a new line of enquiry in a case.

"Very well," Lestrade said when he reached the door, gripping the frame as though he was reluctant to leave. Then he said again, "Very well," and finally made his exit.

Some minutes after Lestrade's departure, Miss Moone emerged from my bedroom once again.

"I am very grateful to you for not giving me up," she said, addressing Holmes.

"Doing so could only have compromised my ability to resolve this matter satisfactorily," Holmes replied without inflection.

"And you still intend to do just that?" Miss Moone asked. I sensed a different question beneath the surface of the spoken one: *Do you intend to prove my innocence?*

"Naturally," Holmes replied in surprise.

I stepped forward to stand directly before our client. "Do not assume that this is only because you are paying for our services," I said, resisting the impulse to grasp her hands. "You would not have approached us in the first instance had you not been innocent of the murder of Ronald Bythewood."

As I said these words, my eyes strayed to Holmes, whose face was impassive.

"I am grateful to you," Miss Moone said again. She ran her fingers through her wild hair. "Though I confess that I feel rather lost. This morning my name has been connected with a heinous crime, and my *nom de plume* – my *other* name – has been destroyed... I confess that I am not certain which is the worse development."

I cleared my throat. "As for the second of these, perhaps it is no calamity at all, in the longer term. Perhaps notoriety might increase the volume of sales of your books."

Miss Moone glared sharply at me, and I regretted my lighthearted statement immediately.

"I accept that all publicity is good if it is intelligent," she said in an icy tone, "but do you imagine that the discourse surrounding Damien Collinbourne at breakfast-tables this morning is likely to be intelligent?"

I opened and closed my mouth, unable to formulate a reply that would be both encouraging and true.

"What seems clear to me," Miss Moone continued, "is that somewhere out there is a man who wishes me ill. He has known for some time of my double identity as Damien Collinbourne – as does everybody in the country, as of this morning. He knew, somehow, of my plans to write a novel inspired by the imagined death of Ronald Bythewood, and he hoped to exploit them. He has stolen my note-book with the aim of exposing me as the author of a real crime rather than a fictional one. Lastly, and in my mind far from least, he attempted to murder me in my own home. When I first came to Baker Street to consult you, I presented you with a riddle that seemed only tangentially to involve me – that is, I was a bystander with a peculiar but tenuous link to the poisoned man. Now it appears that I stand at the very heart of the case."

Holmes nodded in agreement. "It is fascinating, is it not? Do you draw any conclusions about this change in your circumstances?"

I expected Miss Moone to retort that drawing conclusions was Holmes's task, but instead she said simply, "Not yet. I look forward to more information coming to light."

It struck me that she was a remarkable woman – calmer and more analytical than any I had ever known. At the same time, however, it crossed my mind that these were qualities that made her less trustworthy, rather than more so.

"You will insist, I assume, that I must not be seen in public?" she said.

"Quite so," Holmes replied.

"And that I should remain here?"

"I cannot conceive of any location that would be more suitable. Certainly your own home is out of the question, and you have no family in London, and the homes of your friends would all be unsuitable for a variety of reasons."

Miss Moone stared at him for a time, but did not question his reasoning. After a few seconds she confirmed his deductions – if that is what they were, as opposed to suppositions – with a curt nod.

"I am glad that you trust me well enough to allow me to stay here," she said.

Holmes withdrew without responding. I heard his footsteps as he descended the stairs, leaving Miss Moone and me alone.

"What shall I do, while you are both investigating in my name?" she asked.

"You told me yesterday that all events in your life represent a form of research," I said hesitantly. "I'm sure that if you can let your mind settle, this experience will prove inspirational for your work. Is that not how you spent yesterday evening after you retired?"

She exhaled softly. "Yes," she replied, though now I did not know whether or not to believe her.

When Holmes returned, Mrs. Hudson was at his heels.

"Miss Moone," he said, "you have already met our landlady, Mrs. Hudson. She has agreed to stay with you in our absence, while you are confined to these rooms."

Miss Moone offered a slight bow to Mrs. Hudson, whose expression was one of studied neutrality. I could only imagine what were her true opinions of our unusual guest.

"Ah," Miss Moone said wryly to Holmes, "now I see that your trust only extends so far. Very well. I am sure, Mrs. Hudson, that you and I will become great friends, rather like prisoners sharing a cell."

If Holmes noticed the cynicism in her tone, he did not show it. He clapped his hands and then turned to me. "Well, let us make our way to Bythewood's quarters. If we arrive early we will have the opportunity to examine the exterior without the distracting presence of one of Lestrade's men."

"But—" I began, gesturing at the table laden with breakfast-things. My stomach rumbled at the sight of it all.

Holmes was already at the door. He turned and looked at me, one eyebrow raised interrogatively.

Miss Moone moved around the table and, once again, took my seat. She placed both hands on the tablecloth, took stock of the array of food, and beamed with approval.

"Let me just fetch something," I concluded in a weak voice. I crossed to my desk, turned away so that my body would obscure any view of my actions, then locked the top drawer and pocketed the key. Then, without meeting Miss Moone's eye, I joined Holmes at the doorway and indicated that I was ready to leave.

CHAPTER ELEVEN

It was evident at a glance that Bythewood's home on Wyvil Street was in poor repair – even more so than the rest of the terraced buildings alongside it, none of which appeared at all hospitable. Bythewood's property was located almost at the end of the west side of the street, and beyond its corner and to the left of a dilapidated church, I saw a timber yard positioned directly behind it. Even had the yard not been visible, its existence would have been indisputable, as the abrasive sounds of sawing and the calls of workers filled the air.

Bythewood's home was a blunt-faced building constructed of sickly yellow bricks all crumbling at the corners, and the window-sills seemed to rain brick dust even as I watched. There was barely a fleck of paint on the wood of the rotten sash window-frames. Furthermore, the windows on the ground floor and first floor were curtained with drab fabric, and all of the panes except the uppermost dormer window in the eaves of the pitched roof appeared opaque with grime.

A policeman stood conspicuously at the peeling door of the property, his arms folded, surveying us as we approached.

Holmes bounded from the cab to clap the man on the

shoulder. "I trust you have been expecting us? No need to follow us in." Then, without waiting for a response, he pushed past the constable. I attempted the same manoeuvre, but almost collided with Holmes, who had stopped abruptly to examine the door handle. He teased from its fixing a strand of light-coloured thread. Pocketing it, he entered the building. I followed hurriedly, flashing a grimace of apology at the baffled constable, who, in spite of Holmes's instruction, followed us into the hallway.

The corridor smelled strongly of mildew, and I found myself holding my breath as we passed into a murky dining-room. Here, the table was cluttered with used crockery which, in some cases, bore clear evidence of previous meals. Two diagonally opposite legs of the table were set upon warped books of varying thicknesses. The paper of the walls was discoloured, and the only thing that hung from the picture-rail was an outsized mirror that was so fogged as to be rendered useless. Holmes stood before the fireplace mantel to examine a small brass clock that lacked any housing, and I saw immediately that it was worthless – it had only one hand.

"I take it that nothing in the house has been disturbed?" I asked the constable.

The policeman gazed around the room, focusing on the cigar ash that covered the surface of the stacked plates and the tabletop like a layer of fine dust.

"Wouldn't have known where to start looking in all this mess," he concluded wearily.

The conditions in the adjoining kitchen were equally dismal, and the cupboards were bare other than a few packets that were so old that any markings that might identify their contents had worn away. A breeze whistled through a crack in the window above the filthy sink. I raised myself up a little and peered through the window to see a patch of scrubland that reminded me of Miss

Moone's garden. Beyond this area, and without a fence to separate the properties, was the timber yard where I could make out the workers' sawing actions that corresponded with the constant background drone that reverberated through the house.

When I emerged from the kitchen I found Holmes stooping over a sideboard, upon which was set a tray containing one glass decanter half-filled with liquid, and another that was empty save for a residue at its bottom. Alongside these decanters were two upturned glasses which, in contrast to everything else in the room, appeared clean. Holmes lifted the stopper of one decanter and then the other, inhaling and then replacing them. Without comment, he moved on towards the sitting-room at the front of the house, the door of which we had passed as we entered. Before following him, I repeated his actions at the sideboard. The half-filled decanter contained cognac, whereas the empty one smelled faintly of citrus fruit.

The sitting-room was rather more homely than the dining-room, simply by virtue of there being no detritus of meals within it. Dust – or perhaps the remnants of cigar ash – hung in the air, only visible in the knifing of light that penetrated the curtains. However, the two armchairs arranged before the fireplace appeared relatively welcoming. One of these had clearly been favoured by Bythewood: its cushions sagged where the other once-identical chair bulged, and a footstool was placed within reach of its occupant.

On a narrow table beside the armchair was a pile of three books. I bent to read their titles, and drew back with a gasp.

"These are all Damien Collinbourne novels!" I exclaimed. "And it's clear that Bythewood had been referring to them only recently!"

I whirled around as the constable cleared his throat behind me. "In point of fact, that was my doing, sir."

I gazed at him, askance.

The constable's cheeks reddened. "Given this morning's news about the true identity of Damien Collinbourne, I hoped to prove some sort of a link. I took the liberty of locating these volumes and took them down from the shelves."

I turned around to regard the bookshelves that lined the wall opposite the fireplace. Holmes was already in the process of examining their contents, having ignored my exchange with the constable. I could see the three gaps where the policeman had removed the volumes – it was clear that the novels had not been placed together, and two had been located close to the floor, as though ignored.

"It doesn't mean much, I suppose," I said, failing to disguise the bitterness in my tone. "Collinbournes are so popular that you'd have a fair chance of finding a copy in any home you might choose to search."

The constable responded with a wistful smile; he must already have reached the same conclusion. Nevertheless, I leafed through each of the three novels in turn, scrutinising them for any distinguishing marks – but there were none.

Partly to disguise my disappointment, I watched Holmes search the shelves methodically, his head moving smoothly from side to side as though it were on rails. On occasion he took out a book and opened its covers, then promptly replaced it on the shelf. I noted the titles of three of the books he withdrew: one was a history of John Wesley and Methodism, one a collection of biblical Apocrypha, the last a volume of fairy tales.

"What attracts you to those books in particular?" I asked.

Holmes waved a hand dismissively. "A passing fancy, nothing more." He stood back from the shelves, arms folded, and regarded them all together. Then he clucked his tongue and said, "Shall we investigate the upper floors of the house?"

The stair carpet was almost bare in places, and the steps creaked with every footfall. Holmes paused on the landing, gazing at the floor, and I saw that this rubbing away of the carpet continued up the second flight of stairs, which presumably led to the attic, whereas where the carpet continued towards the single door on the first floor it appeared relatively unblemished and its colour was its original crimson. After glancing at Holmes for approval, I approached this door and pushed – then winced as it struck my shoulder sharply. It had opened only a few inches and then stuck fast. I tried again, and this time succeeded in pushing most of my upper body through the gap.

Once again, only a thin slice of daylight entered the room through a single narrow gap in the cloth that covered the left-hand window, and the second window was entirely obscured. The room was large and, I assumed, comprised the entire front half of this floor of the building. The contents explained why the door had failed to open fully. Items of furniture were scattered around the space – I made out two mahogany cabinets, a large mirrored armoire, a spindly *bonheur-du-jour* writing-desk and even a four-poster bed with its columns intact but its upper panel and curtains missing. Clearly, these pieces served no useful function; they were arranged in such a haphazard fashion that none of them were accessible, and the armoire had been placed directly before the left-hand window, blocking most of the meagre light that would otherwise have shone through it. Directly behind the door, and preventing me from opening it any further without great effort, was a low bench that might have suited being placed in a porch, to aid putting on one's boots. The most peculiar aspect of the room was that the furniture need not have filled the space to such a degree; it was only their careless abandonment that made the room inaccessible.

I moved aside to allow Holmes to look into the room. When

he withdrew his head, he simply nodded and then turned to make his way up the narrow flight of stairs leading to the attic. I glanced into the dusty room once again, then pulled the door; as I did, the movement elicited a whirl of dust that rose upon the surface of a nearby table and seemed to travel like a miniature tornado. I shuddered at the sight without quite understanding why, and closed the door fully.

The state of the attic was a great contrast to the abandoned first-floor room. Daylight streamed through the single window in the protruding dormer structure that I had seen from outside; it had no curtains but its panes were clear of dirt. Compared to the other dank rooms within the house, this small space had the light, refreshing atmosphere of a conservatory – and indeed, to my surprise, I saw that upon a low table to one side of the dormer area were two potted plants and a tray of something rather like grass. Though I confess that my knowledge of agriculture is scant, after only a few moments of inspection I was able to ascertain that the potted plants were members of the *Fabaceae*, or pea, family, and that the tray contained some sort of barley. When I announced my findings, Holmes stared at the plants for some time in silent contemplation.

While there was only a single bed within the room – the idea of transporting the four-poster up the narrow attic stairs was absurd – it was carefully made up, with two woollen blankets folded and placed neatly at its foot.

I gestured at these blankets. "It must be deucedly cold at night," I said. "That window's seen better days and must let in a great deal of air if the wind's blowing the right way – or the wrong way, if you take my meaning. What could have driven the old man to use this floor as his bedroom, rather than the first floor?"

"It is an interesting puzzle, is it not?" Holmes responded. "Perhaps it was simply a matter of the furniture downstairs having already filled that room, leading him to take this room as his own out of necessity. However, my brief research shows that this property was unfurnished before Bythewood took it in the winter of the year 1895, which suggests that the items we saw belong to Bythewood himself. It appears that the decision to house the furniture downstairs, and in such a fashion, was a conscious one."

Beside the head of the narrow bed was a small set of shelves which doubled as a side-table. Holmes knelt before it to examine the titles, muttering, "Another Collinbourne, I see." Then, in a rather more animated tone, "Aha!"

I frowned in confusion as he withdrew from the shelves a rather battered clothbound Bible, then sat upon the bed to leaf through its pages.

"Why did you exclaim at finding this volume?" I asked, recalling the titles he had examined downstairs.

Holmes only shook his head in response, and soon finished rifling through the pages. "A mere whim." With an undisguised display of dejection, he returned the book to its rightful place.

I crossed to the dormer window, bowing my head to avoid the diagonal beams that protruded from the plaster ceiling. A cloth fixed upon one of the fastenings had evidently been used to clear the glass. I peered through the window but saw nothing more interesting than an elevated view of the houses opposite – which appeared like smaller versions of Bythewood's home, with the same steep-pitched roofs – and a glimpse of assorted rooftops to the east, as far as the treeline that marked the southern periphery of Vauxhall Park.

Finding nothing of interest, I turned to survey the attic room, but in doing so my forehead struck one of the beams. I swore aloud.

"It is as well that Bythewood wasn't a tall man," I said

unhappily. "Or do you suppose his back became stooped because he chose to live up here in this garret?"

Holmes didn't reply, and took my place in the cramped dormer area. Presently, he turned and strode to the door of the room, bobbing his head at intervals in a fluid avoidance of the beams. Then he marched downstairs again.

When I caught up with him on the ground floor, he was standing at the point where the open dining-room funnelled into the hallway, looking at a series of pegs that were affixed directly to the wall in place of a proper coat-rack. Upon the pegs hung a short tweed jacket, a ragged black tailcoat and a moss-coloured cardigan, and two bowlers were balanced precariously above. Holmes lifted each hat in turn, standing on his tiptoes to peer at the pegs. He took the tailcoat from its place, rummaged within it, replaced it upon its peg, then performed the same action with the tweed jacket. This time, he withdrew from somewhere within its interior a scarf that appeared a similar colour to the cardigan. Without betraying any response to his find, Holmes replaced the jacket and then hung the scarf on the same peg, now draped upon the shoulders of the jacket.

Then, without speaking to me or to the constable still waiting in the dining-room, he walked in silence to the front door and let himself out.

CHAPTER TWELVE

To my surprise and no small sense of perturbation, the following day Holmes informed me that he would prefer to conduct the next part of his investigations alone. Looking back from a latter-day vantage point, it is clear to me that the presence of Abigail Moone at Baker Street was the obstacle to my remaining there. After Holmes's hailed cab had departed, I followed in another.

Holmes disembarked at the foot of Bessborough Gardens, the junction to Grosvenor Road and Millbank, and strode along Grosvenor Road. I lost him for some moments, but then saw him once again at the head of the steps of the Tate gallery. Something struck me as unusual about his posture: his back appeared stooped, and anybody seeing him for the first time would have said he was a foot shorter than his true height. When he turned to look from side to side it appeared a distinctly laboured action, as if moving his neck or manipulating his spine caused him not inconsiderable discomfort. I realised with a start that, like Miss Moone before him, he was playacting the part of Ronald Bythewood.

As Holmes turned fully, albeit stiffly, at the head of the steps to survey the bridge and the river, I ducked behind a stationary hansom cab, not fully understanding my own impulse for secrecy. I understood that Holmes must be attempting to conjure a particular state of mind, and that my presence would have interrupted it – but, equally, was I not a part of the investigatory team? Might there not be some usefulness in my acting as an external observer of the actions of this pantomime Bythewood – that is, could I myself not playact the part of Abigail Moone?

My mind was made up the very moment that Holmes loped into the gallery building. I broke into a jog to cover the remaining distance along Grosvenor Road, chiding myself that Miss Moone had first glimpsed Bythewood each day *within* the gallery rather than out here on the street. I bounded up the steps two at a time, passed through the columns to the right-hand side of the façade, and then slunk around the vestibule counter-clockwise. From the foot of the central hall I saw Holmes padding along the west corridor, his head bowed and his left hand clutching at his left upper arm.

I darted left, following the same route by which Miss Moone had led us on our first visit to the gallery, and passed rapidly through the series of chambers without so much as glancing at any of their occupants or contents. When I reached the Pre-Raphaelite gallery I swung around but saw no sign of Holmes – his slow pace had ensured that I had arrived before him. Giddy and with a thrill running throughout my body despite this entire exercise being a pretence, I slipped into the room beyond the Pre-Raphaelite room and stood in the relative darkness at its far wall in order to observe the view through the wide doorway, ready to leap to one side to avoid being seen should Holmes glance my way.

However, when he arrived his head was still bowed, and I almost believed that he would not be capable of raising his eyes to look at me even if he so desired. As described by Miss

Moone, this replica of Ronald Bythewood then passed around
the periphery of the Pre-Raphaelite room, standing close to each
painting in turn but betraying no interest in any one painting
over any other. I saw one or two other visitors to the gallery
scowl behind his back as he obscured their view.

Presently, he left the room. I dashed across the chamber
and then slowed to a creeping pace as I reached the doorway,
keeping to the left, behind the door frame, to allow me to watch
Holmes's progress out of only my right eye. He did not stop in
the next room, but nevertheless his progress was slow, and it
dawned upon me that I had been gripping the frame of the door
for almost a minute and that people around me were beginning
to watch me with quizzical expressions. Ignoring them, I made
my way into the next room and then directly to the opposite
doorway as Holmes passed through it, growing more confident
that he was so deeply embedded within his role that he would
not turn to look at me.

In the penultimate room Holmes turned left, a slow, deliberate
manoeuvre that seemed to demand great effort. He was now within
the room dedicated to contemporary works, which Holmes – the
true Holmes, standing upright and with his faculties undimmed
– had demonstrated was filled with items of significance to Miss
Moone as well as, presumably, to Bythewood himself.

I watched from outside the doorway as Holmes took his
place on the single bench, then adopted Bythewood's peculiar
sitting posture, slumping forward and gripping both upper arms
with the opposite hand.

His body was as motionless as if it were stone, and I now
found myself confident enough to edge into the room, slipping
along the nearest wall to a position in the left-hand corner,
behind the bench, from which location Miss Moone herself had
watched Bythewood. Here, I was able to mimic absorption in the

two nearest paintings whenever anybody happened to look my way, whilst still keeping Holmes in view.

By all accounts, my friend appeared utterly exhausted, all trace of his usual agility having left him. I felt a flash of annoyance that none of the half-dozen people shifting around the periphery of the chamber appeared to take heed – surely they ought to enquire whether he needed assistance? Nevertheless, I marvelled at Holmes's ability to sink as deeply into a character so very unlike his own.

I looked to the wall of paintings that Holmes faced. There was the milkmaid with her churn, contemplating the wide pond as though in the grip of a dream. Then I gazed at Icarus, whose relaxed posture made him appear almost grateful at having fallen from the sky only to find himself surrounded by water nymphs, no matter his apparent proximity to death.

Then I allowed my gaze to move to the other paintings on the wall. The works depicting human activity included an ethereal vision of Mary's annunciation (I wondered if the flowing blue robe around the Angel Gabriel might have been another prompt to Miss Moone towards water as a suitable cause of death), then two young girls in nightgowns lighting paper lanterns in an overgrown garden, then a whimsical image of a woman shielding a windblown man with her cape as he attempted to light a cigarette in the lee of his battered top hat. Most of the paintings, however, were not portraits; the landscapes relegated their human subjects to a small part of the overall composition. In one, a farm labourer sat beside a brook, sheltering beneath a tree laden with blossom. In another, a barely distinguishable figure emerged from thickets and bracken, the landscape turned golden by the winter sun such that the hillside appeared aflame. Another wintry vision showed a shepherd surveying a small flock of sheep half-immersed in a snowdrift; the irregular stone wall behind the shepherd reminded me of Scottish landscapes. The sole depiction of city life, conveyed with broad strokes and smudges of oil paint, showed people bustling along a narrow street crammed with shopfronts, weaving amid carriages, a narrow church spire in the background. Finally, my gaze settled upon a wide seascape. Yachts and schooners dotted the ocean, though the majority of the canvas was swallowed by the calm sea itself and the streaks of clouds in the dawn sky.

Might one or more of these paintings have held significance for Ronald Bythewood? It seemed likely, but none appeared to be any more striking or important than the others. I watched Holmes, trying to determine whether his gaze was fixed on a specific work, but his stoop-backed posture and baleful, bobbing stare made divining his subject impossible. Anyway, I reminded myself, he was simply playacting the part – he was not really Bythewood. I was in danger of allowing myself to become carried away by the parts we were playing.

Nevertheless, when Holmes rose I stifled a gasp of alarm and then turned to the wall as if scrutinising the painting that hung there, which depicted a young flower-girl displaying a basket of wares in Trafalgar Square. Out of the corner of my eye I saw Holmes get to his feet rather unsteadily, still clutching his left arm. Thankfully, he did not turn in my direction, but instead he followed his preordained path to leave the chamber and enter the west corridor of the central passage.

Which version of Abigail Moone was I to enact? The version who first saw Bythewood on Monday morning and who remained in this room when he left, or the Miss Moone of Tuesday and Wednesday who followed behind him, or that of Thursday who stole ahead of her quarry in order to secure the false poison capsule in the spout of the drinking-fountain?

Again, I scolded myself for my foolishness. Holmes might

well have good reason to play at being Bythewood, but my own charade had not been requested and may have been entirely without merit. I was skulking in the shadows because I was spying on my friend against his wishes – and also due to my growing distaste at the idea of confronting a woman whose nature I could not fully determine, whose presence at Baker Street struck me as being rather like a foreign body within my bloodstream. I had no delusions that I would uncover any new evidence in this process.

So, with a lighter step borne of a new sense of inconsequence, I moved into the central passage of the building. Holmes was not yet at its far end, and I found that I now experienced a thrill at following him, scurrying across the hall to the east corridor, then slipping behind columns to continue to observe his progress. This was a rare opportunity to experience possessing information about an ignorant Holmes. Eventually, I positively enjoyed the act of pursuing him. When he passed through the front vestibule of the building and then emerged into the sunlight, I scampered in his wake like a child.

Upon exiting, Holmes dutifully turned right towards the drinking-fountain. I found myself at a loss to determine where Miss Moone might have stood to view Bythewood using the fountain. The head of the steps lacked any hiding-places, and though I might peer around the base of the southernmost column of the façade, I feared immediately that doing so might appear suspicious to others.

I tried to channel the mannerisms of Miss Moone herself. What would her approach have been? She was not someone who would readily hide in public. More likely, she would behave ever more brazenly, confident in her ability to argue her innocence should anybody accost her, perhaps even feeling contemptuous of the suggestion that her activities were in any way unacceptable.

Having reached this conclusion, I moved into the open to stand well beyond the corner of the building, and watched Holmes pass along the outer wall of the entrance-hall. Despite my decision, I found that it required no small degree of bravado to remain standing in this manner, and did not know what to do with my hands in order to affect an air of nonchalance.

Just as Miss Moone had noted, Holmes's body blocked any view of the drinking-fountain as he bent over it. I confess that my stomach lurched momentarily as the fancy took me that he had ingested the poison capsule – curse my imagination! After several seconds of lapping at the water – or at least miming that act – Holmes rose stiffly once again. I stepped back behind the columns and waited, allowing him to pass and feeling again the intoxicating sensation of having successfully played a childhood game of hide-and-seek.

I suffered no more crises of confidence as I pursued Holmes across the toll bridge, keeping my distance and yet maintaining a line of sight with ease despite the great number of pedestrians and vehicles. By the time we descended to Upper Kennington Lane I felt confident enough to walk directly behind Holmes, at a distance of some twenty feet, without resorting to ensuring there were obstacles between us.

By the time we approached Vauxhall Park I found myself cursing Holmes for his insistence on maintaining Bythewood's slow, tottering pace. I refused to believe that he had learned anything in his dogged adherence to the elderly man's mannerisms. Several times since passing Vauxhall station I had daydreamed of cupping my hands around my mouth and calling out, "Hurry up there, for God's sake!"

Once within the park, though, I resumed my close observation of his movements, as though these moments might really be his final ones, and as if I really was in the peculiar position of anticipating and witnessing his death. Holmes's gait had become ever more unsteady, and frequently he passed from one side of the path to the other, several times throwing out a hand to grasp the trunk of a tree or an overhanging branch, and at one point missing his target and stumbling off the path entirely – at which point I had to stifle the urge to rush forward to assist him. Might Miss Moone have noticed some similar fumbled movements in Ronald Bythewood and yet failed to approach him?

Holmes's meandering became more and more pronounced as he approached the clearing that contained the benches and the central fountain. I held back at the point where the path opened out, my fingernails digging into my palms as I steeled myself to watch Holmes die.

His crossing of the clearing was excruciating to watch. One of the benches was occupied by two elderly women in conversation, and a gentleman wearing a suit and overcoat was passing on the opposite side of the fountain. While each of them glanced at Holmes, none of them afforded him a second look despite the obvious difficulties he was experiencing. Holmes went to the right of the fountain as though heading towards the bench on the opposite side, but then his feet seemed to develop intentions of their own, and he veered suddenly towards the fountain. His abrupt motion startled a group of birds perched upon the fountain, and a couple of them took off, flapping wildly, in my direction. I did not allow my gaze to stray from Holmes, who stumbled away from me a couple of steps, arms outstretched, and I noted that his left hand was closed into a fist. By now, the suited gentleman had left the clearing, and the fountain itself seemed to have hidden Holmes from the two women sitting on the bench – in any case, neither of them so much as looked in his direction.

His stumbling became an outright fall – but then Holmes came to a halt, suspended oddly as though something invisible were propping him up. Then I almost struck myself on the forehead. Of course – he was acting out the moment when a bystander, or conceivably the poisoner himself, had rushed forward. Holmes's head dropped, perhaps mimicking watching the man rifle in his pockets and then extricate the note from his left hand.

Aghast as I was at watching this spectacle, I barely noticed the bird fluttering towards me until it had almost collided with my head. Perhaps it was only because my nerves were in a heightened state that I lashed out with my hand and cried out at the same time, successfully scaring the beast and driving it away; it fluttered far above me and came to roost in the high branches of a birch.

Holmes swung around sharply, all trace of his mimicry of Bythewood's posture disappearing instantaneously.

We stood there, frozen in this odd tableau, staring at one another.

Then Holmes beamed at me, as though we were lifelong friends who had not seen one another in many years.

Somewhat reluctantly, I approached him where he stood beside the fountain.

"You have been following me for the entirety of my performance," Holmes said.

Though I noted that it was not precisely an admission that I had followed him unseen, I replied, "Yes. Are you not annoyed?"

"Not in the least. Did you profit from the experience?"

I hesitated. "I don't know. I will have to consider it. And you?"

"Immensely, Watson, immensely!"

Perhaps it was only the transformation from Bythewood to my familiar Sherlock Holmes, but somehow he seemed more vital than I had seen him for some time. His eyes darted, looking first at me, then at the place where I had been standing, and finally he turned to survey his immediate surroundings once again.

"I suggest that we celebrate our reunion by retiring to some pleasant location to enjoy a light lunch," he said abruptly. Then, without waiting for my response, he clapped me on the back and set off at a rapid pace towards the southern gate.

CHAPTER THIRTEEN

To my surprise, Holmes escorted me across the river to Pimlico, ignoring my protestations that there were equally many fine establishments south of the river. The very moment we entered the restaurant on Lupus Street, he took off his coat, then moved with peculiarly short, slow paces towards the waiting valet and pressed the coat into the man's hands. I offered the valet an apologetic smile as I shed my own overcoat, then followed Holmes into the restaurant proper.

I started by ordering the soup, but then Holmes held up a hand to the waiter and said, "That will be all, other than a pot of coffee."

"What?" I exclaimed, but nevertheless allowed the waiter to withdraw. "I know you promised me a light lunch, Holmes, but this seems rather absurd."

"I promise that you will be fed," he replied.

Knowing perfectly well how much Holmes enjoyed mystique, I left it at that, though my stomach grumbled.

"So, you said that your time spent as Bythewood was fruitful," I said. "Would you care to detail your findings?"

Holmes frowned. "To a large extent, it was not fruitful in

the least. Have you yet had time to determine whether your time spent as Miss Moone was of use?"

"I would hardly—" I began, then thought better of protesting. "It was an interesting experience, to channel another person in that way. But on reflection I confess that I learned nothing that I did not know already."

Holmes nodded. "The simplicity of this case is perhaps its undoing."

I could not help but bristle at the suggestion that the situation might even appear a trivial matter, in any sense. "And yet every piece of evidence that we have unearthed seems to elicit yet another question. Furthermore, we continue to appear to be working backwards, continually anticipating the murder rather than seeking to uncover its cause. It makes me long for a scenario in which we might be shown a body and work from there."

To my surprise, Holmes did not scold me for this assessment. Instead, he nodded again, even more solemnly.

When my soup arrived I felt distinctly self-conscious consuming it while Holmes sat back in his chair, sipping coffee and watching me, yet still I managed to polish it off. However, the moment I set down my spoon he signalled to the waiter and settled the bill.

"Thank you for a most enjoyable meal," I said in a tone of undisguised sarcasm.

Holmes smiled in acknowledgement as though my statement had been sincere, then stood and marched to the front desk to collect our coats.

Outside, we had passed only two or three shopfronts when Holmes stopped and looked up at a rather shabby-looking wood-fronted building with an awning of faded stripes. After a moment's deliberation, he led me inside. When I saw that it was another restaurant, I protested at his choice of premises, but he had already removed his coat and hung it on a stand.

I looked around at the stained tabletops and torn wallpaper and said in a morose tone, "How much am I allowed to eat this time?"

"Feel free to order a main course, Watson."

I scanned the menu, then let my gaze pass over the few customers sitting at other tables, each of whom sat alone. None of the plates of food that sat on the tables before them struck me as at all appetising. When the waiter emerged from a cloud of steam at the kitchen doorway, I ordered only a basket of bread and more coffee.

Feeling certain that nobody of means would voluntarily enter such an establishment, I said, "I suppose this charade is another part of your investigation?"

"Naturally."

Holmes's raised eyebrows seemed an invitation for me to venture a second guess. I paused for a moment before saying, "You suspect that Bythewood may have acquired the habit of stopping at a restaurant serving at an early hour as part of his daily routine, before he entered the Tate gallery." Then, emboldened by Holmes's bowing of his head, I continued, "Furthermore, you suspect… that he may have been poisoned in such an establishment!"

I had failed to keep my voice level – now I blanched as a man sitting at the neighbouring table, who had not removed his hat, turned to stare at us.

"No, on reflection, that would not fit with the existing themes of your novel," I said hurriedly in an even louder tone, saying the first thing that came into my mind.

Though apparently satisfied with this ruse, the man at the next table continued to watch us for several seconds – perhaps he was as interested in the writing of fiction as the uncovering of scandal – before turning back to his meagre portion of beef and potatoes.

I glared at my friend. In a lower register, I said, "If you suspect any one of these premises of poisoning Bythewood, why on earth would you allow me to eat in each of them?"

Holmes gestured at our fellow diners. "If you are at risk, so are each of these gentlemen, as have been each of the patrons every day since Bythewood's death, at the very least. There have been no suspected poisonings recorded these last several days, and no other deaths that are to be treated as at all suspicious. Therefore, Bythewood's death was a unique occurrence. Furthermore, to maintain that Bythewood was poisoned but not targeted specifically would be to introduce yet another element of coincidence to this case."

"What of it?" I replied somewhat defiantly. "Coincidences do happen."

Holmes's upper lip curled. "Sometimes, Watson, I cannot help but conclude that you have gained nothing at all from your years of watching me at work."

The waiter arrived with the basket of bread and our drinks. After some hesitation, I nibbled the corner of a piece of bread. Though I did not truly suspect it of being poisoned, it was certainly on the cusp of staleness. Dismayed, I let it drop back into the basket.

"What is it you hope to learn from entering each of these restaurants? Without any information about Bythewood's activities, are you simply hoping that inspiration will strike you?"

However, before Holmes could answer, I exclaimed, "Your coat! In each restaurant you removed it as you entered. Is this another element of your pantomime?"

"Quite so. You may recall that one of the coats hanging on

Bythewood's coat-rack contained a scarf pushed into its sleeve for safe-keeping. I feel certain that it was his habit to remove his coat and perform this action as he entered any building in which he intended to remain for any substantial amount of time – other than the distinctly chilly Tate art gallery, whose curators have not deigned to provide coat-racks for visitors." Perhaps in response to my expression of incredulity, he added, "It may interest you that caught in the fixings of the front door handle of Bythewood's house I discovered a lime-green thread – from the scarf which he habitually wore. The handle is low enough that a scarf would not become caught on it if it remained tied around the neck and its ends tucked into the lapels of the coat; therefore it had been removed at the point that Bythewood entered his own home. I may go further and state that the scarf was held in his right hand, which he favoured, as he opened the door. Given that he would assuredly remove his coat next, it seems clear that he would then have pushed the lime-green scarf into the arm of the coat he was wearing, in precisely the same manner as *another* scarf was pushed into the arm of the tweed jacket hanging in his home. While it is something of a leap to state that he might have performed the same series of actions upon entering a restaurant, a man of Bythewood's age and routine will frequently display entirely repetitive habits – and let us not forget that the season is clement and the wearing of a scarf was either an affectation or another example of an unbroken habit, as it was hardly necessary for warmth."

My eyes darted as I processed this new information. "Are you suggesting that this is the reason nobody has yet volunteered information about seeing an elderly man wearing a distinctive lime-green scarf, other than outdoors or in the Tate gallery?"

"Precisely that. Moreover, there are a number of routes that Bythewood could have taken that might diminish the chances of him being identified in the street, between the park and his appearance at the art gallery. Vauxhall Bridge is bustling enough that anybody, however striking their appearance, might pass unnoticed – note that nobody other than Abigail Moone has come forth to state that he was upon the bridge even on his return journey, when we know beyond all doubt that he was present. The fact that any witnesses to Bythewood's movements are so far restricted to his own street, the art gallery and Vauxhall Park has suggested to Lestrade that Bythewood made his way directly to the gallery from his home – and yet Bythewood's neighbour attested that his habit was to leave his house at eight o'clock sharp. We can discount the daily use of a cab due to Bythewood's depleted wealth. Unlike the police, we are fortunate enough to have Miss Moone's schedule, which provides us with the time of his arrival at the gallery each day – a quarter past ten. That leaves two and a quarter hours for which we cannot account."

"Do you suspect that the entirety of that time was spent in some eating establishment?"

Holmes shook his head. "After the post-mortem I asked to examine Bythewood's personal effects. His shoes proved to be of great interest. The leather of the upper part showed that they had been purchased new less than six months ago – and yet the soles were worn to the point of requiring replacement, particularly at the ball of the foot, which indicates constant forward motion."

"But consider the man's posture!" I remarked. "Surely he was unable to walk long distances without severe discomfort?"

"That is by no means certain," Holmes replied. "I grant you that his back was stooped, but that in itself need not preclude activity. Even a cursory examination of his body, if you had been looking for signs, indicated that he was limber for a man his age, and his calves were particularly strong. I suppose that next you will remind me of his heart defect – but that supports my suggestion rather than providing a counterargument. Recall that Bythewood took nitroglycerin to combat his weakness, which shows that he was conscious of his ailment and took steps to minimise its effects. It is entirely possible that he considered daily exercise to be an important part of his fight against his condition, is it not?"

"I suppose it is," I said in a grumbling tone. In truth, I had been so occupied with the removal of Bythewood's internal organs that I had given his external appearance little more than a cursory glance. "But what are you driving at, Holmes? Are you suggesting that Bythewood walked in circles for hours before appearing like a genie from a lamp on the steps of the art gallery?

"I merely wish to demonstrate that Bythewood's route each morning may have taken a different, and far lengthier, route than the police suspect – therefore they have been directing their queries to bystanders in quite the wrong area. If Bythewood's aim was to cover a great distance before arriving at his destination for reasons of his health, I propose that he passed along the south bank of the river and crossed it at Chelsea Bridge, then made his way east along the north bank – a journey that would take more than an hour even for a much younger man. Moreover, a route of this nature might reasonably have taken Bythewood past the Thames Bank Distillery, the engine works, the Royal Army Clothing Depot and conceivably also the gas works, at a time long after the commencement of the working day – that is to say, there would have been few unoccupied people within these areas who might have the leisure to observe him passing. At any point along this route, any one of several narrow streets would lead him to Lupus Street and therefore our present location. Naturally, this would be the first opportunity for somebody working in one of these establishments to register Bythewood's presence as a customer – unless he removed the single garment that acted as his most identifiable characteristic."

I released a great sigh. "If everything is as you have described, then what hope can you have of determining which restaurant he frequented?"

To my surprise, Holmes appeared to have no immediate answer to my question. After several seconds of silence, he replied, "Along with the volume of phenol, you will remember that the contents of his stomach included foodstuffs such as bread and pastry – but no meat, which suggests either a moderate diet or a distinctly down-at-heel restaurant. In addition, the autopsy revealed a quantity of alcohol within the stomach, which tells us that it was a licenced premises. For now, that is all the information we have at hand. Nevertheless... I will be frank, Watson, I have begun to despair at my trial-and-error approach, which goes against my every instinct – and that is why I am grateful to you for providing me with a new line of enquiry this morning."

"I?" I said in astonishment. "What did I do?"

"Your appearance in Vauxhall Park, in quite literal terms, provided a new angle on the matter." He rested his chin on his hand and became silent. Then he said abruptly, "I feel bound to inform you that I shall be absent for two or three days, and I trust that during that time you will attend to any needs of our house-guest."

Despite my indignant questioning, Holmes was reluctant to divulge more details, and presently we finished our coffees and left. When he offered me dessert in a third restaurant, I declined.

CHAPTER FOURTEEN

After our semblance of a lunch, Holmes insisted that I return alone to Baker Street to ensure that our guest was still in her rightful place. I asked whether he intended to continue his journeys in Bythewood's footsteps, to which he responded with a wry smile and then replied, "Yes, Watson, but this time I shall proceed *backwards* from our starting-point." With this enigmatic statement, he said a perfunctory farewell and disappeared into the Pimlico crowds. Though I confess I briefly considered following him at a distance, having gained something of a taste for secretive pursuit, I determined instead that I would do my duty.

When I arrived at our Baker Street rooms, Mrs. Hudson met me at the head of the stairs. "Thank goodness you're here!" she cried, clutching at my hands.

I burst into the room and was amazed to find it in utter disarray. Shattered glass covered Holmes's chemistry bench beside the door. All of the books had been plucked from the shelves, and some were strewn on the dinner table, others on the floor, some open and face-down. The bearskin rug had been dragged from its place before the fireplace and now lay in the centre of the room, laden with saucers topped with ash and more broken glass. The punching ball usually situated in Holmes's bedroom stood beside it, placed as if it were a standing lamp rather than a piece of sporting equipment. Abigail Moone was nowhere in sight.

"When did you find it in this state?" I asked, distraught.

"Not long after you left, I suppose," Mrs. Hudson replied.

"What? And did you not attempt to send word to Holmes or me – or failing that, have you called the police?"

My landlady's forehead wrinkled. "Why ever would I do that?"

"Because the place has been ransacked! And Miss Moone has evidently been abducted! And yet your role was to watch her—"

She interrupted me. "And I have done just that." She pointed to the chair before my desk, which had been turned around as if to face the carnage. My desk was the only surface not covered with books or debris. "I watched it all happen, sitting right there."

"My good woman!" I cried. "Were you kept captive?"

"Only by Holmes's instruction to stay in this room."

I stared at her in incomprehension, feeling as though I had gone utterly mad. "But if somebody broke in and turned the place over, surely you can see that Holmes's instruction must be overridden?"

"Nobody broke in."

I gestured wildly at our surroundings. "Then who did this?"

In place of a reply, Mrs. Hudson turned to look at my bedroom door, which was closed. For the first time, I registered sounds coming from within that room. At one moment they sounded like snoring, at another laughter, but then I determined that they were sobs.

"You must approach her very carefully," Mrs. Hudson said. "She has a violent temperament."

Feeling as though I were in the grip of a dream, I did as she instructed, creeping towards my own bedroom door as though a tiger might burst forth at any moment. The sobbing increased in volume, punctuated by groans that seemed drawn from deep within the body.

I knocked twice upon the door and the sounds ceased immediately. Encouraged, I eased open the door just enough to peer inside.

My bedroom was as profoundly in disarray as the sitting-room. The air was thick with smoke, records lay scattered sleeveless on the floor before the gramophone, my bedside table was cluttered with glasses and decanters, and my bed had been pushed askew so that it was angled before the window. Miss Abigail Moone sat on the floor, slumped against the bed-frame, the blankets pulled untidily around her shoulders like a peculiar train of a gown, and she was staring at the half-full glass of red wine held between her knees.

I stood transfixed, knowing that I ought to soothe her somehow, but not having the least idea how to proceed.

Finally, she raised her head, albeit slowly, as if it were as heavy as a cannonball, to look up at me.

"Welcome home," she said in a serious, steady tone.

This broke the spell. I rushed to kneel before her. "My dear lady," I said, "whatever is the matter?"

She responded with a barking, hollow laugh. "Providing an answer to that question would take a considerable amount of time."

I recalled the books strewn about the apartment. "Then you are concerned about your livelihood, now that your *nom de plume* is common knowledge."

She waved a hand in what seemed intended to be an airy fashion, though it appeared to me rather more like the grasping motion of somebody sinking into quicksand. "I suppose that must certainly be a part of it. Doesn't seem as though I'll be publishing more books in the near future, does it?"

"Under another name, perhaps, once this matter has been resolved."

She eyed me suspiciously. "Even then, I would be compelled to divulge my identity to my publisher, at the very least. Has there been a breakthrough in your understanding of the case?"

For a moment I considered lying to her, but she was too intelligent a woman to fall for any ruse. "Holmes appears to have some ideas. But I confess that the situation seems as dark to me as it was the day we began our investigation."

To my surprise, this confession did not seem to displease her. She nodded gravely, the mannerism almost one of satisfaction. "Then my course of action remains the correct one."

"And what is that?" I asked.

Miss Moone raised her glass in a mock salute. "Drinking it all away."

I shook my head vigorously. "That will solve nothing. Miss Moone – Abigail – I beg you, join me in the sitting-room. I would like to talk to you."

"I said nothing about attempting to *solve* a problem," she retorted.

Moving slowly so as not to startle her, I took her by the shoulders to ease her to a proper sitting position, then helped her to stand. As I did so, I saw that the rarely used connecting door that led from my bedroom to Holmes's was ajar, though thankfully the interior of his room appeared unmolested. I led Miss Moone into the main room and shifted a pile of books from Holmes's armchair to make space for her. As soon as she was upon it, she swung her legs from the floor so that her feet protruded over the arm of the chair. I retreated to Mrs. Hudson's position on the seat at my desk.

"Will there be anything else?" my landlady asked.

I turned to her and willed my cheeks not to flush and reveal my embarrassment. "I apologise for the inconvenience already caused to you. I will take over matters from this point."

She subjected me to an inscrutable gaze for several moments, then said in a matter-of-fact tone, "I'll bring up a good dinner earlier than the usual time. She needs some food in her alongside all that wine."

It occurred to me that after my unsatisfactory lunch I, too, was in need of a square meal – but I simply nodded my thanks.

When Mrs. Hudson had left I turned to Miss Moone. She looked as if she had fallen asleep, but presently she faced me and said in a slurred voice, "What's your secret, John?" Then she gestured vaguely at the armchair opposite her. As slow as someone in the grip of a dream, I crossed the room to sit in it.

"Whatever do you mean?" I asked.

"It's not only that we're both writers," she said slowly, as though testing the shape of each word upon her lips before speaking it aloud. "It's the same terror—" She hiccoughed and then grinned foolishly. "*Territory.* Isn't it? Murder and lies, I mean."

"I suppose that there are some similarities between our respective outputs," I said. "What of it?"

"D'you ever wonder why?"

"Why people are compelled to steal from others, or even kill?" I said, frowning. "There are myriad reasons, as you must be well aware. To attempt to summarise them would be sheer folly."

Miss Moone pushed herself awkwardly to something resembling an upright position; though her spine bent awkwardly against the arm of the chair, she didn't seem to notice her odd posture. She shook her head vigorously.

"That's not what I mean," she said in a tone of mild exasperation, as if she were trying to conduct a complex conversation with an infant. "I'm talking about *you*." She jabbed a finger at me to reinforce her statement. "Do you ever wonder about your own fashion – sorry; *fascination* – with all that sort of thing?"

"Not in the least," I replied, though even to my own ears my response seemed to come a little too quickly. "I find myself in the position to chronicle the patient, painstaking work of the greatest mind in London. To reject the opportunity to do so would be a crime in itself."

"So the *chronicling* is the important part? You'd be content to know that Sherlock Holmes's cases were being recorded – even if it were not you holding the pen?"

Infuriation rose within me. It seemed that, once again, Miss Moone's inference was that she might be as well placed as I to play the part of Holmes's biographer. Against my will, images flashed into my mind's eye of the events of some of Holmes's investigations, but with Miss Moone at his side rather than myself. I shuddered.

"The situation is simply a result of the manner in which events have transpired," I said sharply. "There seems no sense in attempting to unravel it."

To my surprise, Miss Moone laughed and then heaved herself from the chair. I pressed myself back into my own seat, uncertain of her intentions – then I scolded myself for fearing her unpredictability. I watched as she moved to the table and poured wine from a bottle into a glass, the bowl of which was already stained red.

In a dreamlike voice, she repeated my words: "There seems no sense in attempting to unravel it."

I watched and waited, unwilling to play her game, whatever it was. Her back was now turned to me.

Gradually, I realised that the rise and fall of her shoulders indicated that she was sobbing once again.

"Abigail…"

Without turning, she said in a muffled voice, "That is not my true name."

"I can hardly call you Damien."

She laughed, but then it became one with her continued sobbing.

"What ought I to call you, then?" I asked.

Finally, she turned to face me. Though the tears had made glistening vertical stripes on her cheeks, her expression was proud.

"I don't know," she said. "I honestly don't know."

She sat again in Holmes's chair, this time with her back straight, almost precisely the posture of Holmes himself.

"Perhaps as a woman I am compelled to question my preoccupations more than any man would," she said, then took a long sip from her glass. "It is no surprise to learn that neither you nor Holmes stop to wonder whether your interest in crime is an indicator of something unsavoury within your own minds. And perhaps, if I had been born a man, I might have directed my efforts towards more practical concerns than the writing of fiction. I suppose I shall never know. Perhaps, too, if I were a man, the stories that I write – which would have been published under my own name – would have caused no eyebrows to raise. In turn, perhaps my stories would have taken no toll on my own psyche."

I shifted uncomfortably at the turn the conversation had taken. "You feel, then, that your work itself serves to diminish your health?"

"No," she replied quickly. "When I write, I am as hale and hearty as you could possibly imagine. It is only *others'* attitude to my work – no, their attitude to *me*, to the mind which produced that work – that wounds me. So what I am interested to learn from you, John, is what it is like to experience no repercussions for introducing depravity to the world via the written word."

My throat had become dry. I eyed the bottle on the table and would very much have liked to have a glass in my hand, but it seemed wrong to encourage my guest's behaviour.

Speaking slowly and choosing my words carefully, I replied, "I confess that I have never considered my work depraved. Nor, in truth, do I consider myself a writer by trade – certainly I am a biographer rather than a composer of fiction."

"You are avoiding the question."

"I do not believe that you asked one."

She sighed. "No. You are right. And it is clear that you would not have the means to answer it if I did. You are uncomplicated, John. That is what I like about you, and at the same time what I loathe about you."

I stood up abruptly, feeling unaccountably rattled. "Despite my failings as a writer and as a human being, I remain a doctor. In that capacity, I would suggest that you stop drinking for a time. Mrs. Hudson will be along presently with dinner. Until then, I would thank you to avoid introducing any more chaos to my home. If you need me for any reason, I will be in Holmes's room with a book."

I went to the bookcase only to discover that all of the volumes still upon it were factual ones. I made a point of selecting the least sensational subject I could identify – a history of the Trekboers of the Transvaal that had eluded my attention for the five years that I had owned it – and retired to Holmes's bedroom with a strong sense that everything in my previously comfortable life had been rendered topsy-turvy.

CHAPTER FIFTEEN

In the morning I woke equally as disoriented as when I had laid my head on Holmes's pillow the night before, though I was gratified to discover that Mrs. Hudson had already seen to the tidying of our lodgings. I scoured the newspapers, but the only reference to our case was a society column speculating once again about Abigail Moone's involvement and noting that sales of Damien Collinbourne novels had soared, though the publisher would retain all money until Miss Moone was located and the confusion over her part in the matter resolved.

Miss Moone and I breakfasted together, but I took the precaution of bringing a book to the dining-table; after some minutes during which I felt her eyes upon me as I read, she stood up and returned holding a volume from my shelves, which she dropped onto the table with a resounding thud that I was sure was intended to reflect her disdain for me.

We spent the day in this manner, reading in opposite corners of the small room. Though Mrs. Hudson made her appearances from time to time, she did not offer to watch Miss Moone in order to allow me to leave the apartment; the patience of even our stalwart landlady has its limit. Miss Moone now seemed to accept her role as prisoner, though hardly with good grace: she muttered to herself constantly, distracting me from my reading, and went continually to the window to stare out at the street, as though she had been kept indoors for two years rather than two days, and as though this were an imposition designed solely to punish her rather than keep her safe from harm.

Only when Miss Moone had retired to my bedroom, carrying a pencil and a pad of paper, was I able to breathe more easily and help myself to the drink that I had forbade myself when in her sight.

The day passed slowly, and though I read much, I learned little about the Transvaal.

The following day, I breakfasted earlier than usual, then retreated to Holmes's bedroom before Miss Moone emerged; I had set up a work desk of sorts at the small table overshadowed by a large mirror, which was ordinarily used by Holmes to perfect his disguises. Here, I made notes with the intention of determining which of our previous cases I might next describe to my readers. However, the constant muttering and, occasionally, the skittering of pencil on paper from beyond the connecting door to my own bedroom served to remind me that a far superior writer was currently residing within my own home, and all inspiration left me.

When we convened for lunch, Miss Moone once again watched me silently until I was forced to lay down my book.

"Has there been any word from Sherlock Holmes?" she asked.

"None at all," I replied, "but be assured that he is doing everything within his power to resolve your situation."

"You have given no hint what aspect of the case he is addressing, or where he has gone."

I helped myself to a slice of ham to mask my consternation, and made a noncommittal sound. Privately, I had been infuriated at Holmes's long absence, and the sense of being trapped in this cage until he deigned to return.

"You do not know?" she said incredulously.

"If it was important that I be informed, Holmes would have done so."

"And conversely, if it is not important that you be informed, he feels no obligation to tell you anything at all?" Miss Moone shook her head in exaggerated wonderment. "I am sure that James Boswell was more involved with the day-to-day affairs of his subject."

I threw down my knife, which produced a clatter on the plate that I regretted instantly; somehow, Miss Moone was capable of puncturing my usually calm exterior.

"I have never claimed to be on equal footing with Holmes," I retorted. "His is the finest mind of our generation. I keep up with him only when it is possible, in the pursuit of duty."

"But he is also your friend," Miss Moone said simply.

I did not know how to respond, and I was grateful when the bell sounded downstairs, providing a timely distraction.

"Perhaps that is Holmes himself," Miss Moone said. I noted her ironic tone and her close scrutiny of my expression.

I scoffed. "One does not need to be a detective to conclude that he would unlock the door and enter his own home rather than ring the bell and wait in the street."

No sooner had Miss Moone withdrawn to the bedroom, Mrs. Hudson pushed open the door to the apartment, staggering a little under the weight of a packing crate that was as wide as her own body. She turned blindly from side to side, appearing dismayed at the table still laden with food and plates; then she bent to deposit the crate onto the carpet.

"Whatever could that be?" I said.

"Do your deductive powers fail you so suddenly?" Miss Moone chided, returning to my side.

"It's addressed to you, that's all I know," Mrs. Hudson said, slightly breathlessly. "That, and the fact that it's awful heavy."

I set to opening the box, resorting to using a metal ruler to lever open the uppermost slats. Within, tucked in a nest of straw, were six bottles of liquid. I lifted one out, and then determined that all of them were identical bottles of cognac.

"I don't understand," I said. "I have not ordered these."

Miss Moone sauntered over and plucked out one of the bottles, examining its label and murmuring the name in an approving tone. Then she said, "Well, I understand."

"You do?"

She grinned. "Given that you make no particular claim over these bottles, I now understand how I will be spending my afternoon."

To my amazement, another crate arrived that same evening, and yet another late the next morning. Each was brought to Baker Street by private carriage, and when I questioned the second and third messenger upon their arrival, each said only that the delivery had been conveyed direct from the manufacturer and that there was no further information to impart.

After I had foolishly relinquished one bottle from the first crate, and failed to hide successive deliveries immediately after their arrival, Miss Moone set to building a stockpile and guarded this supply jealously. She took to remaining in my bedroom for hours at a time. I sat before the fireplace, attempting to make-believe that I was at my club rather than trapped in my home, and trying to ignore the scuffling and muttering from behind the door of my bedroom.

Those same sounds haunted me even in sleep. They grew louder, the chuckling and the skittering of pencils on paper seeming to multiply and surround me.

Then there came a different sound: the click of a door latch.

I sat bolt upright, listening and my head turning from side to side, like a startled dog's. Cautiously, I slipped out of bed and crept to the bedroom door. Despite my apparent alertness, when I opened the door and emerged into the main room I became immediately disoriented, until I reminded myself that I had been sleeping in Holmes's bed, which accounted for my displacement to the 'wrong' side of the fireplace.

I saw no movement and the contents of the main room appeared undisturbed – but soon I realised that I was able to discern *too much*, due to the fact that the curtains behind Holmes's desk had been drawn aside, allowing streetlight to paint the edges of each item of furniture yellow. I tried the window sash; it was secure. The purplish tinge to the horizon, and the otherwise profound darkness of the sky, confirmed that these were the early hours of the morning. Outside the building I saw no movement and little of interest other than a motionless hansom cab, the black horse appearing as frozen as everything else within this eerie scene.

The silence was unaccountably unnerving, after my dreams of constant noise.

This thought inspired another. With a start, I darted to my bedroom door and pressed my ear to it. No sound came from within. On each previous night, the sound of Miss Moone's muttering, or writing, or the sloshing of liquid in a bottle, had continued long past the point I turned out the lamp. Regardless of the hour, and disregarding the misdemeanour of bursting into a woman's bedchamber unannounced, I pushed open the door.

The bedclothes were thrown aside. There was nobody in the room.

Even as I rushed through the connecting door to pull on my clothes of the day before, I heard the sound of another door opening at street level, and then the fainter sound of the cab door opening and closing. I threw on my overcoat, hared out of the apartment and down the stairs with no regard to my safety, then burst into the street and whirled around before spotting the cab receding in the distance. I lowered my head and broke into a sprint to follow it.

After only a short pause at the junction, the cab passed directly over Marylebone Road, and by the time I reached the crossing it was moving at a far greater speed than before. I was already somewhat breathless and despaired of even attempting to catch up. Then, to my surprise, I spied another cab pass in the opposite direction, without any passenger. I hailed it with a wildly waving arm, then darted across the road to leap inside the carriage. Upon my instruction the driver swung his cab around in the centre of the near-empty road, then set the horse going at a fast pace as I continued to shout instructions from my precarious position leaning out of the window. Soon I was elated to see Miss Moone's cab come back into view, and I barked at my driver to reduce his speed.

We passed almost the entire southern extent of Baker Street, then after a right turn we reached Marble Arch and continued south along the periphery of Hyde Park. I bade my driver keep his distance from the cab in front of us, and he seemed to understand immediately the need to avoid attracting suspicion. Along Grosvenor Place we went, then through Westminster. Only when we reached Vauxhall Bridge Road and bumped alongside its tramway did I begin to formulate any ideas about Miss Moone's destination. Would she direct her cab over the bridge, to Vauxhall Park? My mind was racing. What could compel her to leave the safety of the apartment, and at this ungodly hour? Perhaps…

Images of personal effects, or evidence of wrongdoing, that

she may have accidentally left in the park crowded my mind. All over again, my thoughts turned to the possibility that there might be something that Miss Moone wished to hide – in short, that she had indeed been involved in Ronald Bythewood's death. I prayed that it were not so, but if that were not the case, why was I careening after her in the early hours of the morning?

I sighed with relief as the other cab turned left before reaching the bridge. My own cab remained at a discreet distance, and by the time we turned the corner Miss Moone's cab had already passed the junction to Ponsonby Place and now appeared to be slowing. With a start I realised where we were – soon the imposing edifice of the Tate gallery loomed into view, the dawn light lending the Greek-columned façade an orange halo.

I paid my driver hurriedly, thankful that my purse had already been in my coat pocket when I pulled it on. When I slipped out of the carriage at the corner of Ponsonby Place I asked the driver to direct his horse along that street to return to more populous areas, and with a wink of understanding, he did as I asked.

Miss Moone, too, had emerged from her carriage, and now I saw that she was clutching a heavy-looking holdall. To my frustration, the vehicle remained motionless, obscuring her from my view once she had finished speaking to the driver. I kept to the city side of Grosvenor Road, my coat collar pulled up, ready to playact at searching my pockets for my keys, as if I was about to enter one of the houses. I wished that I had had the presence of mind to collect my hat before I had left Baker Street, to obscure my features.

However, when the cab finally pulled away from the kerb, Miss Moone was not looking in my direction. She gazed up at the Tate gallery, her expression unreadable from afar.

I told myself that the building was securely locked. What purpose could Miss Moone have, coming here now? Then I recalled that the drinking-fountain at the side of the entrance-hall would be as accessible as at any other time of the day, and that approaching it now would be far safer than when visitors came and went.

I shook my head in dismay. For all that Miss Moone's presence at Baker Street had caused me discomfort, I had not believed that she was the guilty party in the death of Ronald Bythewood. Now, however, I found myself prepared to believe anything – even the idea that she might be planning to harm yet more innocent people. I resolved that I would follow her, up to the moment she inserted a new poison capsule in the spout, but that I would certainly intervene without allowing her to spring her trap.

As if she had sensed my resolution clicking into place, Miss Moone surprised me by turning around fully and crossing the road, moving directly away from the art gallery. I stood rooted to the spot, blinking stupidly. Then, rather than walking along the length of Grosvenor Road, Miss Moone passed through a gap in the low wall that separated the thoroughfare from the banks of the river.

In an instant I realised that the situation was far from what I had imagined. When Miss Moone's pace did not slow and she moved out of my line of vision, I tried to imagine what was on the other side of the wall. During the final stage of the cab journey we had already passed the army and navy wharves – at this point, surely all that could be there were mud banks dotted with mooring posts?

A terrible image lodged in my mind as I recalled Miss Moone's utter despair during the last few days; her constant drinking; her muttering to herself.

Suddenly, I felt certain that there was only one innocent person whose life was at risk.

I bent forward into a run, crossing the road diagonally and

putting all subterfuge out of my mind. When I reached the low wall I leaned over it, my eyes straining to catch a glimpse of my quarry. I exhaled with relief as I saw her again. Rather than having slid directly down the mud bank, she now walked upon a wooden jetty that stretched perpendicular from the road to a floating pier. Four boats were moored along its length – but already Miss Moone had passed two of them and her pace did not slow. With a lurching sensation in my stomach, it occurred to me that walking to the end of the pier would put her over far deeper water, where the current would certainly sweep her beneath the surface if she were to—

I could not allow myself to conjure the image.

I called out, but Miss Moone did not turn around. There was only a slight breeze, but it was blowing towards me, perhaps carrying my voice away from her. I ran alongside the wall, then leaped onto it to give me a greater chance of continuing to watch her movements as I sped towards her. By the time I reached the foot of the jetty she had passed another of the boats, and then she was out of sight, the bulk of that vessel blocking my view.

I sprinted along the slippery boards of the jetty, stumbling on its uneven surface and at one point almost falling headlong into the Thames myself.

I shouted Miss Moone's name, but even to my own ears my voice sounded small and weak, my throat tightened by panic.

Then I heard a sharp noise. It took me a moment to register that it was the splash of something heavy striking the water.

I believe I have never run so fast as I ran then, despite the swaying and lurching of the jetty. As I neared the end of the boards, my head swung wildly from side to side to locate the source of the sound I had heard.

The froth had almost settled on the surface of the water. I remembered the bag that Miss Moone had been carrying, and in my feverish state I imagined it full of rocks that would ensure that she sank directly to the bottom of the river. I cast off my overcoat, preparing to dive into the Thames.

"John?" a voice said. "Whatever are you doing?"

My arms swung like the blades of windmills; I teetered on the edge of the jetty. When I managed to regain my balance I turned, slow as a somnambulist, to stare into the face of Abigail Moone.

She was standing on the deck of the small yacht that had blocked my view earlier. Behind Miss Moone, clasping the holdall that she had been carrying only moments before, was a young woman who wore a dark dress and whose hair was loose and thrown about by the increasing breeze.

I gazed at them both, still as a statue. Then, when the yacht began to edge away from me, I traced the length of rope tied at its stern to see that it was no longer secured to the mooring post of the jetty, instead trailing in the water. It must have been the weight of the rope that had caused the splashing sound I had heard.

Miss Moone's nose wrinkled as she gazed at me.

"John, are you quite well?" she said in a tone of exaggerated, almost mocking, concern.

"You should be in your bed," I managed to say, and immediately felt an utter fool, as though I were a father scolding a recalcitrant child.

"As should you," she responded curtly, though not without kindness.

Her companion laughed and heaved the holdall through a hatch to drop it below decks.

"I will remind you," Miss Moone continued, "that I am not your prisoner. Nor am I your concern, any longer."

In my befuddled state, I could not summon the niceties of her legal status. She was wanted by the police, was she not? And yet Holmes and I had taken her in, hiding her from those same authorities, which suggested that we considered her freedom to be paramount.

"Where are you going?" I asked weakly.

"It is better than you do not know. This is not the first time that I have been compelled to begin life anew. I suspect I will need to travel further away this time."

"You do not intend to return?" I noted the pleading tone in my voice. "Holmes will clear your name, I assure you."

She smiled indulgently. "Forgive me, but the assurances of men do not hold water – if you will forgive the pun in these circumstances. And anyway, proving me innocent of a crime is only a part of the matter. I prize my freedom and my anonymity. Neither of those can you promise to restore to me, no matter the outcome of your case."

My mouth opened and closed without any words coming forth. Everything that she had said was undoubtedly true.

There was now clear water between the boat and the jetty. Miss Moone's companion emerged once again from the hatch and, retrieving the oars, guided the vessel towards the centre of the river.

"How will we contact you?" I asked, raising my voice to be heard over the hush of the wind.

Miss Moone laughed. "I have my ways of finding things out, just as you and Holmes have yours," she replied. "And if, for any reason, the outcome of the case is not made public by other means, I expect you to publish a full account. Is that clear?"

"Yes," I replied solemnly. "It is clear."

I watched as the boat continued to slide away from me. My mind was still foggy with sleep, and the mist rising from the Thames only exacerbated the dreamlike qualities of our exchange.

Miss Moone spoke again, but I could not hear her words. I raised both of my arms in a mimed gesture to show that I had not understood.

I saw her cup her hands around her mouth to call out, like a character on a variety-hall stage.

"I have left you a gift!" she called.

I watched in wonderment as the dark-clad woman dipped the oars deeper into the water, the yacht gaining speed until Miss Moone's standing figure became first a silhouette and then indistinguishable from the mast and furled sails of the boat, and then all of these were swallowed by the mist.

CHAPTER SIXTEEN

When I returned to Baker Street, having walked the first part of the journey without the good fortune of locating a hansom cab, I was exhausted and my mind whirled with chastisements at having let Miss Moone go free. I could not sleep, and yet in my half-awake state I could do little more than sit at the window and watch the day dawn fully, growing ever more weary as the sun rose. Reluctantly, I climbed into Holmes's bed – which still seemed warm – even as the sunlight streamed through my curtains. Then, just as I slipped into a doze, I was summarily woken by the sound of Mrs. Hudson arranging the breakfast-things.

"Good Lord, whatever has happened?" my landlady said when I emerged wearing my dressing gown over my crumpled clothes.

"I confess that I do not know," I said, offering the lopsided smile of a drunkard. "Except that our house-guest has moved on."

Mrs. Hudson betrayed no sign of remorse. She glanced at the doorway through which I had come. "And no sign of Holmes as yet, I take it?"

"No."

She shook her head in dismay. "It's like a merry-go-round in here," she muttered, and began placing half of the crockery and several of the dishes of food back onto her tray. "There's no telling who'll be where, each time I enter."

I stopped her with a hand on her arm. "Leave those, Mrs. Hudson. As it happens, my tiredness seems to have given me rather an appetite."

Still muttering, Mrs. Hudson moved away from the table, holding the silver tray in both hands as if it were a shield, or as if she might strike me with it.

After she had left I sat at the table and ate, barely registering the taste of the food and yet unable to satisfy my hunger fully.

Once my stomach could hold no more, I retreated to my chair and dozed. My dreams were of hurrying along empty streets, and mist rising from pools of water, and a mermaid with dark hair.

When I woke, I remembered something that had eluded me since I had returned to Baker Street: Miss Moone had referred to a gift.

I went to my own bedroom and examined it in its entirety, but found nothing upon any surface or when – blushing furiously – I searched the tangled bedsheets.

Neither was there anything to be found in the main room, nor did anything seem out of its usual place since Mrs. Hudson had undone the disarray that Miss Moone had caused on her first day alone here.

Perhaps her reference to a gift had been some sort of a trick. It would not have been the first time that I had failed to understand her dark sense of humour.

In the absence of both Miss Moone and Holmes, I had nowhere that I needed to go, and yet it seemed intolerable that I might remain relegated to my rooms now that my freedom had been restored. So, I washed, changed my clothes, put on my coat, and then I stood on the rug before the fireplace, wondering where it was I was going to go. The room seemed more silent than it had ever been; even the ticking of the clock seemed smothered. Within my mind I conjured the sounds of Miss Moone in her restlessness: her murmuring to herself behind my bedroom door; the scratch of pencil on paper. I recalled another sound, too, one that had puzzled me and which had no associated image in my mind's eye. Several times, when I had been sitting here before the fireplace and Miss Moone had hidden herself away, I had heard a faint clicking sound. It occurred to me that the sound had not been replicated when I was within Holmes's bedroom, which adjoined my own.

I exclaimed aloud as the significance of this sound struck me. If I had heard it from the fireplace and not from within Holmes's room, might that not indicate that Miss Moone had moved between the two bedrooms freely? I recalled the first morning when I had returned to Baker Street to find the apartment in disarray; the connecting door to Holmes's room had been ajar. Nothing had been disturbed, and yet…

I dashed into Holmes's room and stood in its centre, whirling to look all around. Then I lunged to push open the connecting door, and stood in my own bedroom, staring back through that same doorway.

My gaze settled on an object that could be accessed easily from my own room without disturbing anything in the main part of Holmes's chamber: the safe. Once again, I summoned the faint clicking sound in my mind. Yes; now I was positive.

I dashed to my own room, chiding myself for leaving my own copy of the safe key within it while Miss Moone was its occupant. Thankfully, the key was still in its usual place within my bedside drawer.

In Holmes's room I bent to the safe, threw open the door and pulled out a sheaf of papers bound with string ties along one side, which appeared far more substantial than the meagre collection that Miss Moone had first asked Holmes to lock away.

I leafed through the pages rapidly, noting at a glance that the document appeared to be prose, written in a slanting, barely decipherable hand. To my alarm, I saw my own name appear more than once. Giddy with indignation, I turned the bundle to look at the front page.

My heart rate slowed considerably. I did not know how to react when I saw the title on the frontispiece, but rage was certainly not within my confused mixture of responses.

It read: *Watson and Holmes: A Study in Friendship*, and below the title was inscribed, *For John*.

The rest of that day was spent in the company of that manuscript, and the less affecting company of the members at my club, who assumed almost spectral presences in the periphery of my vision as I read continually. When I had completed my review of the manuscript I raised my eyes, noticing my surroundings for the first time in many hours. Then I stumbled home, lost in wonderment, and slept in my own bed as well as I have ever slept in my adult life.

When I emerged from my bedroom, the righting of imbalance – which had begun with Mrs. Hudson's changing of my bedclothes to allow me to sleep in my own room – was completed by the sight of Sherlock Holmes sitting in his chair before the unlit fireplace, sunlight illuminating the left side of his face as he read the morning newspapers.

He raised his head slowly as I paced around his chair to stand before him.

"I would like to ask where you have been these last days," I said, "but I recognise the expression you are wearing. I can see that you are on the cusp of pronouncing my own movements and my own state of mind, as is your wont."

Holmes raised one eyebrow. After considering my words for some time, he replied, "No. Do you have any clear idea of Miss Moone's whereabouts?"

Blinking stupidly, I turned to look at my bedroom door.

"I assure you that I have exhausted none of my deductive powers to determine that she is no longer here," Holmes added. "Mrs. Hudson informed me immediately on my arrival that Miss Moone had taken her leave." He gazed over my shoulder at my bookcase. There remained large gaps in my collection where Miss Moone had taken out books and replaced them at random. "Though I can see that she has left her mark."

My cheeks flushed. Though I considered telling him about the wonderful manuscript that Miss Moone had left me as a gift, something prevented me from speaking of it. At that moment it occurred to me that I had no expectation that any living soul other than myself would ever read it.

"I fear that she has gone very far away," I said, "and that perhaps we will never know where."

Holmes nodded, without displaying any suggestion of annoyance.

"Nevertheless," he said, "we can yet do her the service of seeing to its end the case that she brought to our attention."

"Then you have new information pertaining to it? You have not told me where you have been conducting your investigation."

Holmes rose from his seat. "We have little time available to us. We must leave now."

My eyes widened. "What is to happen? Ought I to bring my pistol?"

"If you feel it is necessary, though I fail to see why."

"Then for pity's sake, tell me where we are going!"

"To our lunch reservation."

"To our—" I fell silent, gawping at him. Questions and rebuttals crowded my mind, though the only words that came to my lips were, "But it is only breakfast-time."

Again Holmes scrutinised me, his eyes darting over my person in his search for clues about my erratic behaviour. "It is very unlike you to sleep so very late."

I turned to look at the mantelpiece clock, then I gasped as I noted the time. Somehow, I had slept until a quarter past eleven.

Without another word, I retired to my room to dress for lunch.

CHAPTER SEVENTEEN

Holmes provided no further details during our cab ride to Pimlico. When we entered the restaurant – which was notably less shabby than the ones we had visited before Holmes had begun his long absence – I was surprised to see Inspector Lestrade alone at a table, rising to greet us.

"Care to tell me what this is all about?" Lestrade said in a convivial tone as I shook him by the hand.

"I haven't the slightest idea," I replied. "In fact, I'm rather relieved to know that I'm not the only one of us who is in the dark."

Despite this sentiment, I realised that I was, at least, grateful to Holmes for distracting me from prolonged consideration of the loss of Abigail Moone – and that my appetite had returned in force.

Holmes moved around Lestrade to take his seat at the opposite side of the table, facing the greater part of the wide room. Then he took up a menu and seemed to become immediately absorbed in perusing it.

Self-conscious at my friend's silence, I asked Lestrade, "Has your case been proceeding well?"

Lestrade responded with a bark of laughter. "Your question

assumes that there has been *any* development. I assure you there has not. By all accounts, our man in the lime-green scarf had the ability to transport himself from location to location without the dull necessity of making any journey between those two points. Furthermore, our authoress friend is more of a phantom than Mr. Collinbourne himself."

I had not the wits to continue the conversation without letting slip any pieces of information related to Miss Moone, which Holmes and I had withheld from Scotland Yard. Like Holmes, I took up a menu and hid my face behind it, then felt immensely grateful to the waiter who came to take our orders.

As we waited for our food, Lestrade said to Holmes, "I'm surprised we've placed our order before our companion has arrived."

Holmes smiled. "It will be only the three of us dining together to-day."

"Oh, really? In that case, am I to call you Sherlock Holmes, or Mr. J. Berry, or something else entirely?"

I looked at each of them in turn. "What on earth are you talking about?"

Lestrade laughed. "I had a devil of a time convincing the fellow at the front desk that I had a reservation. I suppose it didn't seem at all plausible that I'd forget who it was that I was supposed to be meeting here. You could've picked a more memorable name, Holmes. A dull one does rather spoil the fun of assuming an alias."

Noting my continued bafflement, Lestrade reached out to turn the folded note-card that was placed in the centre of the table to indicate that it was reserved. I had paid it no notice when I had taken my seat. To my surprise, the name upon it was indeed *J. BERRY*.

I lowered my voice as I said to Holmes, "What is it that

prompts this need for secrecy?" Despite Holmes's mocking attitude earlier, I wished now that I had brought my gun after all.

"You know me well enough to understand that there is little that I do lightly," Holmes replied, the volume of his voice unmoderated. "In addition, I know that you are generous enough to indulge me in my sometimes theatrical whims."

I nodded. "Then what would you have us do?"

"Why, I would have you enjoy your luncheon."

The waiter returned presently and we ate, conversing stiffly about matters unrelated to the case. Lestrade and I exchanged frequent sideways glances, as though we were fellow prisoners and as if the food – while admittedly delicious – was mere gruel.

Finally, Holmes wiped his mouth with his napkin. I realised that I could not recall the last time I had seen him eat a full meal.

I experienced a wash of relief, almost to the point of gratefulness, when Holmes gestured to the reservation card and, as if our former conversation had not been interrupted in the least, said, "As I say, the name was not chosen lightly."

"Then is the name connected with the Bythewood case in some way?" I asked.

Holmes shook his head.

"A more oblique reference, then? Though I fail to see how berries might be involved."

When Holmes shook his head once more, Lestrade exclaimed, "I didn't come here to take part in parlour games, for heaven's sake! Tell us or don't tell us – but if no information is forthcoming I'll thank you for my meal and be on my way. Some people have honest jobs to do, you know."

Idly, Holmes reached out to pluck the reservation card from the centre of the table. Then he straightened and turned the card so that the writing upon it was visible to both Lestrade and me. Something in his mannerism, which lacked any flourish but nevertheless suggested careful consideration of our precise line of sight, reminded me of a conjurer at a child's party.

In a similarly theatrical movement, Holmes placed the forefinger of his left hand over the lower part of the front of the folded card, obscuring the bottom half of each of the letters.

I was conscious of Lestrade leaning forward in his seat. I stared at the card, and then my eyes flicked to Holmes's face. His raised eyebrows made him appear rather like that of a teacher who remained hopeful that a promising student might be capable of making a breakthrough.

After several seconds, I gasped.

"What is it?" Lestrade demanded.

"Don't you see?" I said.

The inspector groaned. "Don't you start. I've just about had enough of this charade. For pity's sake, tell me and be done with it!"

I pointed at the letters – or rather, those parts of the letters that were still visible above Holmes's horizontal finger.

"Each of the letters – J, B, E, R, R and Y – has become another, now that its lower part is obscured!" I pointed at each in turn. "Look, the cross bar on the letter J makes it now appear as a squat letter T. Then we have D, and then C – rather an odd, square-cornered one, admittedly – and then two more Ds and a V."

"Good Lord!" Lestrade said. However, his exclamation was undermined by his unvarying monotone – it was clear that he had reached no conclusion and that he was merely poking fun at me. "And what of it? I take back my comment about parlour games. Even a child would resist being entertained by this rigmarole. I fail to see that the string of letters T, D, C, D, D, V is in any way significant." He hesitated. "Is it something to do with Roman numerals? Though I don't see how the T fits into the pattern."

"The note!" I cried, then coughed and lowered my voice. "Don't you see that Holmes has merely illustrated the possibility of misconstruing *another* message? I am talking of the note found in Bythewood's hand!"

I turned to Holmes; he gave a curt nod of confirmation.

I placed both my forefingers onto my lips, perhaps unconsciously echoing Holmes's mannerisms as I tried to recall the details. "The note read 'D C DID IT'. Is it possible…"

I trailed off as Holmes opened the reservation card and then withdrew a pencil from his jacket pocket. With the card flattened out, he wrote the letters "D C DID IT" in the upper-right quarter of this now larger surface, so that the first D was written halfway across the space and each of the letters rested upon the central fold. He glanced up at each of us in turn, then raised the card and ripped it into four equally sized pieces. I stared at the strips of paper as he placed them onto the tabletop. Then, wonderingly, I reached out to pick up the quarter that contained the letters, which looked very much like the card that Bythewood had been holding, in terms of both its proportions and the peculiar placement and shape of the letters.

"Hold on for just a moment," Lestrade said gruffly. "Isn't it possible that you're creating a facsimile of that note by other means?"

I shook my head vigorously. "It is not only the message that Holmes has produced in this way. Look – the tearing is the same." I turned to Holmes. "Do you have the original upon you?"

Holmes bowed his head and produced from his jacket pocket a small envelope, from which he took the note that had been discovered in Bythewood's fist. After assuring myself that the crumpled nature of Bythewood's note meant that there could be no risk of mixing up the two copies, I held each of them up to examine them in minute detail.

"Look," I said to Lestrade, "it is clear at a glance that the left-hand side of each note is ripped. But beneath the letters is another matter. After being clenched in his fist for a time,

Bythewood's note is crumpled and its edges smoothed, making the lower tear difficult to make out – but now, with this template of Holmes's, we can see something like its original state."

Lestrade took the card quarter from me and ran his thumb along its base.

"The clean tear is due to the deep fold already made in the reservation card," Holmes said, watching us both carefully. "It would have taken the least amount of rubbing in Bythewood's palm to remove any clear sign that the card had ever been attached to another piece at its lower edge."

"But that means that 'D C DID IT' was not the intended message at all!" I said in astonishment, pieces of the larger puzzle finally settling into place in my mind. "Those were actually the upper parts of different letters entirely – a different message?"

"Quite so," Holmes replied calmly. He held out a hand and I passed the quarter-note to him. Then he placed it neatly above the corresponding lower quarter of the unfolded reservation card. "The first issue of importance is the matter of spacing of the letters. We have continually read the message as 'D C DID IT', with spaces in the appropriate places – but now that we understand that the lower part of each letter is missing, the possibility arises that spaces were introduced during the natural act of distinguishing each letter from its neighbour. Let us examine each character in turn. What, for example, might the first letter truly be, to have become a letter D in the message we received?"

I considered his question for a moment. "Why, you have already shown us in your 'Berry' example. An uppercase B split in half produces a D character."

"Good," Holmes responded, once again adopting the manner of a supportive teacher. "But there are other possibilities. P and R have the same upper parts."

I nodded slowly, beginning to enjoy the puzzle. "Very well.

And a letter C…" I trailed off, frowning. "I confess I'm at a loss already. A Greek letter, perhaps? Epsilon?"

"It is simplicity itself, so long as you take into account somewhat deliberate, sweeping handwriting," Holmes said.

With his pencil he traced the C shape, then continued the line onto the lower quarter of card to produce a rounded letter S.

"Note that the bulbous, almost semicircular nature of the letter ensures that the lower part protrudes to the right," Holmes said, "which may account for what appears to be a space between words in the message we were given."

I became conscious of Lestrade bending over the table beside me. "All this is most diverting," he said, "but it still seems like a great deal of conjecture to me. Is there any possibility you might speed up this process and allow us to continue with a discussion of the case itself, rather than mere calligraphy?"

With a sigh, Holmes made three vertical marks on the lower quarter of card. All that he achieved in doing so was to extend the lengths of the two 'I' characters and also the 'T'. "That leaves only the three letter Ds – which we have already noted could each originally have been R, P or B. However, the spacing between the resultant characters once again provides clues. In the word we perceived as 'DID', there is no space after the first D – which suggests that this is a P, or possibly a narrow B. After the second D is a space, which indicates that this began as a letter R, as any hand that produces an S of this distinctive formation is bound to add a flourish to the trailing diagonal of a letter R."

With that, he added the lower part of the R to the card.

"It requires no great leap of deduction to determine that the apparent word 'DID' was originally written 'PIR' – the letter P being a sensible conclusion given that there are so few words that contain the letter pairing 'SB'."

"And there it is!" I exclaimed as Holmes added the lower

part of the letter P. "The word is 'SPIRIT'!"

Lestrade cleared his throat and said rather stiffly, "But that is only if you ignore the first letter, which is another D – or rather, it would originally have been another R, P or B."

I stared at him, marvelling at his blindness to the facts. "But Holmes has already demonstrated that this note was produced by tearing a larger piece of card into four. Clearly, there is another part of the message – another word, which ends with an R, P or B."

"Indeed," Holmes said. "I congratulate you on your reasoning, Watson. Note that the space after the first D is wider than those around the characters in what we perceived to be the word 'DID'. You are quite right that this indicates that there is a true space between words here. Furthermore, I suggest that words ending in R are very much more common than those ending in either P or B."

I stared at my friend in silence. After a few seconds, he raised his eyebrows as if to enquire after my thoughts.

"I apologise, Holmes," I said. "It is only that another idea has occurred to me."

Holmes gave a tight-lipped smile and nodded slowly in a satisfied manner.

Lestrade sat back in his seat, making a harrumphing sound. "I do wish you'd both speak aloud rather than communicating with your eyebrows."

I turned to the inspector. "Don't you see? If we were wrong about the message as we first saw it – if the message in truth related to a 'spirit' of some sort – then the implication of the involvement of somebody with the initials D.C. was produced solely by our own minds. That is to say, that conclusion has no bearing on the case."

Lestrade sat up again sharply. "Then you are saying—"

"I am suggesting that we all saw what we hoped to see –

an accusation. That would be a useful starting-point for any case, would it not?" I said. "And how quickly we each made the link to Damien Collinbourne!" Hurriedly, I added, "Once the detail about Abigail Moone's note-book was revealed in the newspapers, that is. And yet" – I glanced at Holmes, whose expression remained inscrutable – "it was merely a coincidence."

Holmes and I had made the connection to Damien Collinbourne long before Scotland Yard had followed us along that wrongheaded path. I wondered if Holmes ever had truly suspected Abigail Moone, or whether his concern about the accusation that seemed contained in the note in Bythewood's hand was due only to the need to shield Miss Moone from the authorities.

Lestrade shook his head forcefully. "But it is not only this note that implicates Damien Collinbourne – I mean, Abigail Moone. The entry in her note-book detailed the precise manner of Ronald Bythewood's murder."

Holmes gave a long, slow nod of acquiescence, but his eyes remained upon me.

It pained me that we could not speak freely in Lestrade's presence. My mind raced, trying to comprehend whether Miss Moone was now free of suspicion, given the additional knowledge that Holmes and I possessed. Then it struck me – the note-book had been stolen from Miss Moone *after* the death of Bythewood. Even if she was innocent, the fact remained that the culprit must have caught sight of the note-book at a far earlier date, in order to be inspired by her theoretical plan for murder. We could not discount her involvement in the matter quite yet.

I responded with a look that I knew Holmes understood. As Lestrade had so cannily observed, we were sometimes able to 'communicate with our eyebrows', as might any old friends.

For his part, Lestrade seemed satisfied that he had put us both in our places. He rocked back in his chair, glancing around the restaurant. Then he said, "So, then. We now have a *different* message relating to some manner of spirit. What of it?" He wet his lips and looked around him again. Laughing nervously, he said, "Perhaps it is a reference to an after-dinner drink of some sort?"

Holmes smiled. "I shall call over the waiter momentarily, Lestrade. However, before I do so, I may be able to satisfy your curiosity about one or two matters. The note relates to a different sort of spirit entirely."

Lestrade slumped back into his seat, accepting defeat as Holmes steepled his fingers, adopting his familiar lecturing pose.

"Naturally, my first assumption was of a religious or mystical significance," he said. "So, when we visited Bythewood's home, I examined his shelves for any texts that related to such subjects."

"I remember!" I cried out. "You took out books on Methodism and fairy tales, among others. But that means that you had deduced the true message on the note long ago – why did you say nothing to me?"

"A great deal of conjecture was involved, and I preferred to keep my process to myself," Holmes replied dismissively. "As you say, there were a number of texts that may have been pertinent, not least the Bible in Bythewood's attic bedroom. I am sure you recall my dejection once I had examined each of them – none provided any further clues or any particular suggestion that he prized any of these volumes more highly than any other of his books. Furthermore, I unearthed no indications that Bythewood was a member of any religious community, nor any group with more esoteric interests."

"Then what could have been the meaning of the word 'spirit'?" I asked forlornly. Then I remembered Bythewood's name which I had seen written in his copies of Damien Collinbourne's novels. "We concluded initially that the note Bythewood clutched was not written in his own hand... and it strikes me that this conclusion remains the correct one, even now that the message itself has transformed before our eyes." I pointed at the word *SPIRIT* that Holmes had reconstructed on the torn quarters of card. "The original letters were written in a steady hand entirely unlike Bythewood's own. Therefore, we are making conjectures about somebody whose identity we do not yet know. Whoever wrote the message might well have been a religious man."

"Indeed," Holmes said, seeming impressed at my reasoning, "but you accept that it was only reasonable to exhaust all possibilities that the message may have been significant to Bythewood too. Otherwise, why would he clutch it even as he died? Why would it have been torn into quarters, either by himself or another?"

I slumped in my seat. "I confess that I am at a loss, Holmes."

"It is as I have noted before," Holmes said, his enthusiasm undimmed. "One must hold in mind all of the facts of a case at once. To concentrate exclusively on one part is rather like looking only at one-quarter of this handwritten message – that is, the approach is liable to produce an incorrect conclusion. What other pieces of evidence may be pertinent? What aspect of Bythewood's daily routine do we understand in the greatest detail?"

Both Lestrade and I remained silent as we considered the question.

"His visits to the Tate art gallery!" I said finally.

"Exactly so," Holmes said, the teacher evidently now pleased at his struggling pupils' performance. "But what aspect?"

"His route was almost unchanging," I replied quickly. "We know the rooms in which he lingered."

Lestrade turned sharply to face me. "Do we indeed?"

I cleared my throat nervously, and my eyes darted to Holmes, who did not respond.

"We had some early success questioning visitors to the art gallery," I replied hurriedly, "from which we were able to piece together his daily routine. It seemed of little importance at the time, and you already knew that Bythewood was a regular patron of the establishment."

Lestrade scrutinised my face for a long moment, then nodded. "Well, then – what of his movements within that building?"

I searched my memories, though it struck me that it was actually Holmes's recreation of Bythewood's movements that I conjured within my mind's eye.

"Each day, he spent the greatest amount of time in a room displaying contemporary paintings," I said. "He sat facing one wall in particular, upon which hung ten paintings. Holmes, are you saying that you now understand which of them occupied Bythewood's attention?"

"Yes," my friend replied, "I believe that I do."

When it became clear that he was not minded to provide a complete answer immediately, I closed my eyes to summon the works I had seen in the gallery.

"The infants with their lanterns, perhaps?" I ventured. "Or the Annunciation – or the peasant workers occupied in lighting a match?" The memory of this final painting brought to mind my first encounter with Abigail Moone, when Holmes had deduced the details of my visit to the Bryant and May factory in Bow. This in turn summoned an image of my final moments with Miss Moone, as she had drifted away with her friend on the yacht. "Or perhaps it was the seascape titled *Britannia's Realm*?"

Holmes's expression remained indulgent. "It was none of those, though I applaud your capacity to recall these details." Then his chin raised and he looked over my shoulder as a waiter approached. Without consulting either Lestrade or myself, he ordered three cognacs, but then added, "There is not the least hurry, mind you. My friends and I have much to discuss." Then he dismissed the waiter forthwith.

For a time, Holmes seemed lost in his thoughts. Then he roused himself and said, "Bythewood himself was a cognac drinker. You might even call him a connoisseur."

I nodded, uncertain whether this line of discussion represented a continuation of his outlining of the facts of the case, or whether it was merely conversation to pass the time before our drinks arrived.

"I recall you smelling the contents of the decanter in his dining-room," I said finally.

"It was clear immediately that it was an important clue. At least, the type of cognac was unfamiliar to me."

I smiled. I knew well that anything outside Holmes's realm of knowledge by default represented to him a vital development.

Then I gasped and exclaimed, "By Jove! The deliveries of cognac!"

"What deliveries?" Lestrade asked sharply, evidently perturbed at finding himself continually one step behind us. "I've had no reports of deliveries being made to Bythewood."

I shook my head. "Not to Bythewood – to me!"

Lestrade raised both his hands in a gesture of surrender. "Now I'm entirely lost."

"I will explain," Holmes said in a languid, unhurried manner. "As I said, the cognac in Bythewood's house constituted a new puzzle. In conjunction with another aspect of the case, it prompted my brief excursion to Paris—"

"What?" I cried. "You have been in Paris? And what other aspect are you referring to?"

"The painting in the Tate gallery, naturally," Holmes replied calmly.

"For God's sake, man, which one?" I felt like shaking the answers out of him.

Holmes did not react in the slightest. "Perhaps the least diverting of all the works that hung on that wall. It depicted a city scene, featuring carriages in a narrow street."

I nodded several times rapidly, seeing before me the broad strokes that conjured a street bustling with carriages and people. "I recall it. What was its significance?"

"For one thing, it stood out among the other paintings by virtue of its subject. Whereas all of the other works depicted scenes of life in our country – or scenes from mythology, in some cases – this work warranted inclusion in that room of the gallery only because the *artist* was British, albeit an Englishman working primarily elsewhere. His name is Alfred Sisley, and the painting is titled *Main Street in Argenteuil*."

"And Argenteuil is a suburb of Paris," I concluded.

"You could at least have informed me about all these developments," Lestrade muttered.

Holmes ignored him. I imagine he was sceptical that Lestrade would have accomplished anything even if he had been provided with this information.

"So, you can understand why these two intriguing elements warranted paying a visit to that fair city," Holmes said.

"And what did you learn?" I asked impatiently. "And why did you send cognac to Baker Street? Was it some sort of coded message that I failed to interpret?"

"Not in the least," Holmes said gaily. "It is merely that I posed as a British importer of cognac in order to aid my investigation. Fortunately, I was not required to visit the city of Cognac itself, though I would have done so had I not reached any conclusion in Paris. As it is, each of the distilleries in Cognac has an administrative office in Paris dedicated to the export of wares. In answer to your question, in some instances I deemed it appropriate to place an order, to demonstrate my seriousness of intent."

I considered pointing out that his decision had had unforeseen and decidedly negative effects, given the number of bottles that had been sequestered by Abigail Moone, but then I remembered how little Lestrade knew about her recent activities, and held my tongue.

"What I learned was as follows," Holmes said. "The office serving the distillery that manufactures that specific brand of cognac I found in Bythewood's house is situated in Clichy, in the north-western region of the city. The export office is by far one of the smallest I visited, and the gentlemen who operates it, a Monsieur Faucheux, is singularly reluctant to share his company accounts. Nevertheless, from a distance I observed that he had a weakness for fine clothes, and only a short excursion prior to my visit to his office was required in order to secure a tie-pin that would attract his interest upon my calling. The tie-pin having been successfully transferred from me to him, with the appearance of no small display of reluctance on my part, secured our friendship. Then I was able to sample his company's wares and to confirm that it was the same cognac drunk by Bythewood. Better still, on a flimsy pretext I examined the company accounts to determine which wine cellars within Paris stocked that brand – which were oddly few, whereas other cognacs enjoyed widespread availability across the city. It was held by only two cellars in Bois-Colombes, so I next directed my search to those businesses."

I held up my hand. "Holmes, forgive me – what does this place, Bois-Colombes, have to do with the case?"

Lestrade grunted in approval; the same question had clearly occurred to him.

"That is where Ronald Bythewood and his wife Mélanie lived," Holmes replied. "Her ancestral home is in Bois-Colombes, on the junction between the Rue de la Côte Saint-Thibault and the Rue des Bourguignons. Forgive me, Watson – there is so little you know about this case that I now realise that I am dashing ahead at too great a speed. Naturally, when I arrived in Paris I made enquiries relating to Bythewood's circumstances and his standing in the city, in parallel to the matter of the cognac."

"Naturally," I repeated in a weak voice. "It was only that I had assumed that their location might have been Argenteuil, as you seemed to intimate earlier."

"No," Holmes replied bluntly. "Argenteuil is on the opposite bank of the Seine, a suburb entirely distinct from Bois-Colombes. We will come to that presently."

I nodded, resigned to learning about the matter in the order of Holmes's choosing. "Please, continue," I said.

Holmes bowed his head politely. "The reason that we understood so little about the circumstances of Bythewood's fall into relative poverty was that while Bythewood is an Englishman, his wife was a native Parisian – and during their short marriage the couple used the same lawyers that her family – the Desmarais family – had employed for generations. In the three years since Mélanie Bythewood's untimely death, the apportioning of her personal wealth has been mired in legal dispute, and even details of the nature of her death have been zealously guarded by the firm. There is no doubt that Bythewood had little success in securing access to his wife's estate since his return to England, hence his woeful standards of living."

"Then he was not wealthy before the marriage?" Lestrade asked. "His money was all his wife's?"

"Quite so. That is not to say that Bythewood was any sort of pauper before they married. He had been gainfully employed, but he was already nearing retirement when he and Mélanie met in Paris at a society ball, an event which itself illustrates their respective standings – or, at any rate, their position in the eyes of the public. However, the safe embrace of the Desmarais home and its staff, and Bythewood's enjoyment of the patronage of his wife as his own funds dwindled, was cut short after her death – as I have said, the difficulties associated with the apportioning of her wealth meant that he received almost nothing, and so his return to his previous financial state was almost immediate. Determining the precise nature of these legal difficulties has been no easy matter, and I confess that I have been compelled to draw some conclusions based on limited information."

He fell silent, his gleaming eyes surveying the interior of the restaurant.

"Yes?" I said, hoping to prompt him. "Then what are those conclusions?"

Holmes waved a hand. "But I was speaking to you about cognac, before I allowed my story to be diverted."

I sat back heavily and exchanged a glance with Lestrade, who appeared as surprised as I was. It was unlike Holmes to flit between subjects of conversation in this manner.

"That is true," I said reluctantly.

"My visits to the wine cellars of Bois-Colombes produced no further lines of enquiry," Holmes said. If he noticed the dejected postures of both Lestrade and myself, he did not acknowledge them. "That is, I could not link Bythewood to any of them as a patron. As you suggested earlier, I had also checked in the accounts whether any businesses in Argenteuil stocked that brand, but there were none. It was this sparsity that proved the most important detail. I hurried back to my new friend Faucheux at the company offices, and this time I impressed upon him the need to know the *largest* purchaser of the cognac, rather than the small business that sold bottles. When I learned the answer to that question, I knew I had found my way onto the right track.

By far the biggest purchaser of the cognac, and also accounting for the lack of concern about selling it in smaller quantities to individual wine cellars, was a Belgian company which operates under the name Fourcroy. That company uses the cognac exclusively in the manufacture of Mandarine Napoléon."

Upon this pronouncement, he paused and looked at me expectantly.

I frowned, considering this for several seconds before exclaiming, "The other decanter in Bythewood's home – it was empty, but it smelled of citrus fruit!"

Out of the corner of my eye I registered Lestrade's sagging shoulders. Clearly this was a piece of evidence that he had not discovered for himself.

"What is the stuff, anyway?" he asked forlornly.

Holmes looked at me again, so I answered in his place. "An orange liqueur which was reputedly created for Napoleon Bonaparte at the turn of the century. For whatever reason, it has only been produced in large quantities within the last decade. It is a rather potent mixture of cognac, mandarin orange peel and a variety of spices." My cheeks flushed a little. "Some of the fellows in my club insisted I try it. They feel strongly that everybody ought to have a working knowledge of all the varieties of alcohol that are available." I considered adding that as of this moment my research had proved invaluable, rather like Holmes's exposure to all aspects of societal behaviour – but then I decided it was rather a dubious claim.

"This is all very well," Lestrade said, "but was it really necessary to go to all this trouble only to find the source of the man's favoured refreshment?"

Holmes exhaled sharply, indicating his disdain. "Once I had made this connection, everything else fell into place most satisfyingly."

Lestrade's eyes raised to the ceiling. In a laconic tone, he said, "You'd better tell us about it, then."

"Most importantly," Holmes said, "I was able to ascertain by means of a series of telegrams that, before commencing his retirement in Paris, Bythewood had been occupied in a senior departmental position at the Fourcroy distillery near Brussels. This in turn led me to narrow my search down to businesses in Paris which sold its exported brand of Mandarine Napoléon. There were none in Bois-Colombes, but I located a single cellar in Argenteuil. At those premises, I was able to determine that Bythewood had indeed been a regular customer some years ago – a fact that would have been difficult to unearth without the singular information about the Mandarine Napoléon, partly because it reduced the number of patrons in question, but also because Bythewood was identifiable only by my description of his appearance. That is, when he had been a patron of that wine cellar, his habit was to adopt an assumed name."

"And what was that name?" I asked eagerly.

"Ronald Moone."

My jaw dropped. "But that—"

Lestrade interrupted me. "Good Lord! So there is a most satisfying connection to Miss Abigail Moone after all!"

Holmes arched an eyebrow but otherwise ignored the inspector's pronouncement.

"The most salient piece of information," he said, "is that Ronald Bythewood, acting under a pseudonym, appeared to reside for a time in a rooftop apartment in Argenteuil, which happens to feature in that singular painting by Alfred Sisley that hangs in the Tate gallery."

At this juncture, my patient readers, I ask you to shift your attention from this Pimlico restaurant to an unprepossessing apartment in a north-western suburb of Paris, and additionally to retreat back in time by a matter of three years. I promise you that all details will be pertinent to the case outlined thus far, though I confess that some small amount of conjecture has been involved in order to present these episodes to you in a comprehensible and satisfying manner. Widely read Francophiles will note some differences between my account of these events and a highly popular account written by a celebrated authoress known as Noémi Patoche, who has only in the last six months begun to move within Parisian literary circles and whose sudden arrival has itself sparked much debate. (For my part, I suspect that she will never return home, which is a great loss for her own country and her former acquaintances.) While I make no claims that my description is definitive, I trust you will be satisfied that the information from which I have drawn inferences is at least a small step closer to a true account.

CHAPTER EIGHTEEN

Ronald Bythewood jammed his hands into the pockets of his jacket and pressed his back against the tall wooden shutters of the window of the *tabac*. The jacket was loose-fitting and its collar scratched continually at his neck; his cap was no better and seemed at least one size too large, so that he was forced to peer out from beneath its brim, heightening his sense of furtiveness.

Nevertheless, he reassured himself that despite the constant flow of people hurrying along the centre of the street – mostly aproned women carrying baskets and with complaining children in tow – a few others stood in the doorways just as he did. As to what their occupations may have been, Bythewood had no earthly idea. What he had initially taken to be suspicious glares were only the pinched, tired features of hard-working people. As he watched, some of these women ducked into the premises behind them and others emerged, as though the shops were a row of cuckoo clocks.

It struck him that the appellation 'La Grand Rue' held connotations entirely different to the Parisian streets to which he was more accustomed. In the neighbourhoods of Bois-Colombes, all of the streets were wider than this one – yet this street was indeed grand, in terms of the amount of people upon it at any moment of the day.

At the sound of a distant chime, Bythewood instinctively reached for his watch, but then he suppressed the action. Perhaps revealing such an item might undermine his pretence. Nevertheless, the striking of the hour meant that Audibert was late.

He passed another quarter of an hour in discomfort that was both physical and spiritual. He had taken to peering along the street and selecting a distant man at random, then following his passage until he passed Bythewood's position – then cursing under his breath before selecting another man to watch. Occasionally the carriages obscured his view, and when any larger vehicle passed, he lowered his head so that his cap further obscured his features.

Presently, a different sort of vehicle approached. In place of the horses that had passed earlier, the beast that pulled it was a feeble pony with a mottled flank, and instead of a carriage it drew an open cart with contents that clanked and jolted with each uneven paving stone. A scruffy boy, perhaps around the age of ten, sat nonchalantly upon the planks and beams within the cart, bouncing wildly but appearing otherwise undisturbed.

The motley-looking vehicle drew to a stop before the *tabac*. Bythewood turned his attention to the driver, who wore a tatty brown bowler hat and a suit in even worse condition than Bythewood's own. Bythewood finally recognised Audibert's drooping moustache.

"Ha! It *is* you!" Audibert exclaimed in French. "You're a fine sight, Bythewood."

Bythewood gave a low hiss, cutting him off. "It's Moone!"

Audibert gave an exaggerated display of confusion. "Moon? *La lune?*" He gazed up at the cloudless sky.

"My name is Moone. The name on the contract."

"Ah, yes. You know that nobody cares what your name is,

don't you?" He waved an arm to gesture towards the boy sitting in the cart. "Philippe here won't tell."

Bythewood turned from side to side. Nobody on the street appeared to be paying them any notice. It occurred to him that if anybody was conspicuous in this setting, it was Bythewood himself, and certainly not Audibert or his son. He forced his shoulders down and adopted the slouch that he had worked for so long this morning to perfect.

"You're late," he muttered.

Audibert shrugged. "You don't want to go inside? I didn't realise that your interest in the place was restricted by the time of day. Never mind. Off we go again, Philippe!"

Bythewood held up both his hands. In his halting French he said, "No, no. Please, let us go in."

Audibert performed an elaborate bow and hopped from the driver's seat, then clapped both his hands on Bythewood's shoulders. Bythewood winced but forced himself to return a bright smile.

Audibert approached the narrow door beside the *tabac* and, having withdrawn an enormous set of keys from his jacket pocket, fumbled to find one that fit the lock. After trying ten or more, and at a point when Bythewood had once again begun to steal furtive glances along the street, he grunted with satisfaction and shoved the door open.

"Stay and watch the cart, Philippe!" he called over his shoulder.

Bythewood followed Audibert along a dim corridor and then up a flight of stair so narrow that his shoulders touched the walls on either side. As they passed a doorway on the first floor, Audibert gestured at it with his thumb and said, "Old Gareau lives there. His mistress too, some of the time. They won't pay you any mind."

The next flight of stairs was almost pitch black. Audibert's footsteps and his laboured breathing indicated he had reached the head of the stairs. A metallic jangle suggested that Audibert was sorting through his keys again. Bythewood waited impatiently until, finally, a door swung open and a sliver of light interrupted the gloom.

"Your new home," Audibert announced. "Or whatever it is you're calling it." He strode into the room.

Bythewood followed cautiously. Inside, the boards creaked with every step he took. The room was square and blank, and plaster was peeling from the discoloured walls in several places. It smelled strongly of damp.

He crossed to the window and opened the shutters. The sound of horses and voices from the street below increased in volume. If he craned his neck he could see the people hurrying to and fro, but from anywhere further than a pace away from the window, the only view was of the shuttered windows on the opposite side of the street. Bythewood retreated hurriedly when he saw one – no, two – elderly women silhouetted in different windows, who seemed to be watching him dispassionately.

"There's a sink in the back room," Audibert said in a bland tone.

Dutifully, Bythewood crossed the empty room and passed into the smaller one at the rear of the apartment. As Audibert had promised, on the back wall, beside a door that hung lopsided in its frame, there was a sink with a rusty-looking tap above it, the pipe emerging from the ragged plaster as though it had grown there rather than having been installed. Other than that, the only item was a single chair set before the sink, putting the idea into Bythewood's head that the sink performed the dual function of providing both water and also some indeterminate sort of entertainment. One leg of the chair was broken and had been poorly repaired with a bulky mass of tightly wound wicker. Bythewood decided not to sit upon it without further investigation.

"You did say you didn't need a bed," Audibert said.

Bythewood replied, "But there is nothing here at all."

Audibert nodded vehemently, as though this fact were a particular point of pride.

"It does not matter," Bythewood said. He turned around. "Where is the—"

Audibert interrupted him by yanking on the badly hung rear door. "This way, please."

Bemused, Bythewood followed him out of the apartment and onto a metal gantry suspended high above a yard filled with crumbling masonry. He had never before had any trouble with heights, and perhaps what he experienced at that moment was related more to self-preservation than vertigo, but nevertheless he clutched at the underside of the iron steps that led upwards from this balcony and which threatened to strike him on the forehead if he stepped in the wrong place.

"You told me that the rooftop was easy to access," Bythewood complained.

In response, Audibert simply pointed up the stairs, then tramped up them. Each metal step groaned as he put his weight upon it. When Bythewood followed, he was compelled to use both hands and feet to climb, and he told himself several times not to look down.

By the time he reached the flat rooftop, Audibert was out of sight. It was indeed a fine viewpoint. With his hands on his hips Bythewood surveyed the warren of streets, and the spires that punctured them and, to the south, the grand sweep of the Seine and the narrow stripe across it that must be the Pont d'Argenteuil.

"I confess that it seems ideal," he said, still not knowing in which direction to address Audibert. "The distance from the basilica appears precisely the same as from your own rooftop."

He shielded his eyes, trying to determine where Audibert's home must be. Was the Rue de Calais only at the end of the main street, where he had stood for so long in wait?

Audibert emerged from behind a set of chimneys. "You are looking at the wrong basilica, my friend."

"What?" Bythewood exclaimed. He squinted to look at the nearby steeple – the same one that he had seen from ground level, at the end of the Grand Rue. "Is that not the Basilique de la Sainte-Tunique du Christ?"

"It is very *similar*," Audibert replied evasively.

Bythewood could only stare at him.

Finally, Audibert continued, "What you are looking at is the Saint-Denys Basilica. It is very fine, is it not? The Sainte-Tunique is a little over *that* way." He pointed, and only now did Bythewood identify a second spire reaching to the heavens, a couple of streets to the east.

For several seconds, he found that could not respond. Then he managed to say, "But it is vital that the landmarks remain the same. Two steeples, so close to one another! What confusion they will cause!"

An uncomfortable weight had begun to settle in his stomach. With a sickening sense of realisation, it dawned upon him that any leverage he had assumed he possessed had evaporated long ago, without him noticing. The impulse that had compelled him to retrieve his property from Audibert's clutches had only led him to rely more profoundly on Audibert's own judgement. In short, he, Bythewood, was an utter fool.

Partly to distract himself from this dismal revelation, he paced around the rooftop, avoiding the debris on the floor to edge around the chimney-stack. He looked at the bare surface of the roof, the damp patches, the gaps where tiles were missing on the eaves below. He put a hand to his mouth to stifle a moan.

In a weak voice, he said, "You told me that this place was ready for immediate use."

Audibert snorted softly. "I do not recall saying that. I told you very clearly that this apartment has a rooftop ideal for your purposes, which is certainly true. But do not fear, *Monsieur Moone*. It will be complete before the day is out."

"Then you will—" Involuntarily, Bythewood turned in the direction of the street, which remained out of sight, far below.

"I will fetch Philippe presently," Audibert said matter-of-factly, "and we will begin our work. You saw that we have already transported here all the materials we will need. I bought them at personal cost this morning, so I will require payment now, before we begin."

Bythewood pictured the collection of rough slats of wood in the back of the cart. Any construction that resulted from such materials would be a far cry from the secure, imposing structure on Audibert's own rooftop.

Half-believing that this entire encounter was nothing but a bad dream, he bent down to reach into his shoe, where he had secured a roll of notes, having mistrusted the baggy pockets of his rough suit to keep his money secure. He stood stiffly and Audibert watched him closely as he peeled off one note, then another – then Audibert reached out and took another two and nodded as he thrust them into a pocket.

"I had hoped that everything would be in place by this afternoon," Bythewood said in a resigned tone, certain that further disappointment was imminent. "I am expected back at home by six o'clock."

"*Many hands make light work*," Audibert replied. He plodded towards the metal stairs.

Bythewood frowned in confusion.

Audibert turned, saw his expression, and responded with a leer. "Perhaps it will be possible, if you help build it."

CHAPTER NINETEEN

It was a little after half past seven by the time Bythewood reached the tall metal gates of his home on the Rue de la Côte Saint-Thibault. He glanced in both directions along the wide boulevard, then along the crossroads junction with the Rue des Bourguignons. There were only a few carriages on the road, and, to his immense relief, a single pedestrian. He had almost arrived at this junction ten minutes ago, before he had realised that in his dazed state he had neglected to change out of his rough suit, which was even less presentable now that his shirt was stained with oil and one of his trouser-legs torn at the knee. He had dashed away, bowing his head to hide his face from the few people that he passed, and then he had changed his attire hurriedly in an empty side street, cursing his mistake. Now his soiled disguise was bundled up in his satchel. He eased open the gate, teeth clenched at the high-pitched squeal made by its hinges, and immediately slung the satchel behind the bushes lining the wall that encircled the property.

He stood motionless on the doorstep for several seconds, attempting to gather his composure. Then, taking a deep breath, he entered his home.

The smell of food greeted him as he passed into the wide lobby. His stomach contracted in anticipation – he had not eaten since breakfast. Shortly after noon Audibert had sent his son to the bakery, and the boy had returned with bread and cheese that the pair of them had wolfed down with pleasure. They had offered none to Bythewood, and when he had suggested fetching some lunch for himself, Audibert had muttered darkly about Bythewood's supposed hurry to complete their work, and that perhaps it might be completed another day after all, and so Bythewood had let the subject drop.

He passed into the dining-room. The table was set, but nobody sat at it.

As he emerged into the lobby again, Angèle bustled from the door that led to the kitchen.

"I hear you come home, sir," the maid said in the stilted English that she always deployed when speaking to him, despite his protestations. She wiped her hands on her apron. "Is it time that I serve the—"

Only now did she look up and appraise Bythewood's appearance. Her mouth formed a wide 'O'. "Sir – what has happened?"

Bythewood's face flooded with heat. He looked down instinctively, for a moment fearing that he was still carrying his satchel filled with compromising evidence. His shirt was a little crumpled and his trouser creases poorly defined, and he had worn his oldest pair of shoes throughout the day, not wanting to carry a second pair, but he saw nothing in particular that ought to alarm the maid.

"You are hurt, sir," Angèle said, reaching out towards his face but not touching it.

"No," Bythewood replied quickly. "Not at all."

He raised his hand to his face, patting it all over. To his surprise, his fingers came away with their tips painted red.

"It is nothing," he said in a strained tone. "Ink. It is only ink."

He rushed to the wide staircase and bounded up the steps. Then, halfway up, he turned. "Please inform my wife that I have returned home and that I will be ready to dine presently."

Angèle remained frozen in her peculiar posture of alarm, one hand outstretched, the other cupped over her mouth. Bythewood spun and hared up the stairs to reach the antechamber connected to his bedroom. In the ornate mirror above the sink he saw a horizontal cut across his right cheek, from which blood had dripped and then partially dried without smearing. He imagined it was what a rapier wound sustained during a duel might look like. It was no wonder that the maid had been frightened.

After a little cautious probing, he determined that the wound was far less severe than it first appeared. Carefully, he dabbed with a sponge to wipe away the dried drops of blood, as well as the smears of oil and sweat that marked other parts of his face. As he worked he told himself that despite his lack of need of a bed at the Argenteuil apartment, he would require some other items of furniture and some useful tools – the principal of these being a mirror to hang above the rusty tap. He could not afford to leave so many clues about his activities.

"I beg you, accept my apologies," Bythewood said as he strode into the dining-room.

His wife was standing at the far end of the table. She often stated that she did not enjoy dining alone, and always insisted on waiting for Bythewood.

"What was it that detained you all this time?" Mélanie enquired stiffly.

Like the maid, Mélanie always spoke English in Bythewood's

presence, despite his assurances that he was perfectly capable of conducting conversations in French, after a decade working in this country and in Belgium. It had always been a point of contention, and he had long felt that his eventual relenting had effectively reduced his standing within his own home – not that it had ever been substantially greater than it was now.

"Business matters," he said in as airy a tone as he could muster.

Mélanie regard him levelly, one hand placed on her hip. She was still a fine-looking woman, her cheeks flushed and the cut of her red gown revealing her trim figure. Somehow, though, the thick arch of her eyebrows, which suggested simple curiosity or amusement when she was with her friends, seemed to signal mistrust whenever she addressed her husband, and Bythewood could not help but interpret her stiff-necked posture as haughtiness.

"Please, let us eat," Bythewood said.

Mélanie bowed her head and lowered herself into her seat. Gratefully, Bythewood copied the action so that they sat at opposite ends of the table, separated by a distance of six feet. He wished that they might sit closer to one another and on adjoining sides, if only so that she would not stare at him so.

Angèle and a younger maid entered carrying tureens and plates laden with food. Bythewood's stomach performed another somersault. He nodded his gratitude as vegetables and dark slabs of duck breast were ladled onto his plate.

"And were they resolved?" Mélanie said.

"Were what resolved?" he replied in bemusement.

"These business matters."

"Ah. Yes." He hesitated. "Or rather, not entirely. They may yet take a little more of my time."

"So you are presented with a problem, then?"

Bythewood put down his knife and fork, having not yet succeeded in putting any food in his mouth. "I assure you, my love – I am doing everything within my power to overcome these difficulties. You must be patient with me."

Mélanie smiled. In truth, there was nothing in her expression that suggested anything other than sympathy and warm indulgence towards him.

"It is only for your sake that I am concerned," she replied. "Any other gentleman might be more aggravated by these problems that have perpetually beset your finances. But we can rest easy, as we have our home and an allowance that permits us to live as we are accustomed to living."

Once Angèle had filled her glass with wine, Mélanie raised it in a toast.

"Happy anniversary, my dear," she said.

Bythewood failed to stifle a groan, and then he was compelled to mask it with a loud cough. He reached for his own glass, tipped its rim and spilled wine onto the tablecloth, then on instinct perhaps inspired by a visual association, he reached up to touch lightly the wound on his cheek. He made another lunge at the glass and succeeded in swallowing a mouthful of Bordeaux without choking.

"Happy anniversary, Mélanie," he responded, his throat tight with tension.

His mind whirled – what were her expectations of this forgotten event? Precisely sixth months after the day of their marriage he had presented Mélanie with an inexpensive pendant, but she had received it in a decidedly frosty manner and he had never seen her wear it either in public or within their home. His failure to buy a gift for this day, their first wedding anniversary, had not been a conscious one, but even now he felt unsure whether offering one would have been appropriate.

He became aware that his wife was still watching him.

"I am glad that we have decided to do no more than to spend a pleasant evening together to mark the occasion," she said. Once again, there was no trace of accusation in her tone. Bythewood was certain, though, that they had made no such decision – at least, he had not been involved in reaching one. It seemed that she was simply being kind towards him, though this kindness seemed diminished when she added, "Particularly as I find that I have a headache this evening."

Despite the barriers to their communication, and the difficulty in articulating those barriers or, indeed, articulating any true emotions at all, he was grateful to her and he supposed that was a form of love. Furthermore, he reminded himself that his urge to marry her (could it really have been only a year ago?) had been inspired by tenderness as well as a calculation of wealth – and it had been Mélanie who had hastened the formalising of the arrangement. And yet Mélanie must have had her own expectations of him at that time. His façade, that of an affluent investor, had been more plausible than he had could have imagined, and now he was paying for his success by other means, finding himself forced to uphold his pretence in perpetuity.

For several minutes they ate without further conversation, and Bythewood almost succeeded in telling himself that the silence was a companionable one. The food was delicious; warmth and the rich flavours of the duck and the wine seemed to flow into all parts of his body. He told himself that all was well.

"In point of fact," he said before he had even reached a conscious decision to speak, "these troublesome business matters may have the effect of preventing any access to my savings, for a short time."

Mélanie stopped eating and, once again, raised those curious eyebrows.

"I believe I have told you before of the difficulties in the flow of funds from my Belgian bank?" Bythewood continued. Without waiting for an answer, he added, "There are a host of reasons, all too dull to go into at this moment. A result of having worked for so many manufacturers and distilleries in so short a time – my popularity during my working years is the bane of my life, what!" He followed the statement with a barking laugh that sounded to his own ears like somebody else entirely.

Mélanie's eyebrows rose still higher. She voiced no complaint, though the flush of her cheeks seemed more pronounced than ever.

At this point Bythewood began to feel almost giddy. There had been no repercussions to forgetting the date of his wedding anniversary. Perhaps there were no hard and fast rules to marriage at all, as he had presumed.

He concluded, "The outcome is that I'm likely to be rather short for the next several weeks."

Finally, his wife responded with a frown. Bythewood braced himself for a diatribe.

"Short?" she said with only the mildest inflection.

"Yes, short." Understanding dawned upon him. "Apologies, my dear. It's an English idiom. I mean only that there are likely to be barriers to the access of my own savings. So I will have less money available in these next weeks."

"Ah." She nodded solemnly. "So you will need money from me."

"As I say, it will only be in the very short term." He laughed nervously. "That word again: *short*. How silly my language can be. I assure you, Mélanie, that I expect to have unfettered access to my own money very soon indeed."

When his wife returned her gaze to the food on her plate, Bythewood congratulated himself. He passed the rest of the meal forming an inventory of the purchases he would make, using his wife's money, in order to make his Argenteuil apartment a useful base of operations, and, furthermore, a pleasurable respite from the cloying atmosphere in his own home.

CHAPTER TWENTY

Sherlock Holmes paused in his account, my rendition of which I hope is a more characterful depiction of Bythewood's former life. He leaned back in his seat, surveying Lestrade and myself.

"I visited the apartment myself," he said, "this time under the guise of a buildings inspector from the Seine-et-Oise department. This ruse was more effective than I had anticipated – even at a glance at the internal walls, it was evident that the building was riddled with damp and suffering from subsidence. I was welcomed inside immediately. The second-floor apartment is occupied by a mother and child, for the time being."

"They are soon to leave?" Lestrade asked. He looked up from the note-book within which he had made occasional notes with a pencil during Holmes's telling of his tale.

Holmes paused. "The place was very bare, though I am happy to say that I left it in a better state than when I arrived. But yes, I am bound to conclude that they will soon leave."

"Then you presented this woman with money?" I asked.

Holmes's expression remained inscrutable. "The woman in question works in the *tabac* beneath the residential apartments, a fact that resulted in her rent being subsidised, but which has held her prisoner in such paltry accommodation for several years. Her husband died in an accident at the dockside some years ago. Her infant is very thin. Yes, I felt that she deserved charity."

I nodded, my eyes never straying from his face. I had long suspected that Holmes occasionally contributed to charitable causes that he uncovered during his investigatory work, but I could not recall finding such clear evidence of it before now.

"These are inconsequential details," Holmes said bluntly, as though he preferred to move away from this topic of discussion, "and this woman was unable to provide any details about Ronald Bythewood. My examination of the apartment revealed nothing of note, other than the access to a wide area of the rooftop of the building, though she had barricaded the balcony to avoid any risk of her child falling from it. However, a man named Gareau, who lives in the first-floor apartment, confirmed that a man of Bythewood's description had once rented the upper rooms, though he never spent the night there. This cast doubt on my first supposition – that Bythewood had entertained a mistress in these rooms – as did the dismal state of the apartment, which could not have deteriorated so rapidly as to be totally unlike its appearance a mere three years ago. No, Bythewood's use of the rented accommodation was for some other purpose.

"Once again, I was compelled to consider all aspects of the case," Holmes continued, toying with the torn quarters of the reservation card on the table with his index finger. "Any element that stands out, however trivial it appears, may be pertinent to an understanding of the whole."

Lestrade sighed heavily, but I remain engrossed in the conundrum. "Then what other element captured your attention?"

"Bythewood's behaviour in Vauxhall Park," Holmes replied.

Lestrade scoffed, "His behaviour? He toppled over and died,

man! What other behaviour do you expect of somebody who is filled to the brim with poison?"

Holmes ignored the inspector's outburst. "Watson, you will recall that one of the witnesses who proved most useful" – his penetrating gaze indicated that he was referring to none other than Abigail Moone – "described Bythewood veering from side to side before he succumbed to the effects of the poison, and before his heart finally gave out."

"Yes," I replied. Then I glanced at Lestrade. "But as the inspector says, that is nothing unusual, considering his condition."

Holmes nodded. "But before that point he had succeeded in crossing Vauxhall Bridge and taking his usual route to the park without attracting the notice of anybody that we know about. His movements were laboured and his pace fitful, but he remained in control of his direction of movement – until, abruptly, this appeared not to be the case."

My ears pricked up at this. Any reference to 'appearance' was habitually Holmes's invitation to consider quite the opposite interpretation of a situation.

"Then you are suggesting that he was instead approaching something?" I asked. I tried to conjure an image of Bythewood behaving as Miss Moone had described. Holmes was still watching me attentively. "Or perhaps he was avoiding something?"

Holmes gave a tight-lipped smile. "I suspect that the latter is closer to the truth. And what was in the park that might be avoided?"

The word 'people' was on the tip of my tongue, but I knew instinctively that it was not the desired answer. Once again, I summoned the scene in my mind's eye, overlaying Bythewood's documented actions of that day with his customary movements, as though the Bythewood of each successive day might exist at the same moment, or as though his routine each day left ghostly traces that remained visible long afterwards.

I exhaled with relief as answer came to me. With my eyes locked on Holmes's, I spoke a single word: "Pigeons."

Holmes restricted his congratulations to a double tapping of his index finger on the table – though I saw in his eyes a display of satisfaction that warmed my heart.

"*Pigeons?*" Lestrade repeated derisively.

Holmes's eyes gleamed, betraying an altogether different emotion. "Every day, when Bythewood reached Vauxhall Park, he sat on a bench and fed the pigeons. In itself, that may be nothing unusual for an elderly man with little to do each day. But combined with his other characteristics, and his actions on the day of his death, the habit acquires enormous significance."

I held up a hand. "What characteristics?"

Offhand, Holmes replied, "The pea and barley growing in his attic room, for a start, beside the only window that had been recently opened. He selected as his bed-chamber the attic, rather than the much larger first-floor room he left crammed with unwanted furniture, because it allowed views over the surrounding buildings and therefore represented an ideal vantage point from which to observe birds. In addition, there was the clock on the mantelpiece in the dining-room of his house. Do you recall its unusual appearance, Watson?"

"Only that it had only one hand, and it was entirely brass. It looked more like a sailor's compass than a clock. But what bearing does a broken clock have on this matter?"

"We will come to that presently," Holmes replied with a wave of his hand.

His eyes strayed over my shoulder for a moment. Then his eyes flicked back to me. "It was your appearance in Vauxhall Park that inspired my deduction, Watson. I must thank you for that. When I was playacting Bythewood's movements, I looked up as

I veered from side to side, just before the moment of my 'death', and there you were, watching. I was compelled to see myself from your perspective, and to appreciate the presence of the birds that had taken off in alarm, in response to my violent motion."

Before I could respond to this unearned accolade, he continued, "So, why did Bythewood veer away from the pigeons that day, as opposed to approaching them in order to feed them, as would be usual?"

I considered this for several seconds. "Because he was afraid."

"Of what, precisely?"

"Not afraid of the birds themselves, surely," I replied slowly. "In that case… it was what they represented."

"And what was that?"

I blinked and stared at him blankly.

Casually, Holmes extended his finger again, drawing the quarters of the torn reservation card towards him. Having arranged them into their complete form so that the word *SPIRIT* was once again visible, he commenced writing similar-sized uppercase letters on the blank left-hand side, each of the characters spanning the horizontal tear.

Lestrade and I both turned our heads to read the word, which concluded with an amendment to the 'D' shape to the right of the vertical tear. Upon the card was now written: *SILVER SPIRIT.*

"It sounds rather like…" I began.

Holmes arched an eyebrow expectantly.

"Without context," I mused, "I might have assumed it was either the name of a boat, or a racehorse… but in the circumstances I presume it is actually a racing pigeon."

"Indeed," Holmes replied. "This is a fact that was difficult to establish, given that the bird never participated in a formal race – but, as I have been able to prove, it was *entered* for a race, though the bird failed to take part in it."

He stretched languidly in his seat, as though he desired nothing so much as an afternoon nap.

"Incidentally," he added, "did you know that while pigeon racing is increasingly popular in France, it was first made popular in Belgium?"

CHAPTER TWENTY-ONE

As had become his custom, the moment Bythewood entered the apartment, he tucked his satchel into the low cabinet that he had bought solely for that purpose. In truth, there was little chance of anybody knocking at his door, and an even more remote chance of that person spying his fine clothes and reaching any conclusions. Even so, the habit of hiding away his alternative attire at each end of his journey (here, within the cabinet; in Bois-Colombes, in one corner of the coal-shed that he had cleared of dirt) afforded him a sense of inner peace that he could no longer do without.

The apartment was only a little less sparse than when he had first acquired it, but now the sight of its interior warmed his heart each time he arrived. The square main room was dominated by the single most expensive purchase he had made: an ornately patterned Afghan rug that he had discovered at the marketplace. Upon one corner of it was a low table, its top barely wide enough to support a plate and a cup, and beside it a single armchair, facing the window – though the window itself was permanently covered with a gauze blind that allowed in a great deal of sunlight but afforded no view over Bythewood's neighbours on the opposite side of the street. When Bythewood sat in this chair he had no desire to see anything of the world outside – rather, he dozed happily here whenever the weather worsened or when his aching bones demanded more comfort than the wooden deckchair on the rooftop could provide.

He passed into the scullery, within which was a dresser containing all of his crockery as well as his meagre store of food. Objectively, he knew that there was no real impediment to him stocking the cupboard with any food of his choosing, no matter whether or not they matched the working-class persona he had adopted. Nevertheless, he had continually followed his instinct and had bought only modest supplies that could be purchased locally and which he presumed would not be out of keeping with the food in any other of these tiny apartments which were crammed together high above the street. He had soon found that a luncheon of bread and cheese and a cup of inexpensive wine not only sated his hunger, but pleased him inordinately more than any of the fine food that Angèle might provide at home. The only exception to his self-imposed rule was the Fourcroy cognac that he had discovered for sale in a nearby wine shop. He had been so surprised to see it available – as opposed to the Mandarine Napoléon in which the distillery specialised and which formed the bulk of its exports – and it had so vividly recalled his previous life in Brussels that he had bought several bottles immediately.

In the scullery Bythewood filled the small coffee pot and lit the small portable stove, then, while waiting, he filled a metal canister with water from the tap. Presently, he poured coffee into a chipped mug, tore a hunk of bread from a baguette lying upon the surface of the dresser, and made his way out onto the balcony and then up the swaying metal stairs, the canister in one hand and both the mug and bread held precariously in the other.

His birds greeted him upon arrival, calling and fluttering against the wire of the cage.

The loft may have been rather shambolic in appearance, the ends of each wooden strut still rough and unpainted several weeks after construction had been completed, but it served its purpose well. When Bythewood recalled the lofts on Audibert's rooftop, which contained all twenty of Audibert's own pigeons and, in addition, several half-dozen collections belonging to other men like Bythewood, he no longer felt any pang of envy. Instead, he considered his own loft to possess a far more honest, unassuming appearance, and increasingly he considered his six pigeons to be the plucky underdogs, each like a newcomer at a free-to-enter boxing match, scrawny but possessing wily intelligence and lacking any hint of indolence.

"Morning, pretties," Bythewood said affably. Then he kicked at the feet of the wooden deckchair so that it turned to face the loft, and he sat and dipped his bread into his coffee before eating it, feeling certain that few people in the world could be as content as he.

When he had finished his mid-morning snack, he put down the mug and opened the low cupboard at one side of the loft – a piece of furniture intended for indoor use, and consequently the wood had already become warped, not that it mattered a jot. From this he retrieved a sack of feed. He eased back the bolts of the loft door, which were so secure as to be difficult to move, and then he swung the door open to distribute feed from the sack into the trough at the foot of the loft. Then he turned to reach for the metal canister and topped up the water dishes.

His chores completed, he put away the sack and canister and stood observing the pigeons as they fed. Voices and clattering sounds from the street rose from below, and once again he marvelled how well hidden he was when he was up here, and how well hidden was the world below from him. One could easily imagine that the rooftops were the true ground and that everything below was not only unimportant, but actually submerged. Only the steeples rose from this new horizon like limbless trees.

Despite his initial fears, the pigeons' confusion over the twin basilicas had proved surmountable. In this sole regard, Audibert had provided sensible advice when Bythewood had complained about the issue. With his customary shrug, he had said, "You would be required to rehome the pigeons anyway – they cannot be expected to understand their changed location immediately, simply because the distance is not great. It is a straightforward matter. You must house them here on this rooftop for, say, a fortnight. Then make exploratory flights from close by – I would recommend the gardens of the basilicas themselves, to begin with. They will come around to their new premises before long. And if not, surely they will return to my own lofts, which will remain familiar to them."

Bythewood had considered this. "And in that case, I hope that you will return any such bird to me?"

"For a fee, naturally," Audibert had replied, a wide grin forming on his face. "My time is valuable, *Monsieur Moone*."

Thankfully, this eventuality had not arisen. As instructed, once two weeks had passed with the pigeons in almost total captivity, Bythewood had spent the last week performing cautious experiments, taking first one bird and then another to nearby parks, then striding back to the apartment, colliding with pedestrians as he attempted to watch the skies through the strips of light between the narrow streets with their frustratingly tall buildings. For whatever reason, the similarity of the Saint-Denys and Sainte-Tunique du Christ basilicas had caused difficulty for only one of the birds, and yet after an anxious hour of waiting, even that one had returned to the rooftop loft eventually, appearing none the worse for wear.

The birds skittered around Bythewood's outstretched hand but, as usual, five of the creatures seemed to understand that he was reaching out to one of their number in particular; they moved out of the way like chorus-girls parting to reveal a main attraction.

"There, my Silver Spirit," he murmured as the ghostly-grey pigeon came forward to step into his cupped hand.

The bird cooed and nuzzled into his shoulder as he crooked his arm around her.

"To-day is your day," he whispered, and the pigeon made soft sounds that seemed like agreement.

Bythewood reached out to the cupboard and retrieved a cloth sack with a wooden, oval base.

"I know you don't much like it," Bythewood said, "but when you are released you will understand the need for your transportation. In you go."

He propped the sack on the edge of a shelf within the loft and, with almost sensual care, eased Silver Spirit into it, continually smoothing her feathers as he did so. The bird made no complaint and seemed only mildly alarmed at its new, dark confines. Bythewood closed the drawstrings and lifted the sack tentatively. A placid cooing emitted from it, and he beamed with relief.

"Apologies to the rest of you," he said to the remaining pigeons in the loft as he closed the doors once again. "You will have your turn in due course. But we must lead with our best."

The Butte d'Orgemont would ordinarily be a thirty-minute walk from the apartment, but Bythewood's care over his precious cargo slowed his pace a great deal. When he finally arrived at the bare stretch of common he lowered the sack and carefully slackened the drawstrings, little by little, whispering reassurances into the gap. Upon leaving the main street of Argenteuil, Silver Spirit had shuffled within the sack at first, but for most of the second half of the journey she had remained almost entirely motionless.

"We are almost there," he said softly. "Show me that you are well."

As if she understood the exact meaning of his words, Silver Spirit rustled her wings, then looked directly up at him, her narrow head cocked appealingly.

"When we do this next," he said, "I promise not to bump you around so. We will take the train. You would like that, I'm sure."

Another low murmur from the bird reassured him entirely. He tied the drawstrings again and rose. Then, to his surprise, he saw that he was being watched by a woman wearing a headscarf, and at her side a wild-haired girl of about six or seven years of age. The woman held the handle of a bulky perambulator, within which sat a bonneted infant who leaned out from the side, twisting to stare balefully at Bythewood.

Bythewood flushed and looked down at the sack in his hands.

"It is a pigeon," he said. "My own property – I am not a poacher."

They continued to stare at him.

"*Une pigeonne*," he said weakly. He pantomimed looking all around him, one hand shielding his eyes as though he were a sailor in the crow's nest of a ship. "*Où est la Société Colombophile?*"

At first he assumed that the woman had not understood him. Then, the wariness of her expression unwavering, she raised a hand to point to the north-west.

Bythewood bowed to convey his thanks, and hurried away.

He adjusted his direction several times in the next minutes, feeling exposed on the wide common. Then, finally, he found himself scrambling down a steep grassed slope, his toes catching on the roots of bushes and threatening to send him tumbling. He ought to have visited the place long before this point, to determine its exact location.

After a few more minutes of staggering along the foot of the hillside, a gap in the tree line revealed a row of sheds enclosed within an outer wall of wire netting. He hurried towards it, then winced as the sack bounced against his leg, and he slowed his pace again.

Several men were within the enclosure, conversing in low tones. Others stood before the pigeon lofts at its far end, bending or standing on their toes to observe the birds held within. Bythewood entered through a gate in the wire fence and shut it quickly behind him. The men who had been in discussion turned to look at him. Bythewood raised his sack and held it before him as if it were an offering in some sort of ritual.

"You're a newcomer?" one man said in French, speaking from beneath an enormous bristling moustache.

Bythewood nodded. "I have been in contact with a Monsieur Pueyrredón," he said, knowing that he was garbling the pronunciation. "I was told that I must come here to complete some formalities."

"So to-day you are ready to race?" another man said, tilting back his cap in order to examine Bythewood's sack.

Bythewood bowed his head again.

"Then you will certainly win!"

Bythewood smiled, but then it dawned on him that the exclamation was perhaps not intended as a compliment.

"I do not mean I wish to race to-day," he assured the man hurriedly. "I know there is no race to-day. I brought my bird only because I wish to complete a practice flight from the common." He paused, attempting and failing to perform a translation quickly, then added in English, "The more the merrier."

The moustached man frowned. "You live nearby?"

"On the main street of Argenteuil."

"And you have not conducted practice flights from anywhere further than this? That is a distance of perhaps three kilometres – the race will be sixty kilometres at least."

"I know that very well," Bythewood replied, "and the race I intend to enter is the one at the beginning of July. In the time remaining I will perform flights of greater and greater distances. I assure you I am confident of my chances."

"And what makes you so confident?"

Dimly, Bythewood sensed that he was already saying too much, but the men had rattled his nerves, and in defiance he continued, "I am no novice, and neither is the bird in question. She is the offspring of a champion that raced many times in the region around Brussels. If I had remained in Belgium, she would be a champion even now. Rehoming her has proved a minor obstacle, but I am confident that she will surpass the abilities of her father before her."

The man in the cap slapped the surface of a table beside him. "Let's see this girl, then!"

Others had now gathered nearby to watch. Bythewood sensed that he was being drawn into a game, and that while his own nature might appear to be sportsmanlike, it was far from a gambler's. If he was to make substantial money from Silver Spirit, then it would have been better if he had not boasted about her capabilities. Nevertheless, he placed the sack on the table, opened it carefully, and withdrew the pigeon, who nestled pleasingly against his chest.

Several of the men nodded in approval. Bythewood heard muttered remarks: "A fine bird," and, "A pretty thing."

"And you say that she is as fast in the air as she is beautiful?" the moustached man said.

Again, Bythewood told himself to be cautious. He shrugged, affecting nonchalance.

"You are not so sure after all?"

"As you say," Bythewood replied, "I only have information relating to short distances."

"But you have made your calculations."

Bythewood conceded this with a slight bow of his head. The gathered group had grown tighter around his position. Now that they were closer to hand he realised that, for the most part, their attire was decidedly more presentable than the suit he used a disguise. They possessed wealth – perhaps as a result of their efforts racing pigeons. In addition, the bearing of several of them was erect, almost haughty, reminding him more of his neighbours in Bois-Colombes than those in the streets of Argenteuil. It occurred to him that they probably considered him a misguided amateur pinning all his hopes on the winnings of a race. The fact that he was indeed fixated on regaining some of his earlier losses in order to reimburse Mélanie was beside the point.

Abruptly, a sense of contrariness rose up within him. Despite his ugly clothes, he was a gentleman, and furthermore he was equally as experienced at racing pigeons as any of these men.

"Just short of one hundred and ten kilometres per hour," he blurted out, hardly regretting his outburst.

Silence followed.

"You cannot possibly be certain of that, after such short trials," said a tall man at the back of the scrum.

"Indeed I am," Bythewood countered boldly. "Before I left Brussels I conducted many practice flights there. One hundred kilometres per hour was a matter of no exertion for this bird. It has only been the issue of rehoming that has prevented her from racing here sooner."

Some of the men turned to look at one another. Then all eyes returned to the creature held in the crook of Bythewood's arm.

Abruptly, the moustached man turned to face the door of the largest shed – it was as large as a bungalow – and cried out, "Albert!"

Presently, a short man wearing a suit even more dishevelled than Bythewood's emerged from the door, which rattled on its loose hinges. He blinked in the sunlight as though he had been asleep only moments before.

"What is it?" he asked in a distinctly bitter tone.

The moustached man tilted his head to gesture at Bythewood. "Got ourselves a new racer, and a new member of the club along with her. Do the formalities, would you?" Then, to Bythewood, he said, "What's your name, *Anglais*?"

"Bythe—" he began, then caught himself. "Moone. Ronald Moone."

One eyebrow raised, the moustached man said, "And I am Voland. It means 'to fly', which is appropriate, no?"

"Ah yes, Monsieur Moone!" the man who had emerged from the shed said enthusiastically, and Bythewood realised that this 'Albert' must be none other than the M. Pueyrredón with whom he had been corresponding these last weeks. "I have everything ready for you, monsieur." Immediately, he ducked back inside the shed only to return moments later carrying a pasteboard folder and with a cube-shaped wooden box tucked under his left arm.

As Pueyrredón approached the huddle of men he noticed Silver Spirit for the first time.

"*Mon dieu*," he exclaimed, almost dropping the box in his excitement, "but is that not an exquisite creature? She is most welcome here."

"Not just a beauty, but she flies like a bullet," Voland said, a touch sardonically. "If our friend's accounts are to be believed."

"I can believe it," Pueyrredón said, bending to Silver Spirit and stroking the back of her neck with an outstretched index finger.

Feeling distinctly crowded and fearing for the nerves of his bird, Bythewood withdrew her slowly and then eased her carefully back into the sack, though for the moment he left the drawstring a little loose. "If we might proceed with the formalities?"

Pueyrredón blinked rapidly. "Certainly, certainly." He took three pieces of foolscap paper from the pasteboard folder and placed them side by side on the table. "These are the forms for you to complete, or you may take them away with you if you prefer. More importantly, here is your device." He made to present the wooden box to Bythewood, but then hesitated. "I presume you have the money to act as a deposit, as we agreed?"

Bythewood reached into his purse and withdrew the twenty-franc note that he had managed to inveigle from Mélanie the previous week. He had done so on the pretence that the money would be used as a deposit for an entirely different purpose – to secure a new solicitor to operate on his behalf in transferring his Belgian funds, which were almost non-existent.

He heard a collective intake of breath and cursed his lack of foresight immediately. Evidently, he ought to have broken the note elsewhere to avoid attracting suspicion. He pushed the note back into his purse and felt around for coins – but there were none.

"I hope you are able to give change?" he said weakly.

Pueyrredón's posture had suddenly become more erect. "Yes, certainly," he replied. He took the note and, with almost military bearing, he carried it before him to re-enter the hut.

In the absence of Pueyrredón, Bythewood avoided meeting the eyes of the men around him by examining the wooden box. He opened it and withdrew the circular brass clock, turning it in his hands.

"Have you seen one in operation before?" Voland said.

Bythewood shook his head. "I have heard of them."

Voland reached into the box and plucked out a small rubber ring rather like the one that had been attached to Silver Spirit's left leg since she was a squab, though this one appeared far more flexible.

"This removes the need to bring the bird here after the race," Voland said. "The clock will be set running at the point of release, as will all of our own with exact synchronisation. This ring will be attached to the bird's leg, and then when she arrives at your own home you must simply remove the ring and place it *here*." He pushed the ring into a slot at the base of the clock still held in Bythewood's hands, resulting in a dull click. "The clock will stop, and you may then return here to the club with clock and ring in hand, to announce your victory." His lopsided smile indicated his continued scepticism about Bythewood's claims.

"Thank you," Bythewood said, turning the device again in his hands and rubbing its brass surface with his thumb. "It is a modern wonder."

Pueyrredón returned and the group watched as he slowly counted out change, placing each coin in turn onto the tabletop. Bythewood felt that the collar of his jacket was becoming ever more itchy all the time, until his discomfort became almost intolerable. Wanting nothing more than to flee with Silver Spirit and his achievement of membership of the club, he bundled the foolscap forms back into the pasteboard folder, muttering about returning them at another time, and waited impatiently for Pueyrredón to complete his interminable task.

As he left, he felt the eyes of every member of the club upon the back of his head. Silver Spirit, too, seemed agitated, shuddering inside the confines of the sack.

Bythewood allowed himself only a moment's rest. He stood with his hands on his hips, watching Silver Spirit trace wide circles and then flow upwards to scuff against the clouds, appreciating the gleam of her spread wings, the ellipses of her path towards the heights. Then he blinked, nodded in satisfaction, gathered up the empty sack and set off southwards at a brisk march.

He knew some of the men at the club would consider him callous for continuing to perform test flights without a partner on his rooftop at home, waiting to welcome each pigeon and to place it into the loft. However, each time he had returned home the bird in question had always been waiting patiently for him on the perch outside the loft. He had tested this approach with each of the other birds in turn before risking Silver Spirit – but she, too, had proved as obedient as the rest. Furthermore, his own patience had been rewarded. All of Silver Spirit's early promise that he had observed in Belgium, and the inheritance of good blood from her father, had remained evident, despite the long delay in between Bythewood's arrival in Paris and his arrangements to transport his six pigeons safely from Brussels to the loft on Audibert's rooftop. If he knew anything at all about pigeons, he was certain that Silver Spirit was a champion merely waiting for the opportunity to complete her first race. Once she fulfilled that first requirement, and once Bythewood had collected his winnings, along with any profit from wagers on the side, he would lavish ever more money and attention upon her – and she would repeat her feat again and again. In turn, Bythewood would finally regain his independence after having relied upon his wife for an entire year – a year in which she had given him nothing in return save permission to lodge in her family home and gifts of meagre pocket-money every once in a while.

The lane that led from the Butte d'Orgemont was narrow and bordered on one side by a tall, thick hedge, which prevented

Bythewood from continuing to strain his neck to watch Silver Spirit's progress. He chided himself for the pang of fear this absence produced in his chest – even if he could see the sky, she would be little more than a speck, already halfway home. Nevertheless, the tight sensation in his chest lingered. He increased his pace to hurry along the road.

He was disappointed to discover that, after a shallow bend, the lane straightened out once more but seemed to continue endlessly into the distance. This route seemed much longer now than it had on his outward journey. The air was growing colder, too. He told himself he would have to become more hardy if pigeon racing was to become his primary occupation, and his primary means of earning money. For the actual races he would be required to take a train on both legs of his journey, on the assumption that he would be able to make arrangements for some Argenteuil boy to remain on the rooftop to operate the pigeon clock and then convey the ring to the racing club – if any suitably trustworthy boy existed. He pulled his coat tighter and hurried along.

Abruptly, he stopped and spun around to face the opposite direction.

He saw nobody on the path behind him.

He replayed the last moments in his mind. He had heard no sound, at least as far as he had been aware. What was it that he had sensed, then?

The clouds seemed to have lowered and thickened since he had left the common land. Now they appeared almost like ghostly, inverted hills, low enough that he fancied he might be able to reach up and strike them if he had carried a walking stick. The light too, had dimmed, and the hedge cast a blocky shadow over almost the entire width of the lane, as far back as the bend. Beyond that bend was an even murkier darkness.

He waited several seconds, allowing his eyes to adjust. Still, he saw nobody.

By the time he had passed the grassed, untended land and then numerous allotments, and found himself striding between houses on either side of the road, he scolded himself for his earlier fearfulness. Here, the daylight seemed brighter, and some elderly occupants of the houses sat on wooden chairs beside their doors. He raised his cap at one or two of them as he walked past, and they responded with polite nods. Nevertheless, he could not help but turn to look over his shoulder every now and again. Still, nobody followed him.

Presently, the road widened to become the Rue de la République, and the areas through which Bythewood passed became more and more populous. Now people walked past him in both directions, so that whenever he turned to look back in the direction from which he had come, there was always somebody behind him, but then that person would soon disappear into one of the houses or narrow side streets. The fact that Bythewood could not shake the sense that somebody was following him became ever more irksome. He told himself that next time he was required to visit the Société Colombophile, he would instead take the river path as far as possible, and then keep to far wider streets.

The buildings grew taller and, once again, the sun was hidden from view.

When Bythewood reached the Rue de la Grande Ceinture, he hesitated at the point where the footpath veered from the road, representing the quickest means of crossing the railway. He felt sure that he had heard footsteps behind him, but now they had stopped. Moreover, he was absolutely certain that if he set off again, the footsteps would resume.

Having reached a sudden decision, he scurried down the

few steps that led to the footpath, but then immediately turned left to pass beneath the blossom-heavy boughs of a cherry tree. Here he crouched, holding his breath and waiting.

Within moments, he saw a man approach the top of the steps from the direction of the street. His hands were jammed into his long overcoat and his collar was pulled up. He wore a bowler which, though narrow-brimmed, cast enough of a shadow over the face that Bythewood could see nothing of his features. Indeed, the waning sunlight came from directly behind the man, so that he was little more than a silhouette.

This stranger descended tentatively, then stopped at the foot of the steps. Bythewood saw his head turn slightly, as though he were listening for sounds. Ahead of this position the path wound tightly around trees and hedges that marked the periphery of the properties to either side. The man hurried along for only a few steps to reach the first bend in the path, then craned his neck to look around the tall bushes. Bythewood pressed a clenched fist to his mouth to stifle a gasp. He had been right all along.

After the stranger had disappeared around the bend, Bythewood forced himself to count slowly to five before he emerged from beneath the cherry tree. Then he stumbled up the steps, back the way he had come, his mind racing to calculate an alternative route over the railway line in order to reach his apartment.

The remainder of his journey was uninterrupted by pursuing strangers, but that did not mean that he was able to proceed at a fast pace. He paused often, ducking into doorways to survey his surroundings furtively, and he continually sought safety in more populated areas, which resulted in his reaching the bank of the Seine before he dared make his way west and finally north-west, using the twin spires of the Argenteuil basilicas as waymarkers. Then he waited at the corner of the main street, reassuring himself that the movements of people along the street appeared entirely normal, and that those people that were motionless and watching the bustle from doorways were the usual old women, mothers and children. Finally, he permitted himself to rush to the door beside the *tabac*, all the while chastising himself for his overt display of panic.

Once he was inside, he pressed his back against the door and remained there for several seconds before making his way up the stairs to the second floor. It was only now that his thoughts returned to Silver Spirit. He fumbled with the lock of his apartment door, flung it open, then dashed to the balcony and up the gantry steps.

She was there, on her perch, as calm as could be. Her feathers seemed almost translucent in the dim light.

"My good girl," he murmured, reached out to stroke a finger along the back of her neck. "You have no fears, at least."

Silver Spirit cooed attractively as he opened the loft door, and then she hopped inside obediently. Bythewood found himself so affected by the gentleness of the creature that he actually wiped a tear from his eye.

"I'm a silly old fool," he said, now addressing all of the pigeons at once. "We all know that we are alone here, just you and I. That is how it should be."

He remained on the rooftop for several minutes, simply regarding his pigeons. Then, finally, he reminded himself of the time, and he returned downstairs to the apartment. Despite his reassurances to himself, he found himself approaching not the door but the single front-facing window. Carefully, he eased the lower part of the gauze blind away from the frame and then, once his breathing had settled, he knelt to press his head to the glass. From this awkward angle he could see half of the width of the street. His eyes followed one of the passing carriages heading east towards the Saint-Denys Basilica, then his gaze skipped to another horse and carriage heading in the opposite direction, back towards his position. Women bearing baskets weaved to and fro across the street, and tradesmen cried unintelligible words that merged with the rumble of wheels and the clack of hooves.

Then Bythewood froze. On the opposite side of the road, beneath the overhang before an unmarked doorway a little further along from a grocer's shop, he saw a dark shape. At once he knew that it was the same man he had seen on the path leading from the Butte d'Orgemont. He fancied that the man was looking up at him, and yet he found himself oddly unable to retract his head or to rise from his peculiar kneeling position.

He watched, paralysed in this uncomfortable pose, as the dark shape peeled away from the shadows of the doorway. Without emerging far enough into the open to reveal his face, the man turned to the east and strolled away.

CHAPTER TWENTY-TWO

"You have been late each day this week so far," Mélanie said in a mild tone.

Bythewood occupied himself in the act of ladling vegetables onto his plate, then he nodded to Angèle, who topped up the wine in his glass.

"There has been a great deal that has occupied my mind of late," he replied sombrely.

"Related to business?"

He stifled a scowl at her inflection of the word 'business', as though the very concept were a subject of mockery.

"Indeed, yes," he said. "When one has been a loyal employee as long as I was, one finds that obligations to one's former employers last well beyond retirement. My erstwhile employers at the Fourcroy distillery continue to value my contributions."

His wife smiled. "Then I hope that they continue to reimburse you appropriately for your trouble. May I ask what nature of task it is that they have laid at your door?"

Bythewood studied her from across the length of the table, trying to judge the level of this new threat. "Well, I—"

"I only ask because your clothes these last days have reeked of alcohol. Angèle endeavoured to keep the fact to herself, but she is not accomplished at hiding things from me."

Bythewood exchanged a glance with the maid, whose cheeks became as flushed as those of her mistress. Nevertheless, his internal response was one of gratitude. Yes, he had transported a bottle of cognac from the wine shop to his apartment in his satchel, and then he had continued to use the satchel for three days before he realised that the cork of the bottle must have been badly fitted; a small amount of the liquid had seeped from the bottle and into the fabric of the bag. If his usual clothes had acquired the scent of alcohol while they were stored away in the cabinet, he had certainly not realised it – he supposed that the same scent would have been in his mouth and therefore remained undetectable to him. Regardless, it occurred to him now that this mistake may have useful repercussions. If Mélanie suspected him of covert drinking in his hours away from home, then this might preclude her from reaching other, far less desirable, conclusions about his activities.

He turned to Mélanie and offered what he sensed was a foolish smile.

"You are quite right," he said. "It has been necessary to sample their wares in the course of my work."

Mélanie's response was a complex mixture of self-satisfaction and disdain. She smoothed back her pinned-up hair, as if to highlight the differences in their appearances: her the presentable landowner, Bythewood the dishevelled and dependent sot.

"Nevertheless," she said calmly, "this additional work of which you speak appears not to have eased the flow of your finances. Is it the case that these additional sums are being paid into the Belgian account which has caused you so much difficulty to access?"

Bythewood did not reply at once. He sensed that this was

a ploy, and that simply agreeing with his wife would lead him further into complexities of argument that would prove ever more entangling. He reminded himself that it was only a matter of days until Silver Spirit's first race. His goal was so very near, and therefore he was only required to play for time.

"No," he said finally, though he sensed that he had already taken too long over his reply to appear truthful. "It is merely that they are small amounts, with the promise of much more to come. I assure you that that the payments from Fourcroy will be forthcoming, as will access to my existing funds. All the same, I apologise for the difficulty this has caused you."

She shook her head sharply. "These are *your* difficulties, Ronald, not mine. Though I confess that I am glad of my decision to keep our financial affairs separate, despite your encouragements to share our lot. I am certain that my estate is worth rather less than you anticipated – the upkeep of this house is not inconsiderable, and I am sure you are as despondent as I am that so much of my wealth is confined to property rather than ready cash. I ought to have been clearer about the state of things before we married."

Again, Bythewood sensed a trap – but this was one that he had no idea how to navigate around.

With a sigh, he said simply, "I understand what you are implying, Mélanie."

An arched eyebrow was her only response.

Wearily, he continued, "I, too, am sorry that I was not more forthcoming about the state of my finances, a year ago."

Her pinched expression said more than any words. Bythewood marvelled that it was only now that such a substantial truth had occurred to him: that Mélanie had set as much hope in his ability to ensure her financial stability as he himself had placed in her. They were both opportunists, and they had both been duped by one another.

His wife watched him steadily. The ticking of the clock beside the doorway seemed intolerably persistent.

"And yet we can do nothing about the past," Mélanie said in a tone of dull remorse.

Bythewood reached for his wine glass. "Then shall we toast to the future?"

His wife's eyes widened. Scornfully, she repeated, "The future?"

"As I say—"

"You consider that our marriage has a future?" she asked sharply.

Out of the corner of his eye, Bythewood noticed Angèle slink away from her position in the doorway and disappear into the lobby.

"Of course, my dear," he said meekly. "When my allowance is once again accessible, we will be on steadier ground, and there will be no disparity between us…"

His plea trailed off as his wife shook her head, wincing as she did so.

"The problems we have ahead of us are related only in part to money," she said. "If you believe that francs and centimes represent a salve that will cure the many ailments that afflict our marriage, you are a bigger fool than I realised."

Dimly, it occurred to Bythewood that he was of quite the same opinion, and it struck him as ironic that they were so closely in agreement despite their many differences. Yet, when his mouth opened, he produced only a wordless, strangled sound of dissent.

"It will not surprise you to learn", Mélanie said in a louder voice, "that I wish for a divorce."

"No," Bythewood said immediately.

Silence fell. Mélanie continued to stare at him. While he

appreciated this time to absorb all that was happening, he found that some barrier in his mind prevented him from assessing his own true feelings. All that he knew was that his course of action – to race Silver Spirit at last, to garner winnings, to restore his standing in the community and within his own household – remained one that still seemed plausible, if only his wife would allow him to see it through. Moreover, timing aside, his plan remained consistent with his initial hopes just over a year ago, when he had identified in Mélanie a suitable match, in terms of her standing and financial state, if not her actual character.

"No," he repeated, this time more vociferously. "I will not allow it. Our fortunes will soon change, and you will see sense."

Even though he had barely had the opportunity to sample any part of his meal, he rose from the table and stumbled to the doorway, then immediately made his way up the stairs towards his bedroom, his sole intent to prevent Mélanie from sending him any further off course to-night.

CHAPTER TWENTY-THREE

Bythewood strolled with a light step along the Grand Rue of Argenteuil, entering it from the direction of the Société Colombophile at the Butte d'Orgemont, having received his final instructions and directions to the start of the race to be held the next day. This street had long become as familiar to him as any place he had lived in the past. While the rooftop permitted only a view of other rooftops, he found that he had become equally as fond of the scene at street level, as it heralded his arrival and the resumption of his time spent with his pigeons – or, in the latter part of each day, his triumphant return to find Silver Spirit on her perch. The spire of Saint-Denys viewed at ground level between the rows of buildings of the main street now acted as a homing beacon, not only for the birds but for Bythewood himself. Despite its emptiness and shabbiness, the apartment in Argenteuil was now undoubtedly his true home.

He halted on the pavement with his arm outstretched, key in hand. The door was already ajar.

Telling himself that Gareau or, more likely, one of Gareau's women, had likely left it open carelessly, he went inside and locked the door behind him.

Some quality of the air in the narrow corridor was different. Bythewood couldn't account for it, but as he ascended, he grew ever more certain. It persisted even as he passed Gareau's door and climbed the second flight of stairs.

Still, nothing appeared amiss about the door to his apartment. He watched it in silence for half a minute before telling himself that there was no cause for alarm. Nevertheless, he kept his hand as steady as possible as he placed the key into the lock, to avoid making undue noise.

The key would not go all the way in. He tried twice, then took it away and bent to peer into the keyhole. It was blocked from the other side.

He rose sharply, realisation dawning upon him – but at that same moment a creaking sound came from the other side of the door and then it swung open.

Bythewood stared in astonishment. Mélanie stood before him.

With a cordial bow of the head, she stepped back into the room to allow him to enter. Thoughts of escape ran fleetingly through Bythewood's mind, but he dismissed them. He was already within the trap. If he was to get away, he would first be required to gnaw through the ropes that held him tight.

Once inside, he turned on the spot in the centre of the main room. The fact that there was only a single armchair now seemed absurd – should he insist that his wife sit there, or should he take it himself? Deliberating over the matter proved too complex for his addled mind, so instead he simply faced Mélanie, who stood at the opposite side of the Afghan carpet as though they were boxers preparing to meet in the middle of a ring.

"How long have you known about this apartment?" he asked.

"For some time," she replied.

Her eyes shifted up and down, surveying him, and it was only now that he remembered that he was wearing his rough suit and cap. He put down his satchel and kicked it aside. There was no longer any need to keep its contents uncreased.

Mélanie was dressed in plainer attire than was usual for her. Perhaps she had responded to the same instinct that had driven him to adopt his outfit – though if so, her attempt was undoubtedly less successful. When she had passed along the Argenteuil streets, she must have stood out from others in the crowd, easily identifiable by the quality of her clothes, however muted the style.

"And how did you learn about it?" he said, feeling no compulsion to speak in anything but a frank tone. His charade was at an end, after all.

She shrugged. "You are not so good at hiding secrets as you imagine."

Bythewood frowned and turned to the closed door. The key was still in the keyhole on its inner side. "Audibert let you in?"

Her brow creased. "The door was open when I arrived here. It seemed very careless of you."

Mélanie crossed to the armchair and sat in it as casually as if it were a seat in her own home. It was clear that she had been sitting there before his arrival; a mug was set upon the table alongside the chair. When she reached for it and took a sip, Bythewood saw that the mug was already almost empty. He presumed it had been filled with water rather than cognac taken from the dresser, and he could not recall ever having seen his wife make a pot of coffee herself. He would have been surprised if she were even capable of completing such a task.

He considered her answer. It seemed an odd thing for her to lie about having procured the key somehow – and surely Audibert could be the only source of a copy. It occurred to him that he knew little about Mélanie's habits while he was out of the house for such long hours each day, but it nevertheless was inconceivable that she might know somebody as lowly and untrustworthy as Audibert.

"Why did you come here?" he said. "And what is it you want now?"

"To see this place for myself," she said, her nose wrinkling as if to convey her conclusions about the state of his apartment, "and as for your second question, what I *want* remains unchanged. I want a divorce. I trust that this deception of yours will provide me with the evidence required to plead my case."

"How?" he asked, stunned.

"Infidelity," she replied quickly, enunciating each syllable carefully, as though it was a word to savour.

He could not help but laugh. "You imagine I procured this place to entertain women?"

She shrugged. "'Entertain' is a strange choice of word. I suspect the entertainment has been all your own."

He shook his head, more due to wonderment than to contradict her.

She gazed up at him from her seated position, frowning. "Then what was it? I know I should not be curious, but even so I find that I am."

Bythewood laughed again, this time more hollowly, and for the first time he looked towards the rear door, which was visible through the gap that led to the tiny scullery.

The rear door, too, was ajar.

He turned to Mélanie, staring at her stupidly, then back at the door.

"You have not been—" he began.

Interrupting his own question, he leaped towards the door, yanking it open and then bounding onto the metal balcony. The steps complained at his rapid ascent and their creaking echoed even after he had reached the rooftop.

Bythewood stood motionless, goggling at the sight before him.

Though the situation was evident even at a moment's glance, he took the half-dozen paces towards the loft, as slow as a somnambulist.

The perches within the loft were empty.

Six huddled forms lay upon its floor, behind the wire mesh. Five of them were mottled grey-brown, the sixth a ghostly near-white. Silver Spirit's body looked far thinner than he remembered, and her neck appeared longer, curled down against her flank as though she were only resting.

Bythewood slumped to his knees before the loft, sobbing uncontrollably.

CHAPTER TWENTY-FOUR

"And then what?" I asked, impatient to hear more.

Holmes, for his part, appeared too distracted to return to his tale. He looked over my shoulder and I turned to see that our drinks had arrived.

As the waiter set down his tray and placed a filled glass before each of us, Holmes said, "This is one of the few restaurants in London to serve this particular brand of cognac. The manager is a Parisian himself, and is in the habit of bringing across the English Channel a small supply of bottles each wintertime. Perhaps you will recognise the smell, Watson."

I frowned and slid the glass towards me. Though I inhaled the scent of its contents, my sense of smell was evidently less attuned than Holmes's: I identified nothing more precise than *cognac*. However, I understood my friend's meaning immediately.

Holmes saw my concerned expression, but held up a hand. "Your instincts are sound, Watson. As a simple precaution, I suggest that neither of you drink from your glasses."

Without waiting for a response from either myself or Lestrade, he then leaped up from his chair and pounced upon the waiter, grappling him into submission before the waiter could so much as cry out in alarm.

Immediately, an uproar broke out across the entirety of the restaurant. Several of our fellow diners rose to their feet and dashed towards our table, but they were immediately halted as Lestrade, too, got to his feet and brandished his police badge, calling out for them to stay back. Some of the restaurant staff had already gathered in the doorway leading to the kitchens, and presently a burly man in a pinstriped suit pushed his way through their midst and strode towards us.

"What the deuce is the meaning of this?" he said, his eyes darting first to Lestrade, then to myself and finally back to Holmes and the waiter still bent double, both of his arms restrained behind his back.

Ignoring the man, who was clearly the restaurant manager, Holmes addressed Lestrade. "If you would be so good, this would be an opportune moment to call in your colleagues who are waiting outside."

Blankly, Lestrade nodded and then darted away to the front of the restaurant. In very little time, he returned with two uniformed constables. Lestrade's wondering expression was unchanged as he directed them to restrain the waiter, taking over from Holmes.

Once relieved of his captive, Holmes swept one hand over the other as though knocking dust from them. "Thank you," he said, addressing the constables. Then he nodded at Lestrade. "I will confess that he is somewhat stronger than I had anticipated."

Now that two men held him rather than Holmes alone, the waiter was permitted to stand upright. He was lean, with sallow cheeks, and though his hair had been mussed during the struggle, it was clear that he would ordinarily appear a well-presented fellow, with lacquered hair and a handkerchief in the breast pocket of his dark suit. His eyes were dark and gleamed with intelligence and alertness, despite his circumstances. Despite all of this, there was nothing about him that suggested he was anything other than a presentable waiter, down to the fact that he had still not spoken, as if his code of service prevented him from doing so.

"My dear sir—" the manager said to Holmes.

Holmes turned to face him with as placid an expression as I have ever seen upon his face.

The manager blinked as though stupefied. "Explain yourself, man! To come in here and accost a member of my staff…"

Holmes waited patiently for him to complete his statement, but the man's outrage seemed so great that words now failed him. The manager turned to survey the restaurant, only now appearing to notice that all of the former diners had become bystanders to this scene. Turning back to Holmes and Lestrade, having now recognised the police badge held by the latter, he lowered his voice to the level of a stage whisper to say, "I would thank you if you would explain yourself, gentlemen! I have a business to run."

"Very well," Holmes replied. Calmly, he took his seat again.

The manager was agog. "I meant briefly, man! Do not make yourself comfortable – I want you out of here!"

"If you would like an explanation," Holmes replied cheerfully, "then you must be patient. My friends here are no doubt equally curious to understand what has happened."

Both Lestrade and I played our part and nodded our assent. Following Holmes's lead, we resumed our seats. Lestrade gestured to his constables to bring their captive to stand alongside the table. It struck me as a scene from some topsy-turvy courtroom, with the accused adopting the usual position of a judge, looking down upon lawyers and jury alike.

Holmes appeared entirely unmoved by the presence of

the waiter, to the point of ignoring him entirely. He pointed to the intact reservation card which had remained on our table throughout our meal, and upon which was written that peculiar name, *J. BERRY*.

"There is one aspect of this card that both of your failed to notice," he said, addressing both Lestrade and myself, "and the name that I chose was not the only test that it fulfilled."

After considering this for a moment, I said, "Its size, or rather the size of each quarter part, is precisely the same as the note found in Bythewood's hand, is it not?"

I noted that the man held prisoner to my right stiffened at my mention of Bythewood's name. I harboured no doubt that Holmes had apprehended the correct person – though how the pieces of the puzzle fitted together continued to elude me.

Holmes reached into a pocket and once again withdrew the envelope containing the crumpled, torn card bearing the apparent message *D C DID IT*. He flattened our reservation card and laid the two side by side on the table. As I had suggested, the note found in Bythewood's hand was precisely one-quarter of the size of the complete reservation card.

"Quite so," Holmes said, "and moreover the card is of precisely the same thickness, texture and colour. In short, the card found upon Bythewood's person came from this very restaurant. But that is not all that can be determined. Look closer, Watson."

I did as he commanded, and very soon I gasped with recognition. "The writing is in the very same hand!" I cried.

It was clearly the case, once I trained my eye to focus only on the upper parts of the characters in *J. BERRY*. In doing so, the letter B and the two instances of the R were each reduced to an oddly squashed letter D – which appeared exactly the same as those in Bythewood's message.

I turned to face the waiter, whose expression had become

ever more pained as he watched this scene play out before him.

"And this man wrote both of these messages, I presume?" I said.

"That is correct," Holmes said. "This man, Alexander Lennox, wrote the note that was discovered in Bythewood's possession when he died. Furthermore, Alexander Lennox is the murderer of Ronald Bythewood."

For some moments the waiter – Lennox – retained his erect posture, and he faced Holmes proudly, but by degrees I saw his shoulders begin to slump. Either he knew of Holmes's reputation, or he understood that the path that had brought Holmes to perform this arrest meant that there could be no protesting the accusation.

"The timing of our meal was of some importance," Holmes said, once again addressing both Lestrade and me, "as Lennox's work shift is due to end shortly."

Lestrade leaned forward. "And you are saying that this man Lennox abused his position in order to poison Bythewood?" Then he stared at the glass of cognac, which was still untouched before him. "And was this his means of doing so?"

Holmes nodded, ignoring the aghast expression on the face of the restaurant manager.

"But for what reason, Holmes? You don't expect me to cart him off to Scotland Yard merely on your say-so? I mean—"

I interrupted him. "Lestrade, have you not been listening to the story Holmes has told us?"

The inspector's eyes darted. "The Paris affair? All that business with the pigeon fanciers?"

I saw a gleam in Holmes's eyes. "The very same. Alexander Lennox was a member of that particular Société Colombophile, one of those men to whom Bythewood had shown his prize pigeon and inadvertently revealed the creature's capabilities. Judging by the accounts of several other members of the club, Lennox was suspected of more than once following

Bythewood to his apartment in Argenteuil."

"You can't prove anything of the sort!" Lennox exclaimed, and we all turned to look at him now that he had finally spoken.

"I hardly need to do that," Holmes murmured.

"But you told us that Silver Spirit was never actually raced," I protested, "so surely these men were not yet true rivals."

"And I have another objection," Lestrade added. "If Bythewood and this man knew one another from this pigeon club of theirs, then it stands to reason that Bythewood would recognise him here in the restaurant as he was served."

Holmes raised an eyebrow. He replied wryly, "Very well, Lestrade. Would you do me the pleasure of describing the waiter who brought us our meals earlier?"

Lestrade's mouth opened and closed several times before he concluded, "It was this man here."

"You are certain of that?"

The inspector's eyes shifted to the desk beside the kitchen doors, where several other waiters were grouped in a huddle, watching these events from a position of safety.

"No," he said, and let out a long exhalation that seemed to deflate his entire body. "I confess that I did not look at the waiter directly, whoever he was."

Holmes nodded. "A waiter's role is to remain invisible as far as possible, and Alexander Lennox is as good at his job as any other man here."

"Apart from his predisposition towards poisoning," I noted, "which one may argue undermines his professionalism."

To my delight, Holmes responded to my witticism with a chuckle. Then he addressed Lestrade alone. "In truth, the illustration you have so neatly provided has no bearing on this situation. Bythewood encountered this man only once in Paris, amid a group of others, so there would be no reason for him to recognise Lennox here in London, particularly as the circumstances are so removed from that previous event. However, Lennox knew Bythewood's appearance very well indeed."

"So," I said slowly, trying to knit together all of these disparate events, "Lennox knew that Silver Spirit was a threat to his own success at racing... and he followed Bythewood to learn the whereabouts of his apartment – and the whereabouts of his pigeons... and then he killed Silver Spirit, along with the other poor creatures, in a fit of anger. Am I close?"

Again, Lennox struggled in the constables' grip, but did not speak.

"You are more than close," Holmes replied. "You have described the situation perfectly."

"All of this is very well," Lestrade said impatiently, "but what should concern us most urgently are the events here in England. So... just as Bythewood did, Lennox returned to England, assumed work here in this restaurant... and then Bythewood came in unannounced one day, and Lennox recognised him and poisoned his drink. Am I correct?"

"Yes," Holmes replied. "Bythewood became a regular patron of this restaurant, so Lennox was able to plan ahead – though I suspect he did not leave it very many days before making the decision to act, perhaps fearing that Bythewood would recognise him after all. He used the most noxious substance that was readily available to him – carbolic acid, kept for the purpose of cleaning the fixtures in the kitchen. Diluted in as little liquid as a serving of cognac, he believed that it would prove fatal."

I noted his slight emphasis on the word 'believed', and reminded myself that that would not have been the case if it were not for Bythewood's angina.

Holmes half-turned to gesture towards the group of waiters standing at the desk, who responded with alarm, some turning away as if to pretend that they had not been watching. "Then he observed from over there, perhaps, as Bythewood drank the contaminated drink."

He turned to Lennox. "But then an idea occurred to you, did it not? You realised that, even if Bythewood was to die, in his last hour of life he would not understand *why* he was being put to death. That thought persisted and very soon became intolerable to you."

To his credit, Lennox did not crumble under Holmes's scrutiny. Instead, he inhaled deeply and stood ever more proudly, so that the constables either side of him appeared more like ceremonial guards than his captors.

"No matter how you view men of my station," he said in a steady voice, "I am a gentleman, and a gentleman is bound by his honour and recognised by his record. Your allegations are unfounded, naturally, but your insinuations about my character are perhaps worse."

Holmes had listened to this statement with interest, but he now waved a hand dismissively as if disappointed at its contents. "In acting quickly, he acted rashly," he said to Lestrade and me. "He took up a pen and something to write upon – this reservation card – and wrote a message that he knew would be meaningful to Bythewood alone. At this point, Bythewood no doubt already felt out of sorts, but the agony produced by the poison would not yet have produced a burning sensation. He gestured for his bill. When it arrived, sitting alongside it was this note, with its reference to the pigeon Bythewood had once owned: Silver Spirit. Perhaps at this point Bythewood stumbled to his feet. Perhaps he looked around wildly. Or perhaps he dismissed the note as a cruel joke or perhaps he even attributed it to chance, by some convoluted logic. However, he did leave the restaurant – though not before tearing up the note into quarters. What follows is the important aspect: he left the building still holding the torn card, which aroused panic in the onlooking Lennox, who now cursed his rash decision to write the note. Though he may have hoped that Bythewood might discard the pieces somewhere without notice, he could not be sure of it. So, at the first opportunity, he followed Bythewood – or rather, he went directly to a place that he anticipated that Bythewood would go, having observed him at that location on the days leading up to the poisoning."

"The Tate gallery?" Lestrade suggested. He had been nodding eagerly with each new detail Holmes supplied.

I shook my head. "Holmes is referring to Vauxhall Park."

Lestrade's eyes widened.

To Holmes, I said, "So that man in the park who approached Bythewood when he fell – that was Lennox? And he was not attempting to help Bythewood, nor harm him. He wanted simply to retrieve the note, which he feared might implicate him in the crime."

"Indeed. The moment his shift was over, he hurried to Vauxhall Park, in the hope that Bythewood had kept to his usual routine, which partly coincided with Lennox's own custom after finishing his morning shift. Quite why he failed to follow Bythewood out of the restaurant immediately is admittedly a puzzle, though even one of Lestrade's constables might hazard a guess."

As he said these words, Lennox's gaze flicked to one side, to rest upon the figure of the restaurant manager, and a blaze of indignance flashed in his eyes. "I *told* you it was a matter of great importance," he muttered, his earlier aloof stance abandoned.

The manager raised both of his hands in response, as if to represent an apology. I could not help but smile.

Holmes, who had similarly observed this exchange, nodded in satisfaction. Ignoring the accusatory expressions of the constables that still held Lennox, he continued, "Lennox knew nothing about Bythewood's visits to the art gallery, because he was compelled to complete his shift here during that time, but he had previously seen Bythewood in the park, feeding the pigeons. Perhaps that very act was what attracted Lennox in the first place, and caused the Argenteuil association to occur to him immediately. Yes, Watson, you are correct. When Bythewood stumbled – perhaps even revealing that the pieces of the note were still held in his hand, as you will recall that our witness only saw him from behind – Lennox rushed forward and clasped his hands. He succeeded in prising three of the torn quarters of the note from Bythewood's grasp, but inadvertently left behind the fourth, which eventually made its way into our possession."

Lestrade swung around in his seat to look at Lennox. "It seems as though this fellow is unlikely to dispute your account, Holmes. Guilt is written all over his face."

Immediately, Holmes retorted, "That may be enough for Scotland Yard, but I confess that I still prefer to rely upon facts to prove a man's guilt."

I had barely been paying heed to this exchange, despite agreeing somewhat with Lestrade's assessment of the expression on the waiter's face. I continued to stare at Lennox, confounded.

"But none of this makes a dash of sense!" I exclaimed in frustration. "Why on earth would Lennox desire retribution for the killing of this bird, Silver Spirit… if he himself was the killer of the creature? From your story, Holmes, you present the case that Lennox stole into Bythewood's apartment by some means, and that he poisoned the birds on the rooftop."

Holmes's eyes flicked to the waiter. "Would you like to settle this matter, or shall I?"

Lennox only curled his lip in response.

"Very well," Holmes said. "The key aspect that you lack, Watson, is the motive."

"Nonsense," I snapped. "We can all see very clearly that Lennox hoped to prevent Silver Spirit from racing."

"Yes. But why is that?"

"To avoid Bythewood pocketing any winnings. He believed Bythewood's story about the abilities of the bird. He wished to succeed in his own wagers where otherwise he might have lost money."

Holmes pointed at the waiter. "Lestrade, you are confident in your ability to read faces. Would you say that this is a man who might kill a gentle creature simply to secure a handful of francs? I should make clear that his expected winnings from racing his own pigeon would have amounted to nothing close to a life-changing sum, and he bore no substantial debts."

Lestrade scrutinised the man anew, and I followed his lead. Certainly, Lennox's proud stance and his manner of looking at us all along the length of his angular nose seemed to contradict the assertion being levelled against him.

"I suppose not," Lestrade admitted after a pause.

"Then what was the true reason?" I demanded.

"It is certainly the case that he wished to prevent Silver Spirit from participating in that race, and any others that followed," Holmes said calmly, "but his reasons went deeper than simple monetary greed. Rather than gaining additional winnings for himself, Lennox's objective was simply to prevent Bythewood from being enriched. In turn, the reason for that desire was to avoid at all costs the restoration of Bythewood's financial status – because that would have weakened his wife's case of divorce, which rested upon the untruth relating to Bythewood's initial claim of wealth, which in turn had ramifications of her expectations of a certain lifestyle."

I gasped and then stared at Lennox, whose appearance now seemed to change again. No longer an indiscriminate murderer, no longer a killer of animals, he now adopted another guise: that of a thwarted suitor.

"Lennox and Bythewood's wife were lovers!" I cried.

I saw the restaurant manager wince and look over his shoulder. Most of the diners sitting at the nearby tables were still watching our exchange with the utmost interest.

We all stared at Lennox. It was clear that he saw no benefit in attempting to deny the fact; the fire in his eyes confirmed that it was true.

Quietly, Holmes continued, "Now you understand why Bythewood would have been familiar to Lennox, but not the other way around. Within the family home would have been photographs and other likenesses of Ronald Bythewood, no doubt haunting Lennox during his frequent visits to that house. From the Bythewoods' solicitous maid, Angèle Kucheida, I learned that the adulterous affair lasted some months, and I suspect that Mélanie knew as little of Lennox's predilection for racing pigeons as she did of her own husband's. I would be grateful if you would confirm that supposition, Mr. Lennox?"

Lennox's head bowed subtly, and now I detected grief in his laconic manner. "The circumstances in which Mélanie and I met were coincidental," he said, unaware of Holmes's instinctual wince at his use of the word. "We encountered one another at the north bank of the river, where we each found ourselves drawn with the aim of quiet contemplation, finding ourselves there together at a particular hour on most days. It was only long after we had struck up daily conversation, and after the nature of that conversation had taken a turn to the intimate, that I understood that Mélanie's husband was the same man who had recently become a member of the Société Colombophile. I assure you that it was a source of no pleasure to know that my rival was both a racing enthusiast and an Englishman."

Holmes nodded with satisfaction. "Thank you," he said. "In return, I can provide you with some information that *you* may not know. The reason for the continuing difficulties in apportioning Mélanie's wealth and estate following her death was because she had been in the process of amending her will, making it somewhat difficult to determine where the money ought to be directed. Mr. Lennox, I know it will be of little comfort to you to know this now, but a good deal of the money may eventually have found its way to you, and may have done so almost immediately, had you not returned to England. You did so shortly after Bythewood came to the same decision independently, following his wife's untimely death."

Throughout this series of revelations, I had still been attempting to tie together these disparate stories. Finally, I said, "But this still does not explain the note that Lennox wrote, and its reference to Silver Spirit. It still seems back-to-front to issue it as a threat, given that Lennox himself killed the bird which Bythewood prized so highly."

Holmes waved a hand. "To Lennox, Silver Spirit represented an act of retribution. In the first instance, he had killed the bird in order to punish Bythewood for his poor treatment of Lennox's lover, Mélanie. And then—"

Abruptly, Lennox gasped for air. We all turned to look at him as he broke into heavy sobs.

Then he raised his head and bellowed, "And then he killed my love!"

Once again, everybody in the restaurant spun around to stare.

Slowly, I said, "Do you mean to say that Bythewood killed his own wife?"

"Yes!" Lennox wailed. "Is that the behaviour of a gentleman? No matter his upset about his blasted bird. Is that the behaviour of a *human*?"

I turned to Holmes, aghast. "Is it true?"

Holmes placed his fingers together under his chin, his elbows resting on the tabletop. "Certainly, Mélanie's death occurred shortly after Bythewood found the body of Silver Spirit and his other birds. Some degree of cause and effect appears undeniable."

I waited, knowing my friend well enough that this was far from an end to the explanation.

"Again, I believe I have information that may be new to you, Lennox," Holmes said. For the first time, I saw a hint of empathy in his eyes. "You believe that Bythewood poisoned his wife in a fit of spite, to match your poisoning of *his* true love, his Silver Spirit. But I am afraid it may not be so simple as that."

Lennox only stared at Holmes, all colour having drained from his face.

Holmes hesitated, then said, "As I imagine you are aware, Mélanie was transported to the Lariboisière Hospital directly from the apartment in Argenteuil. The newspapers reported that her death, which occurred several days later within the confines of the hospital, was the result of an accident – though in each report this term has the appearance of a euphemism, evidenced by the malign conclusions drawn by Lennox himself. Several statements I gathered served to place Bythewood at the sheds at the Butte d'Orgemont half an hour before his arrival at his apartment, and yet substantial doubt was cast over his direct involvement in his wife's death. My assessment is that members of the Desmarais family, who still enjoy influence in that region, themselves confected this doubt."

"But for what earthly reason?" I asked, still watching the morose Lennox.

In a dismissive tone, Holmes replied, "They relished Ronald Bythewood's association with Mélanie to no greater a degree than this man standing before you. Perhaps, in their own peculiar manner, her family was simply attempting to prevent Bythewood from acquiring his wife's wealth, just as Lennox had attempted to do." He paused, and seemed to scrutinise Lennox afresh. "It was thallium that you used, was it not? And you were no doubt advised by one of your colleagues at the club – who I am sure had no understanding of your true intent – to put it into the birds' water rather than their feed? It is more effective that way, and racing pigeons require a great deal due to their increased respiration. I presume that you could not bring yourself to simply wring their necks?"

"I could never do that!" Lennox exclaimed, then clamped his lips tight together, perhaps due to a realisation that his outburst signified acknowledgement of a far worse crime. His eyes darted uncontrollably and his whole body slackened in the constables' grip. I felt certain that scenes from three years before were at this moment playing before his eyes, recast in the context of this new information.

I too, pictured the scene in my mind's eye. I saw Lennox steal into the apartment in Argenteuil, perhaps having secured a copy of the key from Audibert, untrustworthy as he was. I saw him go to the rooftop and take the birds' water bowls, then – presuming that they had become low more than twelve hours since Bythewood's last visit – return to the kitchen to fill them with water from the rusty tap and to pour in the poison. In his inevitable haste, some of that poison inadvertently rubbed onto the tap itself.

Presently, Mélanie Bythewood had arrived at the apartment, perhaps an hour before her husband. While she waited, she had filled a mug with water from the tap, and this simple act had secured her dismal fate.

The restaurant had now become as silent as the grave, only punctuated every so often by ragged sighs coming from Lennox, which seemed drawn from his very soul.

"My God, Holmes," I breathed. "What a tale. What a pitiable man."

Holmes nodded. "And yet the narrative that you have conjured is only a tale, reliant upon happenstance."

Lestrade struck the tabletop in exasperation. "Speak plainly, man! What is the truth of the matter?"

Holmes regarded him mildly. "Mélanie Bythewood did not die as a result of poisoning, nor an accident. Bythewood told the summoned doctor that when he returned from the rooftop of his apartment, he found her in the midst of a violent fit. Whether she displayed symptoms before that day, I do not know, but the cause of her death was a severe case of meningitis."

Silence reigned once again. I saw that Lennox was trembling uncontrollably.

"Lennox," I said, barely able to look at the man directly, "you now understand that nobody bears responsibility for the loss of this woman you describe as your true love, and that you have killed an innocent man without any cause for retribution." I turned to Lestrade, who appeared as sorrowful as Lennox himself. "I almost feel that imprisonment is unnecessary, given the suffering of the heart that this man will undoubtedly endure."

Lestrade nodded, then blinked rapidly and seemed to regain control over his emotions. "That may be," he said in his customary clipped tone, "but I serve the Queen and enact the laws of this country, which demand that he receive the appropriate punishment – that is, punishment of the mortal body, rather than the mind. Holmes, I thank you for supplying the facts, and you will be required to lay out all the evidence that you accumulated in Paris, at some later date. But for now, I trust that our story-time is over?"

Holmes responded with a slow, solemn nod of assent.

"Then I will say farewell and I will take this fellow to Scotland

Yard," Lestrade said with finality. He rose and nodded to the constables, who guided their captive towards the exit, watched by the restaurant manager, who wrung his hands constantly. Even from behind, the slump of Lennox's body made clear that he was a broken man.

CHAPTER TWENTY-FIVE

Holmes signalled for a cab as soon as we emerged from the restaurant, but after a short period of bumping and swaying in the confines of the carriage, he accepted my suggestion that we disembark at George Street and walk the remainder of the distance to our lodgings. Frankly, I required fresh air. The contents of my stomach roiled, and my head was filled with images of that bare apartment in Argenteuil, and the complexities of the relationship between Bythewood, his wife Mélanie and Alexander Lennox.

"I feel as though, like you, I have only recently returned to London," I said quietly as we turned onto the southern part of Baker Street. "Furthermore, I find that I have no appetite to ever visit Paris or even to leave this city for any reason."

Holmes turned to face me. "You speak as though there were no crimes performed here."

"I know that there are. But the tragedy of the type that you have described..." I shook my head in despair.

We lapsed into silence. Despite my sullen mood, I was grateful that Holmes was at my side, and that we were now returning to our lodgings, where we would no doubt be served tea by our landlady. Within those walls, everything was in its right place.

I recalled the transformations that had afflicted Baker Street in recent days. Just as we were on the cusp of crossing Marylebone Road, I clutched at Holmes's arm in alarm.

"Holmes! Amid all of the flurry of new information, I had entirely forgotten Abigail's part in all of this!"

Holmes withdrew his arm gently, and continued to navigate the bustle of the busy street. When we reached the other side, he said, "And what part is that, do you suppose?"

I did not reply at once, for fear of embarrassing myself with presumptions that would cause Holmes to roll his eyes. "Well, firstly there is the matter of Bythewood's choice of alter ego: the surname Moone."

Holmes stopped mid-stride, but then resumed walking. "I have determined no causal link."

I stared at his back as he walked away, then I strode to catch up with him. "Very well. But now that I think about it... Abigail was our introduction to the case of Bythewood's murder, was she not? It was her fanciful selection of a victim and a method of murdering that victim – Bythewood – that signalled the beginning of this adventure. Are you telling me that there is no correspondence between these details and the events that resulted in his death?"

This time, Holmes did not look up. His pace increased somewhat.

"Holmes!" I called after him. "You must face the facts – Abigail's inventions mirrored the characteristics of the crime, even if they were entirely unrelated. What we are talking about here can only be named 'coincidence' – can you accept and agree to that?"

Now Holmes seemed preoccupied with the paving-stones beneath his feet.

"Holmes," I repeated in a softer tone. "It is no great task to accept that sometimes – some very infrequent times – events may appear to bear some relation to one another, but no relation exists. Anybody in the world might agree that this is true."

Finally, my friend met my eyes. His were dark as pitch.

"Very well," he said slowly. "I accept it."

We stood looking at each other for several long seconds. Gradually, I saw Holmes's expression change. Mirth crept in, and his eyes shone like jet.

"I suspect it is now your turn to experience a revelation," he said.

At first I had no earthly idea what he meant. Then, as gradual as his own change of mood, realisation came upon me. I raised my hands like a parish priest about to make an announcement from the pulpit, then clenched my fingers into tight fists.

"But there is still no satisfactory explanation of the order of events!" I cried.

"Go on," Holmes said, much amused at my distress.

"Abigail…" I replied slowly.

"What of her?"

"She… there was an attempt on her life. That was *real*. It happened. No coincidence could explain away that event, surely?"

"And does any other aspect now strike you as peculiar?"

I stared at him. "Yes! The note-book – it was stolen! Who else but Lennox would have desired to possess it?"

Holmes put a hand on my shoulder, turning me gently so that I faced in the correct direction. Stumbling a little in my wondrous state, I allowed him to lead me along Baker Street towards our lodgings.

"You are entirely correct," Holmes said, "at least in terms of the questions you have finally asked. Yes, the contents of Miss Moone's note-book bore no true relation to the death of Ronald Bythewood – at least, they did not inspire Lennox's method of murder. But both Lennox and Miss Moone were present on several occasions in Vauxhall Park in the days leading up Bythewood's poisoning, both noting the details of Bythewood's routine, for quite different reasons. After the murder had been carried out, and when Lennox learned by some means that Miss Moone was as fascinated in Bythewood's movements as he was himself, he committed himself to learning her identity, and he achieved this by the opportunistic stealing of her bag and purse at the moment she placed it down in order to close her front door. It was only *after* this point that he first read the contents of the note-book, and he reached the mistaken conclusion that her detailed account of an attempt on Bythewood's life, which appeared to describe something very close to the crime he had already committed, meant that she knew about his prior actions – certainly enough to allow the police to mount a more precise investigation that might well lead back to this restaurant – and therefore represented an urgent threat to his freedom."

He became more pensive. "There seems no reason to inform Scotland Yard of this aspect of the case, to avoid Miss Moone becoming any more embroiled than she has been already. What remains important to you and I, Watson, is that Lennox then made an attempt on the life of this apparent witness to his deeds, and poisoned the supply of water to Miss Moone's home."

"My God," I said. Then I quoted solemnly, "'I am in blood stepped in so far, that, should I wade no more, returning were as tedious as go o'er.'"

Holmes only raised an eyebrow in response. "Quite."

I was silent for a time, allowing this new aspect to settle alongside my existing understanding of Lennox's character. Earlier, I had allowed myself to feel a degree of sorrow for him due to the guilt and self-loathing that would haunt him for the rest of his days. Certainly, this new information about his activities made him less a tortured lover and far more a danger to society at large.

"And when that attempt to kill Abigail failed…" In my uncertainty, my words trailed off.

"At some point soon after that, it must have become evident to Lennox that Miss Moone had not been working alongside the police. Indeed, it is equally likely that he familiarised himself with other entries in the note-book, and reached the correct conclusion that these were jottings made in preparation for the writing of novels. It matters not. What is clear is that it was at this point that his approach changed. Instead of attempting once more to dispatch this apparent witness to his deeds, he sent pages from her note-book to the police, in the hope that they might then attribute the crimes to her. As we know, his ploy worked entirely as intended. Abigail Moone became the sole suspect in the police investigation. If it were not for our decision to hide her away, she would have been arrested and the case against her might have appeared – to humdrum and incurious minds – inarguable."

I shook my head in wonderment at this account. "So, the misgivings I had about the case proceeding in a back-to-front fashion… they were all well-founded."

"They may have been mere misgivings in your mind, Watson, but in mine they were inconsistencies – and any inconsistencies in an explanation of a case are intolerable."

Perhaps he noticed that I had taken offence at his implication that I should be ranked alongside those 'humdrum and incurious minds' that might have imprisoned Miss Moone. Whether or not that was the case, his expression softened.

"There is one conclusion that I confess eludes me," he said in a more contrite tone.

"What is that?"

"I still do not see clearly how Lennox deduced Abigail

Moone's involvement in the first place," he replied. "His actions once he had determined that fact are known to us, but not the steps of logic that led him there."

Our own steps had now led us to the door of 221b Baker Street. Without yet reaching for the handle, I turned to face Holmes, beaming.

"Finally!" I exclaimed in delight.

"What?" Holmes asked irritably.

"Finally, I am able to supply one of the answers myself. Do you really not see?"

"I have already told you as much, Watson. Do not make me say it again."

I laughed. "After successfully murdering Ronald Bythewood, Lennox performed an additional act – one that any sensible criminal ought to do immediately after committing a crime in this city. That is the point at which he learned of the involvement of Abigail Moone, and was inspired to follow her to her home – no doubt having recognised her dimly from their mutual visits to Vauxhall Park, each watching Bythewood at the same time."

Holmes reached into his pocket and retrieved his own key to the door. "It does not suit you, Watson, this withholding of information. Your manner has become distinctly smug. I would be grateful if you might say your piece and then allow me to enter my home."

"Here," I replied.

"Yes, my home *here*," Holmes snapped.

I shook my head. "Lennox was *here* when he saw Abigail."

Holmes's eyes darted around the street.

"Do you understand now?" I said, still chuckling. "Lennox's first impulse, to reassure himself that he had not been implicated in the murder, was to watch the door of your own lodgings. His correct assumption was that anybody who arrived here might be a witness to his deeds. And here he saw Abigail, and after that, events transpired exactly as you have described them."

Holmes continued gazing around at the buildings of Baker Street, as if he hoped to determine Lennox's precise hiding-place. Then, without another word, he turned, wrenched the key in the lock and marched up the steps to our shared rooms.

I watched him ascend the stairs. From his body language alone, I knew that my deduction had pleased him greatly – not because of any mental acuity I had demonstrated, but because of the great compliment to his own abilities that it contained.

It pleased me, too, to know that one of Sherlock Holmes's few failures of deduction related to an underestimation of his own reputation, and his own worth.

ACKNOWLEDGEMENTS

In planning this novel, and only sometimes for the sake of its central mystery, I've often been casual about bending the truth. There is no drinking-fountain outside Tate Britain, as far as I know. The contemporary British gallery is reached by a slightly more convoluted route than described, and the room may not even have been labelled as such in 1898, as I worked from a 1914 floorplan.

Within that fictionalised gallery room are numerous errors and conveniences, too. Most noticeably, Alfred Sisley's 1872 painting *Main Street in Argenteuil* has never been exhibited in a British gallery. Both John Henry Yeend King's *Milking Time* and Herbert Draper's *The Lament for Icarus* were acquired by the Tate in 1898, though they were exhibited first at the Royal Academy of Arts. The other paintings described in the novel all had varying, but still reasonably close, exhibition dates – they are: Arthur Hacker's *The Annunciation*, John Singer Sargent's *Carnation, Lily, Lily, Rose*, William Small's *The Last Match*, Alfred Parsons' *When Nature Painted all Things Gay*, John William North's *The Winter Sun*, Joseph Farquharson's *The Joyless Winter Day*, John Brett's *Britannia's Realm* and William Logsdail's *Saint Martin-in-the-Fields*.

As well as a huge amount of historical and medical websites, I'm indebted to Leslie S. Klinger for his annotated versions of the Sherlock Holmes canon, to Miranda Jewess for her exhaustive Holmesian style guide, to my editor, Cat Camacho, for her enthusiasm and unflagging attention to detail, and to my copyeditor, Sam Matthews, for her terrific work honing the final manuscript.

I offer my thanks to my mum, who introduced me to Sherlock Holmes (and, equally importantly, methods of figuring out whodunnit). Finally, thanks to my children, Arthur and Joe, who have finally been impressed by one of my novels, and to Rose, for *everything*, as always.

ABOUT THE AUTHOR

Tim Major is a writer and freelance editor from York, UK. His love of speculative fiction is the product of a childhood diet of classic *Doctor Who* episodes and an early encounter with Triffids. Tim's most recent books include *Hope Island* and *Snakeskins*, short story collection *And the House Lights Dim* and a monograph about the 1915 silent crime film, *Les Vampires*, which was shortlisted for a British Fantasy Award. Tim's short fiction has appeared in *Interzone*, *Not One of Us*, *Shoreline of Infinity* and numerous anthologies, including Best of British Science Fiction, Best of British Fantasy and The Best Horror of the Year. He tweets @onasteamer.

For more fantastic fiction, author events,
exclusive excerpts, competitions, limited editions and more

VISIT OUR WEBSITE
titanbooks.com

LIKE US ON FACEBOOK
facebook.com/titanbooks

FOLLOW US ON TWITTER AND INSTAGRAM
@TitanBooks

EMAIL US
readerfeedback@titanemail.com